L
LIGHT

LAVENDER LIGHT

LIGHT

DAILY MEDITATIONS FOR
GAY MEN IN RECOVERY

◇

ADRIAN MILTON

Adrian Milton

A PERIGEE BOOK

A PERIGEE BOOK
Published by The Berkley Publishing Group
200 Madison Avenue
New York, NY 10016

Copyright © 1995 by Adrian Milton

Book design by Stanley S. Drate/Folio Graphics Co., Inc.

Cover design by James R. Harris

Front cover Picasso etching copyright © 1995 Artists Rights Society
(ARS), New York/SPADEM, Paris.

First edition: June 1995

Published simultaneously in Canada.

Library of Congress Cataloging-in-Publication Data

Milton, Adrian.
     Lavender light : daily meditations for gay men in recovery /
Adrian Milton.
        p.   cm.
     "A Perigee book."
     ISBN 0-399-51939-4 (alk. paper)
     1. Gay men—Alcohol use.   2. Gay men—Drug use.
  3. Recovering alcoholics—Prayer-books and devotions—English.
  4. Recovering addicts—Prayer-books and devotions—English.
  5. Twelve-step programs—Religious aspects—Meditations.
  6. Devotional calendars.
  I. Title.
HV5139.M55   1995
362.29'18'086642—dc20   94-32616
                                                        CIP

Printed in the United States of America

10   9   8   7   6   5   4   3   2   1

This book is printed on acid-free paper.

Introduction

Since ancient times the color lavender has been associated with gay men. Lavender is created by combining blue and red—traditional male and female colors—and then blending them with white, the color of supreme spiritual development. The attributes of lavender, according to Eastern mystical thought, are spiritual knowledge and transformation. Shades of the color lavender are also found in the amethyst, the gemstone associated with sobriety. In ancient Greek, *amethystos* means "not intoxicated."

Studies done at the University of California at Berkeley and at the University of Illinois indicate that one-fourth of adult gay men are alcoholics or substance abusers. There are no reliable figures for gay overeaters, sexual compulsives, gamblers or sufferers of other compulsive-obsessive disorders, but anecdotal evidence suggests the numbers are high.

Most people in recovery use some kind of daily meditation book. Current daily meditation books for men emphasize topics of concern to straight men. There is no gay or lesbian story in *The Big Book*. The special issues relating to gay men, such as confronting internal and external homophobia, coming out, same-sex relationships, civil rights, violence and the lack of positive role models, are not addressed in any recovery literature.

Two of the elements that make a recovery program work are a spiritual awakening through the Twelve Steps and peer identification with other members of the group. If a person does not find a supportive environment in the meeting rooms, it is unlikely he will feel comfortable enough to stay. Instances of prejudice and censorship have been noted by gay men who have been open about their sexual orientation in recovery groups. Many gay men feel awkward sharing their private lives at meetings, because they believe they will be rejected by the group. Without complete honesty and openness, a person's chances of recovery are lessened.

The purpose of gay meetings is to create a space that fosters group identification, helps to create personal connections and encourages fellowship. In other words, a place gay men would want to keep coming back to for emotional and spiritual sustenance. This book of daily meditations aims to serve the recovering gay man in the same way a meeting does—provoke thought, break down isolation, forge bonds and heighten recognition that being gay is more of an identity than a behavior. These meditations are not meant as a replacement for primary program literature but as an adjunct that will hopefully enhance the recovery process for gay men.

I want to thank the recovering men who responded to my questionnaire, contributed quotations and shared their experience, strength and hope with me. Many friends have helped me, but I am particularly grateful to Grant Lukenbill for his professional assistance and to Brother Tom Carey, S.S.F., for reading a draft and making comments. I am particularly grateful to Henry Fournier for his many hours of listening and good advice. I am indebted to my mother for her guidance and love. A special thanks to my lover Patrick, whose encouragement, comments and support have contributed greatly to this work.

Steven~

May the long-time Sun
shine upon you
And
the Pure Light Within you
Guide your way on~

lots of love
Adrean

LAVENDER

LIGHT

January 1

Trust no future, however pleasant! Let the dead past bury its dead! Act in the living present!
—HENRY WADSWORTH LONGFELLOW

Much of our time has been spent saying "If only I had not done this or that" or "I'll never be happy until such and such occurs." Perhaps we think we can never have the lover we want until we have the perfect body. Do we postpone buying new clothes because we hope to lose weight? Are we haunted by regret for past mistakes?

The recovery experience teaches us the meaning of *One Day at a Time*. We may look at the past, but we do not stare at it. We plan for the future, but we turn the results over to our Higher Power. We try to live each day as though it were our last, doing the best we can and enjoying ourselves along the way. The joy is in the journey rather than the achievement of the goal.

When we have a difficult time facing reality, we often slip into daydreams or flights of fantasy. In doing so we are cheating ourselves of the fullness of the moment. As long as we are working our program, we can begin each new day with a clean slate.

Today I will affirm the good that is in my life and concentrate on the present so that I can look back on the day just ended with satisfaction and serenity.

January 2

I would say, if two males or two females voluntarily agree to have mutual satisfaction without further implication of harming others, then it is OK.
— THE DALAI LAMA

It might surprise some of us who were raised in a rigid religious atmosphere to hear a great spiritual leader be so relaxed about homoerotic expression. As we mature, we realize that we have a duty to question any system that limits our full flowering as gay men. We inhibit our emotional and spiritual growth when we unquestioningly accept any teaching. Taboos meant for ancient tribes have no place in modern ethical codes. When a belief system is unable to grow and reflect the present time, then it becomes a meaningless ritual and a system of oppression. Defenders of slavery used scripture to justify it; the same people use irrelevant and mistranslated quotes from the Bible to impose sanctions against gay men and lesbians. Let us turn from these false teachers and embrace those seekers after truth who are loving and open-minded.

We have the individual right to engage in any action that gives satisfaction, provided it does not harm others. We hold our relationships up to the light of fairness, respect and love. Any union that meets these criteria is affirming and holy and has every right to be.

Today I affirm the rightness of my sexual identity, knowing that it is a wonderful part of the mosaic of life.

January 3

In every man's heart there is a secret nerve that answers to the vibrations of beauty.
—CHRISTOPHER MORLEY

All of us are moved by beauty. When we behold a particularly spectacular landscape or observe an exquisite work of art, our spirits are uplifted like those of a miner emerging from the darkness below. He suddenly sees the sky and feels an emotional release. Our lives would be very dull indeed if we did not take time to allow beauty to enter. Our daily routines can be monotonous, and communion with beauty refreshes and reenergizes us.

Beauty is not just a visual manifestation but comes in many forms. It is a quality that exalts the mind and spirit. A person of good character radiates attractiveness. A pleasant face is a joy to gaze upon. A perfectly proportioned body is a reminder of the divine organization in this universe. The more wisdom we gain, the more our ability to discern beauty in everything grows.

Beauty gives pleasure to all of the senses. A rose is wonderful to smell. A merry tune enlivens us. A cat is a joy to stroke. The sweetness of fresh fruit excites our taste buds. Cultivating awareness of the inherent beauty in life helps to dispel the negative and enrich our daily lives.

◇

Today I will suspend judgment and be open to the beauty in all creation.

January 4

When our hatred is violent, it sinks us beneath those we hate.
                              —FRANÇOIS DE LA ROCHEFOUCAULD

As gay men, perhaps we have developed a hatred for "straight" people, thinking that they all hate or have contempt for us. When we think like this, we fall into the same trap as those we condemn. Or maybe we simply "tolerate" straight people and assume that we are superior. The key to becoming a mature person is to recognize people as individuals and not as members of a group.

As recovering people we do not have room to harbor feelings of hatred. If we have been hurt by family, friends or lovers, we should be careful not to get caught up in the "blame game." When we carry around feelings of hatred toward a group or another person, it will eventually consume us and we will become hateful ourselves.

The antidote to hate is love. As difficult as it is, in recovery we learn to forgive those who hurt us. There are practical and spiritual implications for letting go of hatred. We no longer hold on to resentments and anxiety. We are free to be open to love, understanding, harmony and peace of mind. When we let go of hateful feelings, we can become the person we have always wanted to be.

Today I will choose harmony and acceptance over discord and anger.

One reason there is so much drug abuse is that people are not shown other ways to alter their consciousness. All we have is the mall and the video rental shop; that's our cultural experience, our museums.

—KAREN FINLEY

Today the traditional bonds of the family, church and the community are dissolving. These institutions, despite their deficiencies, used to provide people with a secure framework for living. When people are without strong moorings in times of change, they look for certainties. When they do not find them, they turn to drugs or alcohol to fill the inner void.

We are entering a time when old gods are tumbling from their pedestals and the walls of many temples of orthodoxy are crumbling. To make us feel whole, some of us think the only thing left is the acquisition of material goods. However, we can never be satisfied in this way. We must look within to find true security.

Depending on our inner resources is frightening to most of us. We do not like the feeling that the ground is shifting beneath us. Those of us in the program are blessed. We have a set of principles to live by and a community that supports us. The Twelve Steps are tools for self-discovery that provide a firm base for a fulfilling and happy life.

I will set aside some time today for prayer and meditation so that I might get in touch with what is truly important.

Gayness is a gift. I know many people who feel that gay men in particular can be the most powerful force for transformation within our society.
—HIBISCUS (GEORGE HARRIS)

The legends, literature and art of other cultures and periods reveal that many societies saw gay men as vehicles that enabled the spirit to enter into people's hearts and minds. American Indian Medicine men, known as *Berdaches*, were feared and respected for the powers given to them by the supernatural. They were believed to hold the knowledge of gender transformation and other metamorphoses. Gay men have been the shamans and priests of many cultures, from ancient Egypt to modern times. Free to cross traditional role boundaries, gender-variant people were capable of an expanded vision of human potential.

For centuries, most organized religions have condemned same-sex lovers. Yet, ironically, some of the greatest saints have been gay. The contribution of gay people to world spirituality has been immense.

In recovery we have the opportunity to blossom into the fullness of our spiritual nature. As lovers of the arts and the cup bearers of culture, we have given many gifts to the world. Our spirituality moves us to take positive action. We are proud of who we are as we create our singular expression of the truth.

Today I will cooperate with the transforming power within me and be an agent of positive change.

Selfishness always aims at creating around it an absolute uniformity of type. Unselfishness recognizes infinite variety of types as a delightful thing, accepts it, acquiesces in it, enjoys it.   —OSCAR WILDE

Do we wish that everyone around us was like us? Do we give attitude to those who do not share our values and conform to our idea of what is proper? Some in the gay community say that everyone should dress a certain way so as not to attract notice or condemnation from the straight community. This view does not recognize that this world is a place of infinite variety and that everyone has a right to their individual expression.

In this program we encounter all types. Do we condemn someone because of their poor grammar or uncouth manners? Do we belong to some clique that puts down everyone who does not meet with our approval? If so, we cramp ourselves with a narrow and limited outlook. As recovering people, we are all here for the same reason: to heal from a fatal disease. Group unity is essential if we are to make progress.

Opening up to different types broadens our outlook. We often learn from someone whom we judged to be less than ourselves. We even find that we can enjoy the company of people of different backgrounds.

Today I will be open to new people, places and things. I will look to broaden the range of those whom I allow to enter into my life.

January 8

Man is an imitative animal. This quality is the germ of all education in him. From his cradle to his grave he is learning to do what he sees others do.
—THOMAS JEFFERSON

It has been well established that we learn best from example. All children need good guides to help them make positive choices. We tend to copy the behavior of those whom we admire. Unfortunately, very few of us grew up exposed to positive gay role models.

In recovery we have the opportunity to learn from other recovering gay men who have succeeded in their quest for spiritual and emotional growth. We "stick with the winners" when we discover that they have what we want. As we grow in emotional sobriety, we are able to share some of what we have gained. We become part of a healing circle where we learn from one another. It is inspiring to watch our recovering brothers as they face challenges and deal with them in a principled and effective manner.

Recovery allows us to be the positive role models for young gay men. Wouldn't it be wonderful to know that our personal growth and hard work can be an example for someone else?

Today I will share what I have learned by being a good example to those around me.

January 9

There is no good arguing with the inevitable.
—JAMES RUSSELL LOWELL

It is much easier to go with the flow of life than to fight our way upstream. Accepting life on its own terms makes our path smoother. We strive to learn what we can change and what we can not.

Trying to force change in other people only resulted in anger and frustration. Today we leave others alone and work on ourselves. Sometimes we wasted time romantically pursuing someone who was obviously not interested in us. This only set us up for rejection and pain. Now we accept the situation and move on.

We cannot change the past. The past is over, and so as healthy, recovering people we live in the present. We learn that we cannot always win, and we learn to look for the lesson in each loss.

It is okay to make mistakes. Meanwhile, we do the best we can. We accept how we feel and listen to our inner voices. We learn to recognize our limits today and hope to do better tomorrow. If we can make a change, we take the necessary action. If not, we pray for acceptance. We refuse to fight reality anymore. We wear the world like a loose garment.

Today I will respect myself by accepting the things I cannot change.

January 10

God, I offer myself to Thee—to build with me and to do with me as Thou wilt. Relieve me of the bondage of self, that I may better do Thy will. Take away my difficulties, that victory over them may bear witness to those I would help of Thy Power, Thy Love, and Thy Way of Life. May I do Thy will always!

—THE THIRD STEP PRAYER
FROM *ALCOHOLICS ANONYMOUS*

The Third Step teaches us that turning our will and our life over to a power greater than ourselves makes life easier. In the past we misused our willpower and the results were disastrous. Today we take the actions that are necessary for positive achievements and a full life, but we turn the outcome over to our Higher Power.

When we are self-absorbed, we often overlook the obvious and block the flow of creative movement. Letting go frees us from worry and anxiety.

In moments of crisis or desperation we can reaffirm our decision to place our trust in our Higher Power. When we surrender our will and acknowledge our dependence on a power greater than ourselves, our fears are replaced by a lightness of spirit.

I let go of anxiety and stubbornness, knowing that the perfect plan for my life will become clear.

January 11

For both good and bad, homosexual behavior retains some of the alarm and excitement of childish sexuality.
                                                        —PAUL GOODMAN

In early recovery some of us thought we would never have fun ever again. Perhaps our idea of a good time was formed in an atmosphere of hedonism and promiscuity. We associated being gay with substance abuse, wild times and a frantic embrace of sexual stimuli. Eventually, our senses were dulled and each new adventure failed to achieve the desired effect.

Recovery teaches us the importance of a balanced life. We have a wide range of choices, and our lives need never be boring. Our new freedom opens up the potential blocked by addiction and enables us to be better people.

We also learn to treasure the wit, humor and enthusiasm that we share as members of the gay community. The perpetual youth in us is retained by recognizing the power of laughter and maintaining a cheerful outlook. A sense of curiosity keeps us from becoming stale. We are renewed and reformed by the love we find in the fellowship and our new relationship with our Higher Power.

I will try to keep a sense of humor about everything that happens to me today.

In the future everyone will be famous for fifteen minutes.
                                                    —ANDY WARHOL

D o we strive for fame rather than excellence? Is our self-esteem hinged to being a person of renown? Do we envy celebrities? Are we willing to gain notoriety at any price? Do we feel less than others because we are unknown to the world at large? If so, our value system may be skewed and in need of retuning. Fame as a goal can be a source of frustration and bitterness and is easier to attain than to keep.

Whatever we do is best done for the joy of it. We turn the results over to our Higher Power. We feel proud of a job well done, but when acclaim follows, we should accept it with humility. Our true worth is not grounded in the world's opinion of us but in our own sense of integrity.

I am a perfect expression of God's will at work in this world.

Make of yourself a light. —THE BUDDHA

The power of example is the best way to teach. We might be told how to do something a hundred times and not learn it, but we pick it up right away after being shown once. If we have a friend whose drinking or drugging or other compulsive behavior disturbs us, the best gift we can give them is our good example. As we change for the better, they will be attracted to us and want to know what we are doing with our lives. At this receptive moment we can tell them about the program and perhaps plant the seed of recovery.

If we are offended by gossip or backbiting, then we can refuse to participate in such behavior. Being unfailingly kind to those around us sheds goodwill and light on every situation. Practicing rigorous honesty in our affairs with others sets a high standard.

As the ripple of one pebble is felt throughout the pond, so whatever we do is an influence for either the good or the bad. If we wish to change the world, then we must first change ourselves.

Help me to find my true self so that I may be an inspiration to others.

January 14

Plagues and epidemics, like AIDS, bring out the best and the worst of society. Face to face with disaster and death, people are stripped down to their basic human character, to good and evil.

—JONATHAN MORENO

The plight of those sick and dying of AIDS changed the way the gay community thought of itself. Our response to this disease prompted much soul-searching. The time and effort expended on the AIDS crisis spilled over and energized other segments of the gay community. Civil rights, death, mortality and the value of gay lives became subjects of prime interest.

The reaction to this disease has been varied. Some despaired, went deeper into the closet, abandoned lovers and friends and continued to have unsafe sex. Many found new self-worth in caring for the sick, political activism and a greater appreciation of life.

A positive outgrowth of the AIDS crisis is a new focus on spirituality. We have learned to place a greater value on our lives and challenge those who would dispute our worth. Our maturation process has been reflected in a flowering of gay art, literature and films. We have grown as a community as we integrate notions of the spiritual and the physical.

Today I pray that the highest and best in me may be in evidence during the AIDS crisis. Let me be a caring and supportive person and extend my hand to those in need.

Nothing is more honorable than a grateful heart.
—SENECA

Gratitude is the best antidote for all of our fears and uncertainties. Yet sometimes we are so deep into self-pity and depression that we cannot find any reason to be grateful. If we are to find peace of mind, we need to change our attitude. First, let us be thankful we are alive when so many around us have had their lives cut short by disease and addiction. We certainly can be grateful for our recovery. Without it many of us would be dead or institutionalized. From our new point of view, we can be glad for both small and large things—a neighbor's smile, a kind word, a brilliant sunset, the joy of true friendship, a lover's embrace or the deep affection of a pet.

Daily prayer and meditation help us to stay centered and keep the focus on what is really important. Instead of taking things for granted, we build on all that is positive in our lives. Being thankful helps us to heal. It is the sweet balm that soothes away our troubles. When negative thoughts overwhelm us, we pause and make a gratitude list.

**I will begin and end each day with a prayer
of gratitude.**

January 16

Because the part of identity that is "gay" emerges from the most powerful and universal of human drives—the imperative of desire—it is inextricably bound to the torments and delicacies of taboo.
—FRANK BROWNING

Some gay people want to be viewed as "just like everyone else." The reality of our situation, however, is that we are different. We learn to accept difference as neither good nor bad but as an elaborate interweaving of mixed emotions, dreams and contradictions. As gay men, the objects of our desire are other men. This introduces an element of narcissism, rivalry and identification. We relate to our partners in a distinctive manner. Our behavior makes many people nervous, and we will never win full acceptance from everyone.

Because we threaten the status quo, we are viewed as the "other." We have had to create our own communities. This has often forced us to live on the fringe of society. Being the object of contempt further drove us to seek escape in compulsive behavior and substance abuse. Now that we are learning to respect ourselves, we are demanding that society treat us with justice and equanimity. No matter what our social status, manner of identifying ourselves or economic level, we are all people who deserve respect.

Let me remember that all the parts that make up me are worthy of exploration and consideration.

Many hands make light work. —PROVERB

The first word of the Twelve Steps is "We." Without each other we would not be able to maintain our recovery. This program dates its beginning from the first day of sobriety of the second member to get sober. Alone, the founder had difficulty, but when he sought out another drunk and carried the message, his recovery and a long chain of others were assured.

Sometimes we take meetings for granted. We walk in, expecting the chairs to be set up, the coffee made and a speaker booked. Do we take the time to make sure these things are done? What contributions have we made to our group? At our first meeting, someone was there to show us the way. Are we willing to do the same for newcomers?

There are many ways to pass it on—today let us find ways we can be of service. A good beginning would be to answer the phones at Intergroup or chair a service committee for the Roundup. Writing a recovering gay prisoner, attending business meetings or giving someone a ride to a meeting are excellent service opportunities.

It is said that we cannot keep our recovery unless we pass it on. This wonderful discovery has kept countless people sober. Why not make this valuable tool the strong base of our personal program?

My life has been transformed by this program. Help me to carry the message to all who need it.

The abused children are alone with their suffering, not only within the family, but within themselves. . . . They can not create a place in their own soul where they can cry their hearts out. —ALICE MILLER

The behavior of each member of a family affects every other member. If the father drinks, drugs or gambles compulsively or the mother overeats, rages or is co-dependent, the children are going to react. Their basic needs are being neglected. As a result one child may retreat into isolation, another may become angry and rebellious, and another may try to "fix" the situation.

If our needs were never met when we were children, we might spend our entire adult life in the grips of compulsive behavior and a disordered state of mind. We vowed we would never be like our parents, but we find that we end up just like them.

Recovery gives us an opportunity to break this vicious cycle. First we discover what happened and then we process that information. With the help of our Higher Power, our group and professional counseling, we slowly undo the damage that was done. In time we become renewed and empowered, able to forgive and forge ahead.

For today I trust that I can be healed.

January 19

The only thing we have to fear is fear itself.
—FRANKLIN DELANO ROOSEVELT

Many of us have lived lives based on self-centered fear. As gay men we grew up with the fear of persecution and exposure. We returned to the same old fears repeatedly and allowed them to dominate us. We were afraid we would lose something we already had or would not get something we eagerly desired. Fear of rejection, failure, success, pain and loss prevented us from moving forward.

In recovery we have the opportunity to confront our fears. We learn that we are loved by our Higher Power. Then we share our fears with a friend, our sponsor and the group. By identifying our fears, we help to destroy the power they have over us. We release panic and anxiety by centering ourselves through meditation. Helping others frees us of many of these fears by releasing us from self-absorption. Our faith assures us that no matter what happens we can deal with it with the help of our Higher Power.

Today I ask my Higher Power to help me be less fearful and more trusting.

Enjoyment is not a goal, it is a feeling that accompanies important ongoing activity. —PAUL GOODMAN

How much time do we spend postponing enjoying our lives? How often do we say that we will really be happy when we retire? Do we spend much of the winter daydreaming about the summer place we have rented? Do we think everything will be all right if only we can save up a particular sum of money?

In recovery, we try to enjoy the moment. We do the best we can at whatever task is at hand. If we have a task that we consider unpleasant, such as painting a room or cleaning the garage, we bring a sense of fun and excellence to the job. When we bring enthusiasm and interest to everything we do, our lives become more enjoyable.

If we are to get the most out of life, we need to discern what is important and what is not. If we eat a lot of junk food, we will get sick. By the same token if we fill our time with trivialities, we will be left with an empty, shallow feeling. We choose the actions of our lives with care and consideration so we may derive both inner satisfaction and a sense of accomplishment.

Today I will make positive choices that will bring depth and contentment to my life.

January 21

What does it profit a man to gain the whole world and
lose his soul?   —MATTHEW 16:26

When we were active, we tried to fill the void with
harmful substances or inappropriate behavior.
Now sometimes we imagine that acquiring more
material things will take away the emptiness we feel.

In recovery we gain a whole new outlook. We learn
that balance is the key to sobriety and a happy life. We
find that we do not have to have many things to make
us feel worthwhile.

Since ancient times philosophers have stressed the
Golden Mean. We take care of our basic needs and
strive for equilibrium in all things. We are only the
caretakers of the material goods we have received. Our
true goal is to develop a spiritual life. We put the
material into its proper perspective. We let go of
grasping and learn that we are not the things we own.
We gain a healthy respect for our achievements and
share what we have with others. Emotional sobriety
becomes our biggest asset.

**Today I will remember that I am enough, I have
enough, and I do enough.**

**When you're between any sort of devil and the deep
blue sea, the deep blue sea sometimes looks inviting.**
—TERENCE RATTIGAN

Gay teenagers have a very high rate of suicide.
They are taunted, abused, beaten and harassed by
schoolmates and sometimes by their parents. To
prevent this tragedy we become involved in outreach
programs that counsel gay teens. We support curricu-
lums that teach tolerance of gays and lesbians in the
schools and establish peer support groups. Serving as a
volunteer at a gay youth center or answering telephones
at a crisis line is a good way of becoming a positive
role model for young gay people.

We all have had thoughts of suicide from time to
time. When we are newly sober, severe depression may
overwhelm us because we no longer can use a substance
or person to escape our feelings. Coming out is so
traumatic for some of us that we might think death is a
better alternative. The death of a lover may throw us
into despair. If we are HIV positive, we sometimes
have trouble finding a reason to go on living.

We must never give up. Everything changes. When
plagued by suicidal thoughts, we need to get help.
Call a sponsor, friends or seek professional counseling.
Don't give up before the miracle occurs.

**The gift of life is precious. Let me use it to its
fullest extent.**

To find oneself jilted is a blow to one's pride. One must do one's best to forget it and if one doesn't succeed, at least one must pretend to. —MOLIÈRE

When we fall in love with someone, we give a part of ourselves. It is a shock to be jilted or left abruptly. Whether we have been with someone a few months or for several years, there is a process to regaining a sense of ourselves as individuals.

It took time to relax and trust another person, and it will take time to recoup the emotional energy we expended. Because separation is such a trauma, we will want to stick close to the program and keep in touch with our sponsor and friends. This is not a time to isolate. We make plans to see other people and look for ways to be of service to others.

Great care should be taken not to wallow in self-pity or emotionalism. We avoid for a time places associated with our old lover. We don't play music we enjoyed together or love songs about breaking up. We don't, for now, analyze the causes of the separation—this will only give us an excuse to beat ourselves up.

We are gentle with ourselves. We give ourselves special treats and attend many meetings. In time, the painful feelings will subside and our hearts will heal. If we have a friend who is experiencing the end of a relationship, we offer a shoulder to cry on and any other support needed.

Grant me the strength to get through the day. Help me to realize that all things pass in time.

Life is not a problem to be solved but something to be enjoyed.
— J. KRISHNAMURTI

Early recovery is difficult. Problems and dilemmas seem to overwhelm us. How can we reverse this and live a life of joy? Working the Twelve Steps is the answer. The Steps are directions on how to live a healthy and happy life. We find a sponsor for the specific purpose of leading us through the Steps. Attending Step meetings, listening to others share and practicing this program in our daily lives help us to attain emotional sobriety.

Fellowship is another valuable tool. We reach out and ask for help. We begin to socialize with other recovering men. Doing service teaches us to work harmoniously within a group. After meetings we join in helping to clean the room. It is suggested that we get telephone numbers and keep in touch with group members between meetings. As we develop a network of friends who support us, our recovery becomes easier and we begin to enjoy the fruits of sobriety.

By working the program, we heal ourselves and enter into a new life of joy and self-knowledge.

January 25

In jealousy there is more of self-love than love of another.
　　　　　　　　　　　　　—FRANÇOIS DE LA ROCHEFOUCAULD

Jealousy has been called the green-eyed monster. It lives upon doubts and can drive us to irrational and frenzied behavior. Are we jealous because we cannot have a person's friendship exclusively? Do we want our partners to have no other relationships and to devote themselves to us alone? Are we intolerant of our rivals? Do we let jealousy warp our thinking?

When we are suspicious or jealous of our lover, we make both of our lives miserable. Jealousy distorts the strong regard we have for someone else. It can put us into a fury that not only tears at our heart but can destroy our relationship.

As addictive people, we must guard against such strong emotions. In recovery we learn that jealousy is rooted in fear. Fear that we will not get what we want or deserve. Fear that someone else will take what we have.

If we are troubled by jealousy, we ask our Higher Power to lift this destructive emotion from us. We stop obsessing about our desires and remember that we cannot control everything. We learn to trust that all of our needs will be provided.

Today I will choose to be on the side of love and give others the freedom to be who and what they want to be.

The less my hope, the hotter my love. —TERENCE

Pursuing the unavailable has been a habit for many of us. We need to ask ourselves where this tendency comes from. Is it a way of keeping us from establishing a real relationship with someone? Do we fear intimacy and go after certain people we have no chance of ever being involved with? A thorough self-survey will help us understand the source of such behavior. We might discover that there was no intimacy in our family, and as a result we are afraid of it. Or we might have unrealistic expectations that can never be satisfied.

Often we are attracted to people with whom we have nothing in common. Perhaps we enjoy having sex with them but have no other basis for a relationship. A part of us wants to isolate. We are afraid of people and set ourselves up for rejection. It seems easier to be alone than to have to deal with someone else's wants and needs. If we wish to grow and find happiness with another person, we need to rethink all our old ways of looking for love.

**Today I will ask my Higher Power for guidance
in all my affairs.**

**When an angry man thirsts for blood, anything will
serve him as a spear.**   —HORACE

A cting on our anger was an old habit that brought
much destruction with it. We furiously raged at
others or turned our anger upon ourselves. Old
injustices gnawed away at us. We often destroyed our
relationships by outbursts of wrath. Easily aroused, we
overreacted to everything.

Sometimes anger is legitimate. In recovery we learn
to express our anger in a respectful manner. We no
longer shout at or bully others but state calmly what
we feel without making it a personal attack. As children
we thought we would be rejected or abandoned if we
expressed our anger openly. As adults we repressed this
anger and it came out in many insidious forms: jealousy, intolerance, hatred, contempt, sarcasm, self-pity
and anxiety. We let go of resentments that can trigger
our anger.

Before we react to a situation we take a deep breath
and count to ten. We remember that others have their
own problems and are worthy of our respect. Finally,
we learn to express ourselves in a clear and direct
manner. As we sharpen our tools of communication,
we are able to deal with our anger in a constructive and
mature way.

**Today I will not let my anger consume me.
I will acknowledge my true feelings and deal
with them.**

A very great part of the mischief that vexes the world arises from words. —EDMUND BURKE

Some of us were labeled "clumsy," "shy" or "incompetent." Labels have a tendency to stick, and after a while we began to believe what others said about us. We reinforced these messages ourselves by acting as others characterized us. We said, "I'll never get better" or "Why do I always do the wrong thing?"

Let's break this habit. We do this by taking an inventory. We find out who we really are—listing both our defects and our assets. We work actively to destroy any negative self-images. We speak of ourselves in a respectful and kindly way. We no longer put ourselves down, even in jest. We create new expectations and move toward them. By positive imaging we reshape ourselves into the person we always wanted to be. At the same time, we remember that it is progress, not perfection, that is important. *One Day At A Time*, we are growing healthier and becoming better persons. We choose our words carefully, treating ourselves and others with the respect that we deserve.

Today I am a new creation. I work with my Higher Power to move toward a better self-image.

We act as though comfort and luxury were the chief requirements of life, when all that we need to make us happy is something to be enthusiastic about.
—CHARLES KINGSLEY

As addicts we cannot stand being uncomfortable. We are always making adjustments and taking our emotional temperature. Fear grips us when we contemplate change. Sometimes this fear of discomfort paralyzes us and prevents us from taking action. We stay with the familiar because it seems easier.

In recovery we learn that in order to achieve our goals we sometimes have to endure uncomfortable feelings. Perhaps we are afraid to admit that we do not know something. Often we do not want to feel the pain that growth can require. We become easily discouraged if we do not feel good immediately. Over time, as we continue to work the Steps, we learn to take risks. Feelings that once frightened us become guideposts along our journey. We begin to embrace life and all its possibilities. Fulfillment comes from facing challenges and new opportunities.

Today I will remember that feelings are not facts and that taking risks will enlarge my horizons.

Did he break into tears? There are no faces truer than those that are so washed. —WILLIAM SHAKESPEARE

There are some of us who think it is unmanly to cry. We have hardened ourselves and disguise our feelings out of a false sense of pride. We shortchange ourselves when we hold back our natural impulses. When we learn to let go and express ourselves, we are on the road to emotional recovery.

For some of us the first tears we shed will be those of gratitude and relief that we have finally found this program. All our unnamed fears and inchoate feelings come to the surface, and we experience a great emotional release.

In times of illness, accident or death, our woes are lessened and our hearts are softened when we weep. Tears of sympathy for the pain and trouble of others help strengthen our bonds with humanity. Sometimes the thought of a dead friend will bring a mist to our eyes in a tribute to their memory.

Perhaps the most satisfying tears are those of joy. They lubricate the soul and signal the triumph of the spirit over melancholy.

Never let me be too ashamed to weep. A good cry can ease my pain and grief and prepare the way for laughter.

Good-bye. I've barely said a word to you. It is always like that at parties. We never see the people we would like to see or say the things we should like to say. It is the same everywhere in this life. Let us hope that when we are dead things will be better arranged.

—MARCEL PROUST

One of our members tells how he failed to visit his dying grandmother who raised him, because he was on a drunken binge. By the time he sobered up, she had died, and he missed his chance to say how grateful he was for all she had done for him.

In the past we did many things we now regret. We are sorry we acted so badly toward so many people. Remorse over the awful things we did when active will continue to haunt us unless we sincerely work the Steps to the best of our ability. Our inventories reveal a host of defects, oversights and injuries of others. We admit our mistakes and resolve not to repeat them. We do our best to make amends. We take care of what needs to be done as soon as possible. We are present for our loved ones and coworkers.

**Today I am present for the wonder
and awe of life.**

February 1

Once I thought I would meet somebody who would take me away from all of this. I realized after a while I was stuck with myself and no one was going to take me away from anything.　　　　　—QUENTIN CRISP

D o we daydream that someday we will meet someone who will make our life complete? Even if we enter into a near-perfect relationship, we still have to live with ourselves. Are we too dependent on other people for our happiness? No relationship with anyone, whether a lover, friend, parent or sibling, can provide for all of our needs.

The situations in which we find ourselves are mostly of our own creation. How we react to them is definitely up to us. The more we grow in our recovery, the more willing we become to take responsibility for our own well-being.

No matter where we go in this world or with whom we go, we take ourselves. Closeness and sharing with others is good, but we need to keep a breathing space between ourselves and those near to us so we can grow into the people we are meant to be.

Help me to respect my own individuality and independence. Today I will take a private moment to get to know myself better.

February 2

**I never travel without my diary. One should always
have something sensational to read in the train.**
—OSCAR WILDE

K eeping a journal helps us to chart our progress. It
is an excellent idea, beginning in early recovery,
to chronicle our impressions and reactions from a sober
viewpoint. When we review what we have written, we
can see how far we have come. A journal serves as a
record of where we are. We can see if we are keeping
our house in good order and, if not, take the necessary
steps to change.

Doing a written inventory gives concrete form to the
stream of consciousness running through our minds. A
careful reading of what we have written reveals patterns
of behavior and gives shape to the jumble of thoughts
and feelings that cloud self-understanding.

If at any time we feel confused, it helps to jot down
on paper a summary of all the elements in the situation.
Seeing everything in writing can clarify matters and
help us find the trouble spots.

Some people like to write the names of close friends
and family members and note the status of their relationship with each. From time to time they check the
list and see how things are going with the important
people in their life. Writing is a tool that can simplify
the present and can provide us with a record that gives
insight into our growth and progress.

**Today I ask for the discipline necessary for
self-awareness.**

Believe there is a great power silently working all things for good, behave yourself and never mind the rest.
—BEATRIX POTTER

It is possible to have great faith without believing in the outward forms of religion. Debating theology can be an endless source of strife. A great teacher suggested that when we want to pray we should retreat to the privacy of our room. In the silence of our inner self we commune in unity with our Higher Power.

What is most important is that each individual get in touch with a power greater than himself and know that power is working for his good. Realizing that there is a force in the universe larger than ourselves is a humbling experience. The gift of sobriety is a demonstration that some force wants to save us for better things.

One of the many benefits of sobriety is the ability to make choices. We can choose between right and wrong. Our conscience is our guide. At the end of each day we take an inventory, noting both the positive and the negative. We resolve to do better and say thank you for our recovery. We relax, get a good night's sleep and let go of all our cares.

Today I have faith that the universe is in good working order and that everything is unfolding as it should.

February 4

The object of art is to give life a shape.

—JEAN ANOUILH

We take our cues in life from many sources. Sometimes a story reflects our own thoughts and feelings. A particular film might speak to us and help us to see ourselves in an objective manner. A song can make special a moment in time or stir our soul. Seeing a beautiful dancer makes us more conscious of the way we occupy space. The light coming through a stained glass window may draw us closer to transcendence.

Art is an expression of man's desire for immortality. It is a spiritual marker of our time here in this world. The films we watch, the books we read and the images we observe are powerful influences. We should carefully choose what we allow to influence us. If we rely on TV or magazines for all of our information and inspiration, we will be flooded with mediocrity. It takes some effort to seek out quality. What we put into our minds is comparable to what we eat—certain movies or books can have the same effect as junk food.

**I am thankful today that my life is being shaped
by a spiritual outlook.**

February 5

Being queer-bashed at home is just as deadly as—and perhaps more terrible than—being assaulted by strangers. The difference is that this is violence we have the power to stop. —VICTORIA A. BROWNWORTH

Domestic violence is not something found only in the straight community. Yet we are afraid that if we acknowledge that it also occurs in the gay community, our struggle for equal rights will be hindered. Like most people in our society, we have absorbed the message that force makes right. If we are feeling frustrated with our lover, we sometimes lash out physically and verbally. Lack of understanding or poor communication also leads to conflict and harassment. Internalized homophobia can cause us to abuse the one we love.

In recovery we are learning to be gentle, loving people. When there is violence in our relationship, we seek help. If we are a victim, we need to realize that we do not have to suffer such abuse. If we are the perpetrator, we must refrain from such behavior and get professional assistance. We are all responsible for our actions.

I do not have to remain a prisoner of my old habits. Let me be a caring and considerate lover.

February 6

If someone is not feeling comfortable with the gay community, they are not feeling comfortable with themselves.
—MICHEL ROUX

It is important to challenge those who attack our community. They lie about us, deal in false generalizations and try to trivialize the integrity of our struggle. Those who attack or condemn gay people usually are trying to compensate for their own lack of self-esteem. They need a scapegoat in order to feel better about themselves.

The noted therapist John Bradshaw states that people attracted to extreme fundamentalism have a need to control everyone and everything. He characterizes adherence to that type of religion as a form of addiction. The men and women who are most virulently homophobic are those who are uncomfortable with sexuality and insecure about their sexual identity. They project their unhealthy attitude onto gays and anyone else who does not conform to their standard.

Sometimes gay men also make generalizations about the community that reveal residual self-hate. Our community needs healthy self-criticism, but unless we temper this criticism with love and tolerance, we fall into the same trap as our enemies. Today, as sober people, let us think of ways we can be a positive force in the gay community.

Today I choose to be loving.

February 7

I was seized by the stern hand of Compulsion, that dark, unseasonable Urge that impels women to clean house in the middle of the night. —JAMES THURBER

We have all been victims of compulsion. Something seemed to force us to commit what seemed to be an irrational act. Sometimes this was the urge to drink, drug or eat until we lost consciousness. Perhaps we were driven to wash our hands constantly, gamble away our life savings or try to control other peoples' lives. After each binge we were filled with remorse and vowed never to repeat this behavior. Yet our obsessions returned, and we never could find satisfaction or peace of mind.

We lived in dread of discomfort or the unexpected. To break this cycle of self-destructiveness we learn in recovery to rely on a power greater than ourselves. Turning our will and our lives over to our Higher Power takes away the need to change our mood anytime we feel uncomfortable.

Working the Steps, attending meetings and seeking professional help when necessary are the tools that help us break the hold these disturbing preoccupations have on us.

I dedicate this day to going with the flow. I relax and trust in the divine order of life.

February 8

Success means successful living. A long period of peace, joy and happiness on this plane may be termed success.
—DR. JOSEPH MURPHY

Many of us measure success by how much acclaim we receive or the amount of material goods we possess. However these things do not guarantee happiness.

Happiness results when we do satisfying work, maintain harmonious relationships and have the time to do the things we want to do. If we are in doubt about which career direction to take, we pray for guidance and the answers will come. How we react to people and events determines our peace of mind. We eliminate criticism and argument. We set our priorities and pursue them with enthusiasm.

Today as recovering men, we are winners. We have a second chance to live joyful and productive lives. Through working the Steps we eliminate negative thinking and acquire spiritual and psychological well-being.

I release from within me all the power and wonder that will guide me toward my abundant good.

Gays are in the vanguard of that final divorce of sex from conventional notions of sin. If we can take sex out of the realm of sin altogether and see it as something to do with personal relationships and ethics, then we can finally get around to another phase of Christianity which is long overdue. —ANNE RICE

Our society gets upset over sexual scandals but seems to tolerate high levels of violence, cruelty and poverty. From this we can deduce that something is wrong somewhere. Preachers seldom rail against war, but they are quick to pounce on anyone who steps outside certain proscribed sexual boundaries. This distorted and obsessive focus on sex has caused many of us to feel sinful and unclean.

When we were in the grips of our addiction, we did not have the tools to clearly see our essential goodness. Now that we are living a life based on spiritual principles, we have enough self-esteem to defend our sexual orientation against the ignorant and the biased.

As long as we are not harming ourselves or others when we have sex, then we can sleep with a good conscience.

I will not let the limitations and prudery of others inhibit the exploration of my sexual potential.

Some people think that doctors and nurses can put scrambled eggs back into the shell.

—DOROTHY CANFIELD FISHER

Because of our addiction and codependency, many of us developed serious illnesses or came close to dying. Our mental and physical habits were destructive and we did ourselves a lot of harm. If we are to repair the damage we have done ourselves we need to take responsibility for our health.

One of the first things we do in recovery is get a physical checkup from a doctor. We then take a careful look at our diet to make sure we eat moderately and nutritiously. A regular program of exercise will go a long way toward keeping both our bodies and minds in fit condition. The proper amount of rest rejuvenates us and keeps us alert. Practicing meditation helps relieve us of stress and anxiety. We learn to listen to our bodies and seek help when necessary. We participate in our own healing and do not passively expect the doctor to perform miracles.

We move away from self-abuse to self-respect. We choose how we will develop and cooperate with our bodies so that we can achieve wellness.

I will be sensitive to my body's needs and heed any warning signs that I might be off balance.

February 11

The spiritual life is part of the human essence. It is a defining characteristic of human nature without which human nature is not full human nature.
—ABRAHAM MASLOW

The search for life's meaning and a Higher Power has been with us since time immemorial. We find evidence of burial rites indicating a belief in an afterlife well over 250,000 years ago. Shrines and altars also date from that period. Humanity's theological and philosophical concepts have changed over the centuries and have been adapted to cultural conditions. However, an underlying premise seems to be that our interior life is just as important, if not more so, than our external life.

Because we are each different, every man must seek his definition of spirituality within himself. We work toward constructing a belief system that can transform us and bring us closer to God-consciousness.

When we neglect the spiritual part of our nature, we become lopsided and brittle. Life lacks the depth and richness that accompanies the seeker after truth and wisdom. We remember that we are not just our physical bodies but are also part of a universal scheme.

Today I will be thankful that I am on a spiritual journey and will draw on the magnificent resources that I am finding within myself.

February 12

We are taught not to think decently on sex subjects and consequently we have no language for them except indecent language. —GEORGE BERNARD SHAW

Many of us carry around shame about our sexuality. We have been conditioned to think of it as something "dirty." Reducing sex to just a physical level limited us. The more sex we had, the less satisfied we felt. Some of us depersonalized our partners and used them as objects for our pleasure. Our genitals ruled us and we tried to perform like supermen. Most of the information we had about sex came to us through pornography—leaving us with unrealistic expectations.

In recovery we grow weary of this narrow view. Admitting that sex can be spiritual as well as physical is the first step toward healing. We recognize that the sex act can be affectionate, intimate and loving. We treat our partners with respect. Sometimes we simply embrace or touch our lovers, knowing that every encounter does not have to lead to orgasm. Above all we affirm the sacredness of our bodies. We claim the love that is due to us and our partner.

Today I will call forth words and images that connect my sexuality with my spirituality.

February 13

We cannot help the birds of sadness flying over our heads but we need not let them build their nests in our hair. —OLD CHINESE SAYING

Many of us in early recovery are surprised to find that we are often depressed. The cause is usually biochemical and is a result of the body adjusting itself to sobriety. We have trouble thinking clearly, and our sleep patterns are disturbed. Our minds are troubled by self-destructive thoughts, and extreme mood swings make us feel we are on a roller coaster.

If this condition persists, it is suggested we seek the help of an addiction counselor or a therapist. But on our own we can do several things to ease the problem. We make sure we eat properly and get plenty of exercise. We keep busy, refusing to give in to depression—we go to a movie, explore a neighborhood we have never visited or take up a hobby. We do not isolate—being alone will make us more miserable. Research has shown that exposure to sunlight helps to lift depression. Therefore, we expose ourselves to as much sunlight as possible, and if it is winter, we can try light therapy.

Helping others is another effective way to forget our own woes. We make a gratitude list and count our blessings. Prayer and meditation keep us focused on our primary purpose, which is staying sober, *One Day at a Time*.

Today I ask for the strength and courage to face whatever the day brings.

February 14

The ideal companion is one to whom you can reveal yourself totally and yet be loved for what you are, not what you pretend to be. —CHRISTOPHER ISHERWOOD

It takes time to build a relationship. While in the throes of our addiction we did not have the patience necessary to establish intimacy. We thought that sex was love. For many of us it was impossible to go beyond romantic myths. We were easily disappointed. If someone did not measure up to our expectations immediately, our first impulse was to look elsewhere.

If we are looking for a long-term relationship, we have to ask ourselves some questions. Do we share a set of common values with our lovers? Are we proceeding on the same assumptions? If we decide to continue, can we face the realities of everyday living?

Our addictions were based on fear. Now we need to discover trust. Trusting involves taking a risk. We acknowledge our lovers as persons of worth and learn to feel secure in the relationship. To achieve trust we develop a clear line of communication and honesty. We strive to overcome jealousy and possessiveness. This process cannot be hurried. We take a spiritual approach by bringing our Higher Power into our relationship. As we practice kindness, courtesy and respect we learn to live with differences and accept our lovers as equals.

Today I will take a risk and allow my love to unfold naturally and honestly.

February 15

What Oscar Wilde and the court were contesting was not the evidence, but who had the right to interpret that evidence. It is no accident that the line "the love that dare not speak its name" haunted the trial, and has stayed with us ever since. It is not the love itself which was on trial, since even the law, since even our parents, acknowledge that some men do have sex with other men. What was on trial was the right to speak (invent and articulate) the name of that love. The question was, and is, who speaks, and when, and for whom, and why.
—NEIL BARTLETT

So often we are told not to "flaunt" our homosexuality. Imagine telling a straight person not to show their love for someone of the opposite sex! This hypocritical double standard is no longer acceptable to many gay men and women. When we openly speak about our "lover" at the office, proclaim our identity in the courts and the media and stop hiding who we are to anyone, we are expressing the true meaning of gay pride. Because we know the worthiness of our cause, we no longer allow others to narrowly define the boundaries of the proper expression of our sexual identity.

Today I will speak out loudly and clearly for my basic rights.

February 16

Religion is for those who believe in hell, spirituality is for those who have been through hell. —ANONYMOUS

We were told early in recovery that the Twelve Step program is a spiritual one. For many of us this caused confusion because we did not know the difference between religion and spirituality. Eventually we came to understand that we were not asked to believe a set of institutionalized dogmas or to hold to proscribed practices. We discover that spirituality is about what we do more than what we believe. Most of us have to rethink what we were taught as children. As addicts we dismissed our Higher Power because we felt rejected or abandoned.

In recovery we come to realize that we are loved and cared for and that we are deserving of abundance and joy. Self-seeking begins to fade away, and we derive great satisfaction from helping others.

Having survived much, we are grateful for our recovery. We saw the horrible places that addiction took us, and we do not want to return. The breath of new life that fills us in recovery stirs our spirits and keeps us vigilant. Communion with fellow recovering members and with our Higher Power enriches our spiritual outlook.

Let me never forget the bondage of addiction. I rejoice in the freedom of recovery.

Always rise from the table with an appetite and you will never sit down without one. —WILLIAM PENN

B ecause of the nature of our addictive personalities, we often feel that we do not get our full share of things. An empty feeling inside drives us to try to fill ourselves up, and in the end we dull our senses and lose our appreciation for what really matters. Too often we see the glass as half-empty rather than half-full. By practicing restraint and moderation in our daily habits, we achieve balance and serenity.

Often we give up one compulsive behavior only to overcompensate in another area. This is when we need to use the tools of the program. The same principles that applied to our primary addiction are useful in combating other compulsive behavior.

Our experience has taught us that we cannot rely too heavily on people and things to make us feel complete. Satisfaction depends on the achievement of a fit spiritual condition. Whenever we feel tempted to overindulge, we will ask our Higher Power for help. Eventually we will develop good habits which will serve us well in times of stress and temptation.

Today I will work on my spiritual development so that I may experience the fullness of life.

February 18

I wish to infuse myself among you till I see it common for you to walk hand in hand.   —WALT WHITMAN

Because we have been discriminated against and often brutalized, gay men need a healing and nurturing environment. As compulsive-obsessive people, our difficulties were compounded by our self-destructive behavior. Finding a safe space is difficult, but at meetings we can feel free to express ourselves fully. Little by little we learn to accept and appreciate ourselves and other gay men. We grow in strength and courage. We resolve to express ourselves openly. As our self-esteem grows we go out into the world and proclaim ourselves proudly.

By learning about our gay forefathers, such as Walt Whitman, we are inspired to emulate their heroic actions. Every gain that gay people have made is the result of individuals taking actions. Today we can ask ourselves how we can contribute to the greater good. As we realize that gay people have a history, we lose our sense of isolation and claim our place as full citizens of the world.

Let me strengthen the bonds that link me to my gay brothers and sisters.

Vows made in storms are forgot in calms.

—ENGLISH PROVERB

When we are suffering or in trouble, it is quite human to pledge never to do anything that would bring us to that awful place again. In the depths of our addiction we may have cried out "God, help me and I will never drink or drug again." Perhaps after a heavy binge of overeating or a period of sexual compulsivity we vowed to reform. Whatever our affliction, when we felt better, we soon forgot the consequences of our behavior and repeated these actions over and over.

Those of us who have this disease cannot make promises lightly. We have been saved from a wretched fate. We must maintain a fit spiritual condition so that we do not relapse. Going to meetings, sponsoring newcomers and speaking at institutions and rehabs keeps the memory of our past behavior green for us. There are countless stories of people who have slipped, thinking they would indulge just a little, only to end up dead within a few days. This addiction is a life-and-death condition that requires us to be serious about our recovery. We need to reaffirm our commitment each day by asking for our Higher Power's help in staying sober. At the end of the day we express our gratitude for another day in recovery.

Today I am learning to listen to the wisdom learned in recovery.

How many cares one loses when one decides not to be something but to be someone. —COCO CHANEL

An American visitor to the Himalayas tells how he was separated from his traveling companions for a few weeks. At one point he was standing alone, gazing up at Mount Everest, and his sense of identity suddenly dropped away. At that moment he stopped thinking of himself as an American or as a gay man. His sense of identity as a son, a brother and a lover slipped away from him. For a short time he saw himself as pure self. After this experience he realized that all the things he thought of as essential to his being were only peripheral. His true self was beyond description. He felt an immense connection to everything in the universe.

Is our own self-esteem tied up with a particular profession? Do we think of ourselves as a lawyer, doctor, dancer or fireman first? Are we endlessly striving to attain a higher social status or more titles on our office door?

The truth is we are pure spirit that inhabits a body. Our first task is to become a realized person, and all else will follow in good order. We carefully use our social, professional and familial roles as vehicles for spiritual realization making certain not to confuse our outward masks with our real essence.

Help me to remember that my life lived in love and service will be a happy and fruitful one.

February 21

As long as you are trying to be something other than what you actually are, your mind merely wears itself out. But if you say, "This is what I am, it is a fact that I am going to investigate and understand," then you can go beyond.   —J. KRISHNAMURTI

For much of our lives we lived in denial. We pretended that our drinking, drugging, overeating and other compulsions were not a problem. Trying to keep up the facade that everything was okay became a tedious chore. Most of our time was spent propping up the falsehoods that were the foundation of our disease. But eventually we no longer could lie to ourselves. Finally we had to admit the truth and face reality.

One of our great tasks in recovery is to dismantle the many barriers to the truth that we have erected over the years. Taking a Fourth Step inventory is the beginning of a lifelong search to discover our true selves. In the process we let go of artifice. Understanding and accepting who we really are lifts a great burden from us.

Self-acceptance has been a difficult struggle for most of us. Our energies have often been exhausted by feelings of guilt, shame and denial. Recovery enhances our ability to feel comfortable with all the aspects of our self, including our sexual identity.

**Today I will make a commitment to the truth,
knowing that growth and positive change
depend upon it.**

I don't have anything against work. I just figure, why deprive somebody who really loves it? —DOBIE GILLIS

Sometimes we find ourselves in dead-end jobs that do not engage our attention. Too often in this situation we cheat ourselves and our employer. We do not do our best, probably because we are working to fulfill somebody else's goals. When we are working to fulfill our own dreams, we embrace work with enthusiasm.

Maybe we don't know what we want to do. Perhaps we are at our present job by accident or because we thought it is what we "should be doing." Let us examine our motives. What are our goals in life? Are we going to lose precious time watching the clock and waiting for the next paycheck?

Whatever we do, we should learn to seek satisfaction in a job well done. Since we spend so much of our waking life at work, wouldn't it be nice to enjoy it? Finding what we are good at and pursuing our goals is one of the rewards of recovery.

I will work today toward fulfilling my dreams.

Most folks are about as happy as they make up their minds to be. —ABRAHAM LINCOLN

Bad things happen to everyone. We need to accept this fact if we are to move beyond complaining and self-pity. If a situation persists that causes us discomfort or unhappiness, perhaps it is time for an inventory. Do we take some pleasure in always feeling sorry for ourselves? Do we think that life has been unfair to us? A measured look at reality will tell us that there will always be someone worse off or better off than we are. Are our expectations unrealistic? Do we wallow in fantasies of wealth and fame instead of making an effort to do the best we can today?

Much of our depression came from the abuse of substances or self-destructive behavior. A Fourth Step inventory will uncover the causes of our discomfort and give us a realistic view of ourselves and the world around us. An inventory that is thorough will include our positive attributes. Now that we are embarked on a new way of life, we can become the people we always wanted to be. We can let go of old ideas that limited our outlook and kept us from living happy and fulfilling lives.

Let me remember that my response to people and things is my choice. Today I choose to emphasize the positive.

February 24

A healthy body is the bedchamber of the soul, a sick body is the soul's prison.　　　　—FRANCIS BACON

In the past we often abused our bodies. Perhaps we harmed ourselves through poor diet, drug and alcohol abuse, lack of sleep and little exercise. We became prey to disease. Our poor physical condition affected our mental processes.

When we come into recovery, we are advised to get a physical checkup. Then we plan a diet and exercise program that can restore us to health. It is a mistake to think that we can separate our physical recovery from the mental and spiritual progress we are making in this program. Science has shown that stress can weaken our immune systems and affect our health. To reduce stress we exercise and practice meditation daily. We get the proper amount of sleep—taking naps when necessary and learning to listen to our body when it tells us that we are tired. We take responsibility for our health and well-being—doing what is needed to stay in the best physical shape possible.

Today I will remember that my body is the temple of the spirit and worth respect and care.

February 25

There is no dependence that can be sure but dependence on one's self. —JOHN GAY

Many of us have spent years clinging to people for support or affirmation. We had no sense of ourselves as individuals. Our self-worth was determined by the opinion of others. Some of us were lost in unhealthy relationships. We made unreasonable demands on friends and lovers to satisfy our every need. As adults we sometimes clung to our parents in an immature way.

In this program we learn what healthy dependence is. Mutual dependence is one of the comforts of a relationship, but it must be tempered with a sense of one's own duties and self-worth. When our partner does not act the way we want, we do not pout or nag until we get our way. We check our attitude and expectations. Sometimes we have been overly dependent on others and wanted them to solve all of our problems. We blamed them when things did not turn out the way we wanted. Today we must take responsibility for our own life.

We turn away from excessive emotional and mental dependence on others. We abandon self-pity and self-deception. We seek balance in all of our relationships. Ultimately, dependence on our Higher Power is the surest path to true independence.

I will become more aware of my inner self as I strengthen my relationship to my Higher Power.

Amazing Grace! How Sweet The Sound!
That Saved A Wretch Like Me!
I Once Was Lost, But Now Am Found,
Was Blind But Now I See.　　　—JOHN NEWTON

Despair, loneliness and a sense of defeat plagued us before we entered this program. We felt trapped. Our lives had become miserable and unmanageable. People began to avoid us. Nothing we did seemed to turn out right. Our spirits withered and our horizons shrank. Our minds had become warped by obsessive behavior.

Perhaps in our bottom we simply cried out "Help" and the grace of our Higher Power descended upon us. It is a mystery why some of us receive this gift and others die or linger on in the limbo of addiction. Certainly we were not making any progress on our own.

Grace opens us up to the gift of recovery. We must not take it for granted. We keep renewing ourselves by attending meetings and working the Twelve Steps. We surrender our need to control everything. We learn to let go and relax.

Gratitude for the gift of recovery inspires us to share what we have been given. Let us look for opportunities to carry the message to others.

Today I will let the radiance of God's grace lead
me toward compassion and gratitude.

February 27

We simply had to be number one people to hide our deep-lying inferiorities. —BILL WILSON

False pride governed much of our lives. At the root of this pride was fear—fear that we would be judged harshly by others. To disguise our anxiety, we became contemptuous and disdainful. We were hard to please and had placed unreasonable expectations upon others. We took an arrogant delight in any of our good fortune. We tried to convince ourselves that we were better than others. Our pride led us to make serious mistakes. Our conceit prevented us from asking for help. We feared all competition and dreaded all rivals. When we hit our bottom, we were filled with shame and remorse.

Now that we are living life grounded in spiritual principles, we let go of selfish behavior. In time we develop humility. We stop trying to dominate others and learn to be an equal among equals. We recognize the value of people who are different from us and we learn from others. We use the principles of recovery as a guide in our relationships.

Today I will cultivate a loving and respectful attitude toward others.

February 28

"I can forgive, but I cannot forget" is only another way of saying I cannot forgive.

—HENRY WARD BEECHER

When we hold onto resentments, they turn inward and poison us. If we go through the motions of forgiveness but hold back on some level, we stifle our growth. It may take time, but we must make a genuine effort to forgive those who have harmed us. The best way to begin the process of forgiveness is to pray for the person we resent. We also look at our part in the situation and see if we need to make amends.

To let go of the past, we forgive ourselves as well. We take an inventory and acknowledge past errors. We then move on to a new way of life. Forgiveness can help heal and restore us. We look at the past, but we do not stare at it. Forgetting is good medicine. Once we have forgiven ourselves and others, we can practice giving greater love and compassion.

I ask my Higher Power for help in overcoming old resentments. I work the Steps in order to move forward into a new life.

Being gay can be an enormous childhood trauma, and that trauma can be a spur to creativity. I grew up believing that to be gay was unspeakably bad, and only in music could I overcome this difficulty and express the way I really felt. And people would applaud my displays of feeling without ever knowing what might be behind them. So it's like the way a pearl gets created: this grain of sand gets lodged inside and ends up producing a wonderful work of art.

—DAVID DEL TREDICI

The difficulties of growing up gay are enormous and separate us from other children. Early feelings of isolation, rejection and loneliness had a great effect upon us. We sensed that we were on the outside looking in. Often we developed a perspective on the world that enabled us to question the status quo.

We are a distillation of all our experiences. Our gayness is a primary influence. We can take all the childhood pain and suffering and transform it into a unique tool for bringing a new approach to everything we do.

I will examine both the positive and negative ways my sexual orientation has had an effect on me.

March 1

The promised land is the land where one is not.
—DENYS AMIEL

When we were active, we supposed that anywhere was better than where we were at the moment. Many of us kept moving from place to place thinking that was the solution to our problem. We blamed everything on the people around us and the circumstances of our daily lives.

In recovery we learn to live with ourselves. We look within when we are disturbed and try to locate the true source of our worry and anxieties. We ask our Higher Power for the help to squarely face the important things we have to deal with in our lives.

Inner discontent surfaces in all areas of our lives. We think about who we are not rather than who we are. Changing externals and acquiring things does not fix us. A gratitude list is a good tool to help us seize the moment and to look to the day at hand for satisfaction.

Today I will affirm the present by accepting reality and counting my blessings.

March 2

It is well to lie fallow for a while.
—MARTIN FARQUHAR TUPPER

Farmers plant certain crops in a field, plow it over and then let it lie unused for a period of time so that the nutrients can be restored to the soil. Likewise, the human mind requires some downtime to relax and make room for new thoughts and ideas.

In the past we escaped from the stress and rigors of daily life by misusing food, drugs, alcohol, sex or by being obsessively preoccupied with another person. Now we realize that these behaviors robbed us of our vitality.

Today we are leading full and productive lives. Sometimes we are so eager to make up for the time we wasted in the past that we do not set aside periods for rest and relaxation. Not every hour needs to be planned. Perhaps we can enjoy sleeping later than usual one morning or just walking aimlessly on a pleasant day. Spending time playing with a pet and acting silly is a good way to release our cares. Meditation is like giving the mind a leave of absence.

We also need vacations and holidays away from our regular routine. Our minds and bodies are similar to machines. If we run them constantly, they will break down. We return to our regular schedules after a time of inactivity with our batteries recharged, ready to do the best job we can.

Today I will recognize my need for rest and relaxation by setting aside some quiet time.

Character—the willingness to accept responsibility for one's own life—is the source from which self-respect springs. —JOAN DIDION

Character development begins early in life. The attributes and features that distinguish us as individuals are formed by a wide variety of influences, from family and friends to schools, and by the time we are adolescents, we have been molded in definite ways—both healthy and unhealthy.

Sometimes we have been affected negatively by our environment. Perhaps a drunken father, an overeating mother or a narrow-minded teacher transmitted inappropriate and negative messages. Everything that happened and how we reacted marked us. If we were not given clear moral guidelines early, we have difficulty as adults.

Before we got sober, we often acted improperly because we did not know better or because we were in the grip of our disease. Now we take responsibility for our behavior. By doing the Fourth Step, we discover our defects of character. In the Sixth Step we prepare to let these defects go and place our trust in a Higher Power to show us a better way. A sense of self-worth and dignity comes to us the longer we stay sober and continue to work the Steps.

Help me to remember that the forming of my character lies in my own hands.

Nowadays we don't think much of a man's love for an animal; we laugh at people who are attached to cats. But if we stop loving animals, aren't we bound to stop loving humans too? —ALEKSANDR SOLZHENITSYN

Most people who live in cities today are quite removed from nature. We rarely come into contact with animals, and when we do, we are often frightened by them. Our distance from animals causes us to ignore their importance. We occupy the same earth as they do, and each of us is a part of a larger system. Indifference to the fate of animals can lead to planetary imbalance.

Many people tell how something special was awakened in them when they became close to a cat, a dog or some other creature. Research shows that contact with animals has a positive, healing power on the elderly and the ill. Petting an animal lowers our blood pressure and produces an effect similar to meditation.

Animals relate to humans differently than we relate to each other, and our understanding is widened when we enter their world. They accept existence unquestionably—expressing their joy and sorrow openly. Relaxing with or watching an animal is a wonderful way to let go of our daily concerns.

Today I will remember my relation to all living creatures and do my best to show love and respect.

Scientists and mystics throughout history have realized that every human being is the carrier of complementary life energies—yin and yang, poetic and rational, feminine and masculine—that interact in everyone regardless of sex.　　　—JUNE SINGER

Because of cultural constraints or fear of rejection, many of us have suppressed aspects of our personalities. Some of us thought we had to act "butch" to gain acceptance, and we eliminated anything from our lives that might betray softness or vulnerability. Others imagined that because they loved men they had to assume a female persona to justify their desire. As healthy recovering men we accept ourselves as we are—affirming our right to fearlessly expose our true feelings. We impoverish our psychic well-being when we do not recognize that a wide range of impulses exists within each individual.

We explore the undeveloped aspects of our nature and take on new roles. We are not afraid to do "woman's work," nor do we limit ourselves by shirking the practical and the rough.

By avoiding labels, whether self-imposed or attached to us by others, we release the energies that allow us to realize our full human potential.

**Today I embrace and accept the totality
of my being.**

March 6

Time is but the stream I go a-fishing in.
—HENRY DAVID THOREAU

When we were young children, a summer afternoon seemed like an eternity. As we grow older, we wonder where time goes. How are we using our time? Are we just "killing" it, or are we spending it wisely? Do we mostly dwell on the past and daydream about the future?

The way we use our time will determine who and what we are. If we constantly gossip, we will become bitter and cynical. Spending hours in front of the TV will leave us passive and out of shape. If we isolate, we will end up forlorn and alone.

Today let us make a conscious decision to use our time rather than just letting things happen to us. Including a period of prayer and meditation centers us. Planning nutritious meals and exercising keeps us healthy. We strengthen our human connections by calling a friend in the fellowship or writing a letter.

We can neither stop nor rush time. Life has its own order and rhythm. There is a time for work, love, relaxation. Paying attention to our mental and physical states will tell us when it is time to slow down or to get moving. We savor the good moments and pray for patience and endurance during troubled times.

Today I will govern time, not be governed by it.

**Although the world is full of suffering, it is also full
of the overcoming of it.** —HELEN KELLER

It is only natural to feel sadness over disappointment
and loss. However, if we cannot shake these feelings
and we sink into despair, we might find that we are
suffering from depression. We often discover in recovery that our addictions did mask a deep depression.
Sometimes this malady had been with us all of our
lives, but we did not have the necessary information to
recognize it.

Some of the symptoms of depression are a loss of
interest and pleasure in our jobs, sex or family lives.
Other indicators are difficulty in remembering, concentrating or sleeping. Perhaps we have lost our appetites
or have turned to overeating. Sometimes we cry for no
reason or have long periods of feeling blue. Other
warning signals are unusual irritability, an attitude of
indifference or a loss of self-esteem.

If we suffer from any of these symptoms for more
than a few weeks, we should seriously consider getting
professional help. Depression is a treatable disease and
we do not have to suffer. We must not let embarrassment or shame keep us from getting help.

**If I am having a rough time, I will ask for help
and guidance.**

I wash everything on the gentle cycle. It is much more humane.   —UNKNOWN

Life flows more smoothly when we are gentle with ourselves and others. Overworking leaves no room for us to rest or relax and causes us to burn out. If we are harsh and critical toward people or behave ourselves in a loud and annoying manner, others will avoid us. If we are rigid in our spiritual search, the truth will elude us.

At whatever task we work, we try to pace ourselves so we achieve harmony and balance. A kind, amiable manner dispels fear and timidity and draws others to us. Speaking in a quiet, dignified way makes certain that our voice is heard. If someone has made a mistake, we do not scold. Keeping an open mind, we are courteous to those who differ with us.

We are gentle with our bodies and our environment. We try to be alert for ways to reduce the wear and tear we inflict on our planet. We move through the world as though we were wearing a loose garment.

Today I will carry myself in a calm and poised manner so that I may contribute to the world's supply of peace and harmony.

I've always thought that the stereotype of the dirty old man is really the creation of a dirty young man who wants the field to himself. —HUGH DOWNS

Our society focuses on youth, excluding those in their middle or later years. Magazines, movies and television bombard us with images of beautiful young people. On one level we have all internalized the idea that the world belongs only to the young and the rich.

As gay men we must be especially wary of buying these stereotypes. We get locked into categorizing people according to physical type and cannot enjoy the company of or make love to any but that kind of person. In doing so we close ourselves off to many exciting possibilities. Some young people are insulted, rather than flattered, when an older person makes an advance toward them. On the other hand, many gay men only find those younger than themselves attractive.

We need to examine where our ideas come from and how much we are conditioned by the world around us. Do we regard our lovers as trophies? Are our emotional needs not being fulfilled because we have a limited outlook? Do we judge others because we do not approve of their choices?

Today I will open my heart to the endless possibilities for meaningful and loving relationships.

Dogmas and definitions rationally insisted upon are inevitably hindrances, not aids, to religious meditation, since no one's sense of the presence of God can be anything more than a function of his own spiritual capacity. —JOSEPH CAMPBELL

If a council of elders in this fellowship convened to define our image of God, there would be bitter arguments and constant strife. Our conception of our Higher Power grows out of our experience in life. For each of us this is different. No one can force us to adhere to something that is not an integral part of our spiritual quest.

Our search for truth leads us to a course of action that is relevant to our circumstances today. We can build on the ideals of the past, but each person investigates the mysteries of life on his own. A combination of trust, independent observation, reason and critical thinking are the tools we need on our search. Our conclusions will guide us along our spiritual path.

As we practice the Twelve Steps, pray and meditate, and give service to others, we develop a faith in a power greater than ourselves. Ideologies and theologies do not trouble us as we discover that living in the moment, *One Day at a Time*, draws us closer to a mystic understanding of this cosmos we inhabit.

Today I will pray for the flexibility that leads to true understanding.

March 11

The collective unconscious has contents and modes of behavior that are more or less the same everywhere and in all individuals.
—C. J. JUNG

Sometimes we get so caught up in our individual wants and needs that we forget we are part of a larger whole. We have responsibilities toward our families, friends and communities. We are part of an interconnected system. Cultural differences can hide the fact that all humans have the same basic needs for love, meaning and a sense of purpose. When we lose touch with this reality, we diminish our human potential.

Our perspective changes when we contemplate nature and consider our relationship to the rest of planet. Do we have the right to pollute? Do our needs supersede those of other living creatures? Do we treat our environment with the respect it deserves? Are we part of the solution?

We sometimes become consumed with our daily activities and neglect our spiritual life. Today we practice setting aside time for prayer and meditation so that we can keep in touch with those eternal truths that sustain us.

Today I will try to be a responsible traveler through time and space on this wonderful planet.

Every time a homosexual denies the validity of his feelings or restrains himself from expressing them, he does a small hurt to himself. —PETER FISHER

We are told in this program that we are only as sick as our secrets. One of those secrets may be the fact that we are gay. Coming out, whether before or after recovery, is a major step and can cause much fear and stress.

When we do make the decision to come out, we often gain a sense of relief. At first we may just tell one friend or a family member. Some people will reject us, others will be indifferent, and some will be supportive.

Once we are out, we can seek fulfillment of our social, sexual and emotional needs that were stifled by being in the closet. At gay meetings, we have a ready-made support group which understands and shares our concerns. As time goes by, we come out on even deeper levels: at work, politically and in the larger social community. When we stop hiding, we take away the power that secrecy has to prevent growth. The less playacting we do, the better it is for us. We accept our identity and take pride in it. We then integrate our gay identity with all the other aspects of our selves.

Today I will reject the secrecy and shame of the closet and come out on one more level.

March 13

My only regret in life is that I am not someone else.
—WOODY ALLEN

Are we in danger of daydreaming our life away,
wishing we had been born elsewhere, to different
parents or in another time? How futile! Many of us
have spent a great deal of time saying "if only" this or
that were so. We absolved ourselves of responsibility
for the quality of our lives because we perceived that
we were handed a raw deal by fate. We found ourselves
unable to deal with life's realities. Our vision was
distorted by the lens of envy and self-hate.

In recovery we have the opportunity to be someone
else other than the addicted, compulsive person we
were. A clear mind and a newfound sense of purpose
allow us to set goals and work toward self-fulfillment.
Through our working the Steps, speaking with our
sponsor and our regular attendance at meetings, the
gap between our ideal and our reality narrows. In time
we come to love and accept ourselves for who we are.
Our low self-esteem is replaced with a healthy ability
to assess both our good and bad qualities.

**I give thanks that I am now becoming the person
I always wanted to be.**

March 14

We are here on earth to do good to others. What the others are here for I don't know. —W. H. AUDEN

Sometimes we get so caught up in ourselves that we begin to act selfishly and ignore those around us. We think that we must keep what we have for ourselves, whether it be knowledge, money or skills. We fear that the supply of everything is limited and that we will not get our share. Some of us hoard things physically, while others rarely give of themselves on a personal or public level.

This narrow view doesn't get us very far. When we close ourselves up and refuse to share our abundance, our world shrinks and we live tiny, fearful lives.

The paradox is that the more we give, the more we get. As we give of ourselves, we open space inside to receive. When we help another, it makes us feel good. Every opportunity to share is a chance to grow and learn. In giving we receive benefits that are immeasurable.

Let me remember that the love and the good I have received cannot be stored and are best acknowledged when they overflow to others.

Another unsettling element in modern art is that common symptom of immaturity, the dread of doing what has been done before. —EDITH WHARTON

We are given suggestions when we come into the fellowship about how to work the program. These suggestions are the accumulated wisdom of those who have gone before us.

Sometimes, out of stubbornness, we decide these suggestions do not apply to us. Some people have come to regret ignoring the suggestion not to get involved romantically during their first year of recovery. In doing so, they had difficulty establishing a relationship with themselves and ran the risk of grave emotional turmoil. Others felt that certain Steps did not apply to them. Still others thought they could flirt with temptation and associate with people who were active or frequent places that were slippery.

We need to acknowledge that our old ways did not work. If they had, we would not have come to this program. We try a new way of life and have the faith to take a chance. We use our common sense but do not close our minds to the practical knowledge offered us. We do not have to reinvent the wheel. The path to sobriety has been trodden by many before us, and their experience, strength and hope will guide us in the right direction. When we let go of our willfulness and follow suggestions, startling changes occur that make us grateful we could step back and listen to others.

◇

Today help me to keep an open mind.

March 16

If a tree dies, plant another in is place. —LINNAEUS

What will be our legacy when we are gone? Will people remember us as mean spirited and closed-minded or as persons of goodwill and love? We are not here just for our own self-enrichment. We are a part of the great cycle of life.

Today we ask ourselves how we can contribute to the world around us by adding a measure of good. Planting a tree, even though we will never see it fully grown, is an act of service and of faith. We can cheerfully volunteer to replace hospitality people at our home group when a new term opens up. If our parents have died, we can help to keep the family together by hosting a reunion. If we have lost friends to illness and death, we are careful not to shut out new people. Cultivating new friends is a lifelong activity.

Renewal is a basic building block of life. There is a powerful urge in all of us to leave the world a better place than we found it. Realizing that we are part of a spiritual chain that links all created matter helps us to show respect to the environment and those who inhabit it. Let us use our resources wisely. A simple thing, like not littering, can be as important as saving a species. When we respect the environment, we are respecting ourselves.

Today help me to work for harmony with the world around me.

March 17

Men talk of "finding God," but no wonder it is difficult; He is hidden in the darkest hiding-place, your heart. You yourself are a part of Him.

—CHRISTOPHER MORLEY

This program speaks of "God as we understand Him." This novel concept allows a degree of freedom that is rarely found. We are not constrained to believe any dogma or adhere to any particular notion of the divine. Our search for communion with our Higher Power is not limited by preordained boundaries, and we can initiate our contact with the spiritual without any pressure.

We look into ourselves to discover who we really are and in the process begin to know God. As we grow and change, our idea of who and what God is will alter.

When we were active, we surrendered to our "lower selves." Now that we are recovering we align ourselves with our "higher selves." It is important to let go of old negative images of God and become comfortable with a power greater than ourselves who is a friend. When our Higher Power touches our heart, we feel as one with the universe.

Today I will reflect on my Higher Power and how my life has been touched by spiritual gifts.

March 18

The first great gift we can bestow on others is good example.
        —THOMAS MORELL

When we first came into this program, we were amazed at the people we encountered. They seem so healthy and full of joy. We wanted to find out how they got that way. We learned that those who came before us owed their success to working the Steps.

We seek out people we admire and develop a network of recovering friends. We find a sponsor whom we respect and ask for help. We develop a relationship with our sponsor and become open and willing to learn a new way of living. When we are troubled by something, we find out how others have handled similar situations. We listen at meetings and learn from other people's mistakes and successes.

As we grow in recovery, it is our responsibility to pass along what we have learned. We reach out and share our experience with the newcomer. The best way we can be of service is by being a good example. Others will be attracted to us naturally, and we will become part of a larger circle of love and healing.

**Today I will practice the principles of the
program to the best of my ability.**

March 19

If you are gay, all you have to do is to live a lie, to hide, to refuse to affirm or to be yourself, to choose non-being and non-loving—a living death.
—REPRESENTATIVE GERRY STUDDS

As gay men we pay a great price for being who we are. Growing up in the shadows, hiding our true identity, takes a great emotional toll. It is difficult for anyone who has not experienced this to understand what we have suffered. We are told, be gay, but don't flaunt it. In other words, stay in the closet. We are told to negate our very being.

Thankfully, we have the safety of gay meetings at which to express who we really are and share our deepest concerns with like-minded souls. As recovering people we have an obligation to respect and support our fellow recovering brothers. We especially need to avoid gossip, backbiting and personality conflict within the fellowship. If we are not for ourselves, then who is for us?

Our healing from stigmatization and oppression comes through working the Steps. We are given the confidence and self-respect that we need to affirm our place in this world. As we grow stronger in the conviction of our worth, we reach out and nurture those who need our help.

Help me to love myself as a gay man and help others recognize their own worth.

March 20

Spring has returned. The earth is like a child that knows poems.
—RAINER MARIA RILKE

By the end of the winter our bodies are tired of the cold, fatigued from wearing heavy coats and frustrated by being shut up indoors. Our weary spirits long for sunshine and movement. When the first burst of spring appears, our hearts leap with hope at the coming renewal of the earth. Nature calls us. We marvel at the beauty of our world and long to be outdoors.

This is a good time to think about our part in keeping this a safe and healthy planet. This new season reminds us that we are connected to everything in our environment. We have an obligation to make a positive contribution to the earth and its well-being. Planting a garden, cleaning a vacant lot or educating ourselves about ecology help us to discover our place within the universe.

Spring is also an excellent time to take another inventory and renew our commitment to the program. The new season refreshes us as we express our gratitude for the second life we have been given in recovery.

The stirring of new life creates a sense of awe and wonder in me. Today I strive to be in harmony with my environment.

March 21

Trust in God, clean house and give it away.

—ANONYMOUS

Sometimes we make things more difficult than they need be. We waste hours or days worrying about the outcome of something over which we have no control. There are times when we get ourselves worked up into a lather over something only to find that it was not important. We rush around, chasing after phantoms, and lose sight of our real needs. Perhaps we are addicted to drama and are unable to allow an unpleasant thing to pass without doing battle.

This is a simple program for complicated people. Often the best thing to do is slow down and relax. Prayer and meditation develop our trust in our Higher Power. The answers to all of our problems will be found as our spiritual life grows.

When we are troubled, it is best to keep busy. By cleaning the house or doing other physical chores we dissipate much of our tension and anxiety. Helping others also goes a long way toward letting us forget our own concerns, whether large or small.

We create a life of dignity and serenity as we learn to simplify things. When we focus on the basics, we gain clarity and give ourselves more time to enjoy the wonders of creation.

Today I will do my best to keep things simple.

To love oneself is the beginning of a lifelong romance.
—OSCAR WILDE

I n recovery we can truly begin to love ourselves—not in a narcissistic way but by an honest recognition of our self-worth. This also applies to feeling good about being gay. Growing up, we were surrounded by negative messages about our sexuality. Often we internalized the hatred around us and became self-loathing. Some of us were taunted, called names and physically attacked. We saw that society did not value difference, so we donned masks and hid our true selves.

Initially our addiction provided a release from our fears, and we felt somewhat better about ourselves. But as our disease progressed, this release was usually followed by a physical or emotional hangover. We retreated into fear and depression.

Recovery has taught us our true worth. We know that the old Gay Liberation slogan "Gay is Good" is indeed true. In our inventories we include a list of our positive traits. We surround ourselves with people who respect and nurture us. We gently let time be the healer. Self-love is a process.

Today I will affirm my worth as a human being and a gay man.

The intoxication of anger, like that of the grape,
shows us to others, but hides us from ourselves.
—MALABAR PROVERB

When we act out our anger, we usually are masking
our true feelings. Instead of throwing a temper
tantrum, we might better ask ourselves: Has someone
hurt my feelings? Am I disappointed? Did I let myself
down? Am I holding someone up to impossible expectations? Am I wrong and don't want to admit it?

If we want to uncover the true cause of a troubled
situation, we stop blaming whatever or whoever let us
down and we cool off. Anger darkens the mind and is
the enemy of understanding. Anger is like a momentary
madness, and if we do not control it, it will control us.
The greatest remedy for anger is delay.

Even if we are right, our position will suffer if we
defend it in the heat of anger. The program asks us to
consider that people who have harmed us may be
spiritually sick. The best course is to pray for the
person who has offended us and show them the same
compassion we would a sick friend. We take our own
inventory, not others'.

**Help me to take a kindly and tolerant view of
everyone, especially those who have offended me.**

March 24

There is a law in life: when one door closes, another opens.　　　—JOHANN WOLFGANG VON GOETHE

Change is often painful and frightening. We may feel a loss of control and be tempted to revert to self-destructive behavior to mask our feelings. Perhaps how we react to change is the problem. Do we try to cling to old ways and patterns when they no longer work? Are we unwilling to admit that a once close friend has grown distant? Are we so stuck in our routine that we close ourselves to surprise or new possibilities?

This program teaches us to be less controlling. It opens us up to the energy of life and helps us to move into the unknown. Once we let go of the past, we can move on and accept things as they are. We take care of today's tasks. We set aside our fear of change and move with the flow. We welcome the new as an opportunity for continued growth and learning.

Today I will move with the flow and remember that to resist change is to die spiritually.

If wrinkles must be written upon our brow, let them not be written upon our heart. The spirit should never grow old. —JAMES GARFIELD

Many of us had terrible fears about aging. We dreaded the changes that occur in our bodies. We feared being rejected or alone. Ours is a youth-oriented society, and gay men are not exempt from this obsession. We placed great value on physical appearance. As we grew older, some of us became frantic. We foolishly tried to copy every new fashion, hoping to be included and accepted. Because we have suffered so many rejections by society, the thought of being rejected by other gay men was unbearable.

Today we are aware that many young people, gay or straight, judge people superficially. We accept this reality and we do not waste our time pursuing the unavailable. In recovery we surround ourselves with people who are supportive and loving. We reach out to others and accept them as they are.

We do the best we can to maintain our physical condition but accept that aging is a part of life. We do not deny ourselves the fruits of growing older. Whatever our age, we see that we are a part of a beautiful tapestry. Keeping a fresh and open attitude allows us to fully participate in all the wonders around us.

I thank my Higher Power for the gift of life and my place in it.

March 26

Observation, not old age, brings wisdom.
—PUBLILIUS SYRUS

Sometimes we race about so madly that we do not see what is passing under our own eyes. Are we so self-centered that we do not notice what is going on around us? Are we indifferent to the plight of those less fortunate? Do we care only for our own advancement? Are we so isolated that we have become insensitive to our friends and families? Have we allowed ourselves to become the victim of abuse for so long that we do not even notice it anymore?

Today we begin to train ourselves to observe accurately everything around us. When we open our eyes and ears, our universe is expanded. We do not always have to participate. We can remain silent or refrain from action. We sharpen our powers of observation as we listen to others in the program and watch them grow and change.

Developing our powers of observation will open up a world of wonder and enduring pleasures. As we open up more and more to the whole range of life, our experiences become richer and more fulfilling.

Help me to pay attention to people and things around me.

Acceptance appears to be a state of mind in which the individual accepts, rather than rejects or resists; he is able to take things in, to go along with, to cooperate and be receptive. —DR. HARRY M. TIEBOUT

We first learn acceptance in this program when we admit our powerlessness over addiction, other people and circumstances. We let go of trying to dominate and control everything. We are freed from futile struggles and focus on what is important. Once we learn acceptance, much of the strain and conflict in our lives disappears.

Acceptance does not mean we submit to a degrading experience. We have the right to correct any abuse that we can change. It does mean that we do not struggle against the facts or reject reality. Progress comes when we stop trying to control the uncontrollable. We relinquish self-will and embrace a new way of life. We cooperate with our Higher Power by being open and receptive. We give up fighting people and things. In surrender there is victory.

Knowing that the path to freedom lies in nonresistance, I will practice acceptance without reservation.

Out of comradeship can come and will come a happy life for all. —HEYWOOD BROUN

By nature many of us tend to isolate. We become fearful and withdraw from people. Sometimes we get so caught up in the pursuit of our careers that we forget the simple joy of fellowship for its own sake. Our mental and spiritual health is enhanced when we reach out and make contact with others. We must be careful not to limit our circle of friends and acquaintances too narrowly.

Today we can say hello to someone we often see but never speak to or go to coffee or a movie with someone new. We might want to call an old friend we haven't seen in a while and make a date to get together.

Relaxing and having fun with other people adds an extra dimension to our lives. Now and then we just want to "hang out" and enjoy the company of friends for no other reason than that we love them and enjoy being with them.

Let me be open to making full and loving contact with others.

There are some people that if they don't know, you can't tell 'em. —LOUIS ARMSTRONG

Trying to reason or communicate with certain people is just not possible. Perhaps we have a friend who is drinking or drugging and does not want to hear the message offered by this program. We might find ourselves in an argument with a homophobe and suddenly realize that no amount of talk is going to change this person's mind. Maybe a relationship is bogging down because one of the partners refuses to grow.

We have to learn when to cut our losses. Sometimes we find ourselves in a no-win situation and are wasting our time. If so, we should try to gracefully disengage. We do not have to have the last word. A dignified retreat is better than a bloody skirmish. On occasion it is better to say nothing than to add to the negativity.

Today let me pray for those I am in conflict with and move on.

A real book is not one that we read, but one that reads us. —W H. AUDEN

Recovery makes us more receptive to learning. Because we practice listening to those with whom we share recovery, we are attuned to important messages when we encounter them.

Going to Step meetings is extremely beneficial. At least once during the reading of the Step, something will speak directly to a past or present situation. Sometimes we hear something read and we will experience the shock of recognition. A truth about ourselves is revealed that expands our world view.

Some people worry that program literature is equivalent to brainwashing. Others have commented that perhaps our brains need a washing. Immersing ourselves in program literature will give us a new perspective on life and help steer us toward our goal of being happy, joyous and free. In our reading we encounter the wisdom of those who have gone before us. Their struggles and joys can illuminate the path of recovery and make the journey one of adventure and wonderment.

Today I will read something which will further my recovery and uplift my spirit.

March 31

Moderate lamentation is the right of the dead; excessive grief the enemy to the living.
—WILLIAM SHAKESPEARE

The death of a friend, lover, sibling or parent can trigger unexpected emotions. It is difficult for us to accept the fact that life can never be the same again. Although change is a basic fact of life, we still feel empty, and the pain can be overwhelming. At times like this, the future can seem grim. Allowing ourselves to grieve is therapeutic. It is proper to grieve and shed tears for those who have died. It cleanses the soul and helps us to say good-bye.

Intense feelings of hopelessness and loss can cause despair. Rather than trying to handle these feelings alone, we should seek help. Feelings of grief do not leave quickly. Mourning is a process that can take months or years.

One death can remind us of other deaths. Our own mortality comes sharply into focus. No matter how hard we try to stay away from sickness or accident, we will someday die. Contemplation of our own death helps us to commune with our Higher Power.

Death can draw us closer to the living. We begin to value others more. Living one day at a time takes on real meaning in the face of death.

Let me have the courage to grieve and express my feelings as I move forward on life's journey.

April 1

To really know someone is to have loved and hated him in turn. —MARCEL JOUHANDEAU

Most murders are committed by people in an intimate relationship with their victim. In the majority of cases the crime is committed under the influence of drugs or alcohol. Passions run high among lovers, friends and families. The closer we are to someone, the stronger our emotional connection becomes. We expect more of those we are intimate with, and if they fail, we are embarrassed. If they say something silly, we feel it reflects on us.

Because we are so attached, we are sometimes afraid of losing our identity. This is particularly true of two gay men who are lovers. We need to take special care to preserve our individuality. Each person should be free to spend some time away from the other, either relaxing, seeing old friends or cultivating an interest.

We have a similar relationship with our parents. We try to excel to gain their approval. Yet we are often afraid of surpassing their achievements, fearful that we will make them insecure and humiliate them.

By working the Steps, we will be able to accept the moments of emotional turmoil common to any intimate relationship. We take special care to be gentle and loving to those near and dear to us.

Today I will practice restraint and self-discipline. I will extend loving thoughts to all those I am close to.

April 2

Problems are only opportunities in work clothes.
                                              —HENRY J. KAISER

P roblems never arrive on schedule. They usually arise when we least expect them. If we allow these problems to overwhelm us, our spirit shrinks and we lose an opportunity to learn. When we respond to a challenge by using the tools of this program, we often discover that we are stronger than we imagined. Faced with adversity, we draw on our inner resources. We might also be surprised to find that help can come from unexpected quarters, such as a stranger or someone we thought did not care for us.

Often, a problematic situation sends a message that something is wrong with our attitude or behavior. It gives us hints about where we need to make adjustments and can spur us on to action to prevent a repetition. Our problems only get worse if we deny them or are unwilling to take action. In times of calamity or great difficulty we also learn our limits and how powerless we are over people, places and things.

Once we have squarely faced a dilemma, we can take the necessary steps to cure the situation. We then let go and turn the results over to our Higher Power.

Help me to face any obstacle and look at it as an opportunity to grow.

April 3

Finality is death. Perfection is finality. Nothing is perfect. There are lumps in it.   —JAMES STEPHENS

Sometimes we think we can carve a moment of time into stone. We don't want things to ever be different, and just when we think we have mastered life, something comes along that makes us realize we were only on a plateau. We will be striving to improve ourselves until the day we die.

Like an artist working a piece of clay, we are always molding and shaping ourselves. Some lumps will be more difficult to smooth out than others. In recovery we have discovered the challenge that goes with change. In every situation there is a lesson to be learned.

The only thing we can do perfectly on a daily basis is the First Step. *One Day at a Time* we can stay away from a drink, a drug, codependent behavior or sexual compulsion. We accept our humanity and do the best we can each day. If we step back and look at ourselves, we see that we have assets and flaws—like everyone else. No one is perfect. We can strive for excellence but must accept that we cannot achieve perfection.

I will be gentle with myself, accepting each day as it comes.

April 4

Talk not of wasted affection! Affection never was wasted. —HENRY WADSWORTH LONGFELLOW

It is so easy to forget to take the time to show our love and regard for the people in our lives.

When our lover leaves for work in the morning, we can give him a warm embrace and a kiss. In the evening, a foot massage will show how much we appreciate his being there. Giving flowers, preparing his favorite dish or listening attentively to his problems and concerns are all tokens of our deep affection.

We show our friends how much they matter to us. We make opportunities to say something kind or to draw attention to their good points. We can express our fondness by always being warm and loving—we take the time to be of help, do a favor or give emotional support.

Sometimes we are so close to members of our families that we take them for granted. We can demonstrate our love by giving a big hug, remembering a birthday or running an errand.

Many people in our lives touch us—the stranger at a meeting, the old friend from college, the courteous clerk at a store or the teacher who gives us extra attention. Today we make a list of all the people who bring happiness into our lives and try to return to them a little more of ourselves.

Today I will say "I love you" to those close to me and send loving thoughts to all the people in my life.

April 5

God is an intelligible sphere whose center is everywhere and circumference is nowhere.
—THE BOOK OF THE TWENTY-FOUR PHILOSOPHERS

Science has reaffirmed the ancient truth taught by all mystics: that we are not separate from anyone or anything in all creation. To remain aware of this immense reality is difficult, so the conscious mind funnels this information to us in small amounts and occasional insights. Sometimes we are aware of the larger spiritual dimension, but most of the time we are completely caught up in the affairs of the world and the particularity of our egos.

It is an illusion that God is somewhere separate from us. Our Higher Power resides within us. The laws that apply to the cosmos are the same laws that guide our daily existence.

Have we limited our spiritual search to one day a week? Perhaps we forget about such matters till we are at a meeting. Do we separate the spiritual from the political, social and business aspects of our lives? Do we forget our common humanity with our brothers and sisters? Have we mistreated or snubbed someone because we thought they were less important than us? Are we indifferent to the environment?

Today we have a choice. We can follow a narrow, selfish course or live a life of spiritual awareness.

Help me to realize my spiritual link to my Higher Power and all the wondrous manifestations of creation.

April 6

My government gave me the medal of honor for killing many men and they gave me a dishonorable discharge for loving one.
—LIEUTENANT LEONARD MATLOVICH

It is sometimes difficult to express the love we hold for another man. Growing up in a society that devalues our existence can prevent us from openly expressing our true feelings. The pressure to conform sometimes warps and twists our personalities, and we lose touch with our most basic and decent impulses.

The prejudices and oppression of society at large have lessened somewhat in certain areas in recent years, but we still have a long way to go toward full social acceptance. Because we have internalized society's homophobia, we must be careful not to believe the negative messages that continue to be heaped on us.

Sometimes the first place we see men acting toward each other in a loving manner is in the rooms of recovery. We find in these rooms a safe space where we can learn to act honestly in a loving way. We come to know that "real men" can love each other physically, emotionally and spiritually. Our recovery becomes more solid when we recognize our self-worth and tune out the lies and distortions we grew up hearing about gay people.

Today I will affirm myself and be loving toward all of God's creations.

Trust that still, small voice that says, "This might work and I'll try it." —DIANE MARIECHILD

T aking the first step in any new venture is always the scariest. We repeatedly go over the various options available to us. Often fear holds us back and sometimes paralyzes us. For years our addictions kept us living in terror, and our lives shrank because we were consumed by dread of the unknown. We had to know the outcome of everything before we could act. Afraid of risks, we stayed with the familiar even if it meant being unhappy or unfulfilled.

Perhaps we did not apply for a new job because we thought we weren't good enough, or didn't ask someone out for a date because we thought we would be rejected. When we allowed fear to stop us from trying something new, we often regretted what might have been. Today whenever we are gripped with panic or are worried about the consequences of a particular action, we can stop, calm ourselves and turn to our Higher Power for guidance. At such moments we remember that we have taken the Third Step. A prayer asking for direction and help will give us the confidence we need to take action.

Today I release my doubts and fears. I form the habit of making giant swings into faith.

April 8

Perhaps the new sexual abstinence will lead to new forms of gay life. Now time is available (indeed is required) to elaborate the arts of courtship.
—EDMUND WHITE

Most gay men never developed the art of courtship, since sex was so readily available. We cruised the bars, baths and byways of the gay world with a devotion to youth, pleasure and beauty. This was exhilarating and, for a time, liberating.

Circumstances have forced a change in the way we relate sexually. No longer is it responsible to jump into bed with someone without first knowing something about them and setting certain boundaries. This can be awkward when we are not used to such behavior. Learning new ways takes time.

We must shift our emphasis from immediate gratification to more subtle modes of communication. Our fears of intimacy and dependence on fantasy need to be overcome if we hope to deepen our relationships. Getting to know a person and revealing ourselves to them takes patience and consideration. If we allow the process to happen, the rewards will be great.

Today I am grateful for a new way of life that leads me to a deeper understanding of myself and others.

April 9

The rose and the thorn and sorrow and gladness are linked together.   —SAADI

When we were active, we tried to manipulate our feelings so that we would feel good all the time. When we succeeded, we tried to recreate the same effect. This usually backfired, but we vainly repeated our efforts. Trying not to feel any uncomfortable feelings consumed much of our energy.

In recovery we learn that we can have several feelings all at once. Some are joyful, some are painful. Trying to sort them out can be confusing. Someone can die and we are sad yet relieved that their suffering is over. We might be glad for a friend's success yet be envious as well. We can feel regret for time wasted when we were active yet look back with nostalgia at some of the exciting moments we experienced before recovery.

Learning to accept the ambivalence inherent in life is a sign of emotional maturity. We may not like what we are feeling, but we can be confident that we have the strength to meet any challenge. Our feelings are like the many colored threads of a tapestry—they are all needed to complete the picture.

Instead of trying to control my feelings today, I will go with the flow and just watch them. Let me look for any lessons that might be learned or signals that may need heeding.

You must forget everything traditional that you have learned about God, perhaps even that word itself.
—PAUL TILLICH

Most of us grew up thinking of God as an old man with a beard who was punishing, angry and jealous—much like a stern parent who sits in judgment of us. Because we were often angry and upset with this idea of God, we might need to discard it completely.

Recovery frees us to explore our inner self and choose our own Higher Power. We might modify the idea of God we grew up with or we might come up with a completely new notion. This process takes time, and we may go through several permutations before we settle on a concept of God that works for us. The important thing is that this Higher Power will spring from the ground of our being.

We will each come to our own understanding regarding our Higher Power. "God" means many different things to the people in this program. It is important that we respect the right of others to believe in what works for them. It is also essential that we do not try to impose our beliefs on others.

As a recovering gay man, I know that I can choose a Higher Power that affirms and loves me.

April 11

Unless certain attitudes change there is no way for me to function in this society doing what I want to do. If some of us don't take on the oppressive labels and publicly prove them wrong, we'll stay trapped by the stereotypes for the rest of our lives. —DAVE KOPAY

If we are to be mature gay men, we must stand up and be counted. Are we riding on others' coattails? Are we unwilling to take the necessary risks to achieve social change but still desirous of reaping the rewards?

It takes courage to advocate what we believe in. However, there are times in our lives when we are called on to defend certain principles that affirm and proclaim our basic identity. When we do not, we live narrow, shrunken lives, denying ourselves our full potential.

If we depend on other people to secure our rights for us, we might never get them. Sometimes the struggle requires us to speak up when we would rather be silent. We remind ourselves that we are not alone. We have the support of other struggling gay men and women. In addition, the strength we receive from our recovery group gives us an extra boost when we face a world that might not understand us.

I ask my Higher Power to be my guide as I take a stand for what is right.

April 12

Living with a saint is more grueling than being one.
—ROBERT NEVILLE

In our enthusiasm for this program, we sometimes can become preachy and rigid. We forget we cannot write the script for someone else's life. Although ours is a path that has worked for us, we need to remember that each person must work out his own destiny. There is no single path for everyone.

If we wish to attract people to our way of life we teach by good example. If someone is meant to be in recovery, they will find their way in time. Meanwhile we show love and compassion to those who are still suffering. When a person we love is drinking, drugging, eating, gambling or acting out in any other way, we carry the message but we do not harangue, deride or condemn that person. Such behavior will only fuel their denial and drive them deeper into their problem. No one responds well to judgmental lectures. Instead of speaking about their behavior, we share our experience, strength and hope.

Today I will do my best to carry the message of this program and turn the results over.

April 13

If you want a quality, act as if you already had it.
—WILLIAM JAMES

Coming into this fellowship exposes us to a whole new way of life. We see people living by a set of principles rather than acting on impulse or following their emotions. At first we are bewildered and think we will never be able to live up to the standards of the program. Then we learn the truth of the old saying "bring the body and the mind will follow."

If we are unused to giving service or think it is beneath us, we learn to volunteer to help make the coffee or go pick up the literature from the central office. Setting up chairs is a good antidote to arrogance and pride.

Perhaps we are in the habit of lying. *One Day at a Time* we act as if we are honest people. Soon we prefer the truth to dishonesty. It is possible we are ashamed of our sexual identity. We reverse this feeling of shame by being as open and honest as we possibly can about who we are.

"Acting as if" gives us time to learn what the real thing is. If we move in the direction we want to go, before too long we will find ourselves becoming the people we always wanted to be.

Today I will focus on one aspect of my character and work on any blockages to progress I may find.

April 14

Reproduction and children and the promise of an afterlife are utilized by some as magical devices to cope with the fear of death. To many, the homosexual, who does not appear to be wearing these amulets, evokes this fear.

—DR. GEORGE WEINBERG

Once Allen Ginsberg had the opportunity to father a child with a woman friend. He thought about it and decided not to because he realized that it was his ego he wanted to perpetuate. Many people do not feel fulfilled unless they have children. This is a remnant of the biological imperative to pass one's genes on to the next generation.

Today, with an overpopulated planet and strained resources, fewer, not more, children are needed. Perhaps the best way to satisfy the parental urge is to adopt one of the many unwanted children who are cast off each day. We should question our motives before bringing another person into being.

Gay people do not need to justify their existence by reproducing. Perhaps destiny has meant us to be childless and free of that responsibility so that we can focus on our spiritual progress.

Today I will be alert to the possibilities of being a caregiver.

April 15

We have a new employer. If we take care of God's business he will take care of ours.
—THE BIG BOOK OF ALCOHOLICS ANONYMOUS

The causes of many of our economic woes are toxic attitudes toward work and money. Our low self-esteem tells us we have no right to enjoy what we do for a living. We equate work with drudgery and end up punching a time clock, hoping that retirement will let us do the things we really want to do. Fear of poverty often keeps us chained to dead-end jobs that offer no fulfillment or creativity.

One of the Promises states that if we work the Steps, fear of economic insecurity will leave us. We will come to believe that a power greater than ourselves is looking out for us. We bring a spiritual outlook into economic matters. Money is a form of energy, a part of the movement of the universe. When we are in proper harmony with the flow of life, our economic needs will be provided for.

Another Promise tells us that we will intuitively know how to handle situations that used to baffle us. A hunch or a strong feeling will guide us into work that will be meaningful. When we are doing the right thing, money will come to us.

Today I will find the right work for the right pay.

April 16

The universe is duly in order, everything in its place.
—WALT WHITMAN

Some days we might wonder how we are ever going to get through the rest of the day. We might become overwhelmed by anxiety and stress caused by conflict with others or situations that we have no control over. Often we seem at the breaking point, and the world becomes a frightening, chaotic place. It is then that we pause and step back, so we can gain perspective on what is happening to us.

We use the tools of the program. We make a spot-check inventory. We call our sponsor or a friend. We find a quiet place where we can sit alone and breathe deeply.

By meditating, we get in touch with the center of our being. This anchors us and enables us to see clearly. If possible, we make contact with nature. Observing the stars at night lets us know that we are part of something bigger than ourselves. Being by the ocean and watching the tide rise and fall soothes and calms us. Climbing a mountain gives us a different perspective. We see our interdependence with all creation and have faith that all is right with us.

Today how can I best use the tools of this program so that I stay calm and centered?

April 17

Humility, like darkness, reveals the heavenly lights.
—HENRY DAVID THOREAU

On the new path we are following, humility is an essential virtue. Without it we lack a true perspective of our place in the universe. Before recovery we were often consumed by false pride that isolated us from humanity and prevented us from communicating with our Higher Power.

Coming into this program is a true act of humility. We admit that our way did not work. We become open to growing through the practice of the Twelve Steps. When we do not know something, we are humble enough to ask. Sometimes wisdom comes from a person we consider beneath us. We need to learn that there are many voices and all have some value. When we close our mind to other points of view, we seriously limit ourselves. If we are rigid or uncompromising, we leave little room for growth.

We refrain from personal judgments, negative criticisms and unkind comments. We let go of self-will and its ill effects. Humility prepares us to know the will of our Higher Power and to surrender to it.

Let me be humble enough to look and listen for the help that I need.

April 18

The sculptor himself must feel that he is not so much inventing or shaping the curve of a breast or shoulder as delivering the image from its prison.   —ANAIS NIN

In the past we were slaves to our addictions. Our finest qualities were submerged in a well of fear and compulsion. Recovery frees us to begin an exciting journey of self-discovery. An honest appraisal will reveal both our good and bad traits. Self-acceptance becomes the base for significant change.

Today we begin to choose the kind of person we want to be by eliminating old negative self-images. Just as an artist pares down his work to the essentials, we need to strip away the artifice and debris accumulated when we were active.

Oscar Wilde said, "My life is my art." This is an attitude that permits us to see ourselves as flexible expressions of our inner being. Our characters are not set in stone but are open to improvement and change. The most valuable tools for sculpting ourselves are the Twelve Steps. The greater our self-awareness, the more likely it is that we will unlock the image of the divine self that resides within us.

Today I will make my best effort to reflect the truth, beauty and goodness that are the ground of my being.

April 19

Nature is full of freaks, and now puts an old head on young shoulders, and then a young heart beating under fourscore winters.   —RALPH WALDO EMERSON

We are never too old or too young to come into this program. If we show up at a meeting, we are probably not there by accident. In the beginning, some young people make the mistake of comparing their stories to those of older members of the group. They have not yet learned that it is not a question of how much we drank, drugged, acted out inappropriately or overate, but how this behavior made us feel. In recovery we identify with people's insides, not their outsides. Many have gotten sober in their teens or twenties. It is not necessary to lose everything before we receive the gifts of this program.

Older people may feel it is too late for them to get sober. They see all the wasted years and give in to despair. But experience has shown that people can recover at any age. For both older and younger men it is important to find a group that has some members near their age so they will not feel isolated.

No matter what age we are when we enter recovery, we can only get better. Finding a group with a good age mix benefits everyone. We can all teach one another something no matter how young or how old we are.

Today I will make room in my life for people of all ages.

April 20

Ozone and friendship will be our stimulants—let the drugs, tobacco and strong drink go forever. Natural joy brings no headaches and heartaches.

—ELBERT HUBBARD

There was a time in our lives when we thought we could not live without our primary addiction. Some of us thought more food would fill us up, but it never did. Others imagined that just one more sexual escapade would bring the satisfaction that had been eluding us. Still others looked for drugs or alcohol to appease their cravings. Even though we knew we were out of control, we were afraid to make a change.

When we made a commitment to let go of our compulsive behaviors, we imagined that our lives would be empty. But today we realize that as recovering people, we are living fully for the first time. Now that we are no longer slaves to our addictions, we have real choice. The morning takes on a whole new meaning when our minds are not clouded by physical and emotional hangovers. We enjoy simple things, such as taking a walk, chatting with a friend on the phone, caring for a pet or playing a game. Our values change, and we find joy in developing friendships based on mutual respect.

Today I will remember to be grateful for the new life I have been given.

My addiction was an acting out of my shame. Each drunken episode, which started as a way to feel better and overcome shame, escalated into behavior of which I was ashamed. —JOHN BRADSHAW

Shame is a painful emotion caused by feelings of guilt, a shortcoming or improper behavior. In order to avoid this pain, we "acted out" in self-destructive ways that only made us feel worse. Sometimes this guilt was the result of our own actions, and sometimes it was imposed on us by our family or society. Perhaps one parent was an alcoholic or another an overeater. Whenever the parent found the pain of addiction unendurable, feelings of shame were transferred to the child.

Many of us suffer from internalized homophobia and harbored feelings of guilt and shame for many years. We saw ourselves as flawed and were plagued by critical and contemptuous inner voices. These voices kept us from our authentic selves and drove us further into compulsive behavior.

In recovery, by using the tools of the program, we learn to affirm ourselves and move toward a fuller self-expression. We may need the help of a professional or a spiritual advisor to guide us in finding the exact cause. If our shame arises from our actions, we make amends whenever possible and resolve not to repeat such behavior.

Today I will reject false feelings of shame and construct a positive image of myself.

April 22

Craft must have clothes, but truth loves to go naked.
—THOMAS FULLER

No matter what we do, if we are not honest, recovery will elude us. First we had to admit that we were powerless and our lives had become unmanageable. Most of us found this difficult because we supported our addiction with a web of lies. We fabricated stories to justify our irresponsible behavior. We spent a lifetime fooling ourselves and others.

Suddenly we are asked to let go of this bad habit. It takes time to break old patterns. When we humble ourselves and make a commitment to tell the truth, life becomes easier. When we are tempted to lie, we remind ourselves that when we tell the truth, we don't have to remember what we have said and we don't forget what we have said.

By sharing openly at meetings, we rid ourselves of denial, end a life of pretense and become ready to listen and learn. When we let people know our inner thoughts and feelings, we end our isolation. Being honest is like opening a window and allowing a fresh breeze to come into our lives.

I will be vigilant about telling the truth, knowing that my recovery depends upon it.

April 23

It's but little good you'll do a-watering last year's crop.
— GEORGE ELIOT

Too often we waste time reliving or regretting the past. We look backward and forget to pay attention to the present. Memories haunt us, and we focus on what we could have done. This program suggests we examine the past, not stare at it. We can use the past as a reference point, to help us learn, but we must not let it divert us from the day at hand.

We also sometimes ignore the present because we fear the future. Perhaps we daydream, thinking everything will be better tomorrow. Projecting into the future cheats us of the moment.

Our goal is to live in the moment. We pace ourselves and take one step at a time. We pay attention to what is going on around us. We savor the details of daily life, enjoying the good parts and accepting the bad. We do what we can and save the rest for tomorrow. What lies behind is over. What lies ahead is unknown. We are grateful for all the good that has happened to us over the years and hope that the future will be pleasant—but our chief concern is doing the best we can in the here and now.

I will focus on living in the now and turn the past and future over to my Higher Power.

April 24

Most fathers can't talk about *any* feelings, let alone their responses to homosexuality. —JAMES M. PINES

Sometimes we forget that our fathers are a product of the society in which they were raised. As gay men, we particularly feel the loss of a bond with our fathers. In many cases, our fathers were also addicted people, and this further separated us from them. Sometimes we were rejected outright because of our sexuality.

Our society does not give men permission to show their feelings. As a result it is difficult for fathers and sons to establish any real communication. When the son is gay, the chasm can widen and leave both people feeling isolated. The son usually feels abandoned and the father is disappointed.

We have a chance in recovery to repair our relationships and to come together with our fathers. If both parties are willing to grow, a common ground can be forged. When this is not possible, we accept the situation as it is and pray for improvement.

Today I will do my best to be a loving son.

Each one sees what he carries in his own heart.
—JOHANN WOLFGANG VON GOETHE

Our view of the world is conditioned by who we are and where we have been. Our experiences in the past mold and shape us. If we grew up in a cold, unloving and suspicious family, then that is how we see those around us. If we have experienced oppression and intolerance, then it is likely that we will possess those defects as well. Sometimes, because of what has happened to us, we are bitter and angry. In an attempt to escape these feelings, we act out compulsively and make our problems worse.

Recovery gives us a chance to break the long cycle of dysfunction and addiction that we have inherited. When we bottom out, we are given an opportunity to renew ourselves. Working with our sponsor and fellow recovering brothers, we learn the purpose and benefit of each Step. Our hearts soften, and we are given a vision of a new way of life.

Today I will be grateful for the second chance I have been given.

Better to shun the bait than struggle in the snare.
—JOHN DRYDEN

This program teaches us to be careful about people, places and things. Sometimes we have difficulty letting go of old relationships that are harmful to us. We have become dependent on people who are not supportive of our needs. If we are to continue to grow we need to side with our recovery. As we make spiritual and emotional progress, we do not settle for less than we deserve. We set boundaries and affirm our true worth. We seek emotionally healthy friends and lovers.

Similarly, we learn to avoid places that stimulate our addiction. We replace bars, parties where there is heavy drinking or drugging, bathhouses and porno bookstores with meetings, professional associations and spiritual groups. Developing alternatives to dangerous situations is necessary if we are to find a new way of life. Perhaps we can take the initiative and throw a party or make a meal for our recovering friends.

Sometimes a particular song, an old habit or erroneous ideas can trigger our compulsive behavior. Some behavior, such as losing our temper, might get us so stirred up that our resolve to stay sober is weakened. We make a genuine effort to avoid situations that put us on shaky ground. We ask ourselves if our actions are leading us toward or away from recovery.

Gratitude for my new life keeps me vigilant. I make choices which enhance my recovery.

April 27

Some people are so afraid to die that they never begin to live. —HENRY VAN DYKE

We respond in many ways to death. Some of us focus on it morbidly and live in terror of the prospect. Others refuse to accept death and deny it by such actions as refusing to make a will. When we acknowledge we are mortal, we enhance the significance of life. If we want to live life to its fullest, we need to be prepared to die.

Acceptance of death can be a difficult task. We can see its necessity yet still love life. But if we see life as a freely given gift, we can learn to surrender it without complaint.

On a psychic level we long for death because it represents an end to suffering. Yet our life force is so strong there is often a battle between these two drives. As recovering people who have a history of avoiding reality, we seek to align ourselves with the life force while respecting the inevitability of death. Death is a mystery. It may be the last sleep or the first awakening.

I will give myself roses today and let others place them on my grave.

The iron chain and the silken cord are both equally bonds.   **—FRIEDRICH VON SCHILLER**

Many things can bind us: a bad habit, too great a dependence on one person, a shameful secret, certain luxuries, constant worry or a terrible resentment. We need to free ourselves from the bonds that tie us down and claim the freedom that is ours. We find our rightful place in this world by working the Twelve Steps. As we move forward, we clear up the wreckage of the past.

Building a solid foundation in this program helps to release any unpleasantness from the past. We envision it fading from memory and drifting out of sight. Now we are free to do what is before us. We live a life filled with the spirit. We do not worry about tomorrow. We trust our Higher Power to guide us. We know our finest work and best efforts lie before us.

By breaking the chains from the past that bind me, I let love rush in and fill the empty spaces.

A good conscience is a soft pillow.   —JOHN RAY

The Tenth Step suggests that we continue to take personal inventory, and when we are wrong, to promptly admit it. By doing so, we grow in self-knowledge and are no longer condemned to repeat the same self-defeating behavior over and over. To keep on an even keel, we guard against the kind of behavior that leaves us with an emotional hangover.

This program gives us tools that make living *One Day at a Time* easier. If we feel disturbed by something that happens to us during the day, we stop, take a deep breath and assess the situation. We remember the principles of the program and try to put them into practice by acting with thoughtfulness and restraint. We refrain from emotional tirades which only backfire and destroy our serenity.

Before we go to sleep, we review the day just past. We list our liabilities and assets. We survey our relationships and ask if we have harmed anyone. If so, we become willing to admit our fault. By developing this habit of self-survey, we find it is easier to correct our behavior when we go off course. When we end the day at peace with ourselves and others, we have a good night's sleep and are prepared for tomorrow's challenges.

Help me to be kind, courteous and loving toward everyone I meet today.

April 30

The creation of a thousand forests is in one acorn.
—RALPH WALDO EMERSON

Many of us never knew the meaning of the word "process" before we came into a Twelve Step program. We wanted to go from A to Z in one leap. We were too busy going someplace to enjoy the moment. Perhaps we overburdened ourselves with too many unrealistic goals and ended up accomplishing very little.

It is comforting to know that we only have to take one small step at a time toward any goal we set. We perform the task at hand in the best way we can at that moment. We will make mistakes, and we accept this as part of being human. Sometimes we may lose our way and falter. At that point we begin anew, knowing that perseverance brings results. Our goal is progress, not perfection.

We are learning to appreciate each day's progress and to enjoy our accomplishments. We do what we can and then rest. We do not beat ourselves up for not achieving everything we set out to do that day.

In time we will see that gradual effort eventually produces results. At the end of the day, we take an inventory and tally up the positive things we have accomplished. We know that with the help of our Higher Power we can eventually achieve whatever we set out to do.

I will set a goal and take one small step toward it today.

May 1

Just as the lives of lesbians and gay men are enhanced
by a knowledge of their history, so too will the field
of history be enriched by a reclamation of the homosexual past.   —MARTIN DUBERMAN

As recovering people we find great value in examin-
ing our personal history. We learn what forces
shaped and molded us into the people we are today.
Armed with this knowledge, we are better equipped to
evaluate the effect of the past on us and to face
the future.

Most young gay people grow up thinking they are
the only one in the world with romantic and sexual
feelings toward members of the same sex. A sense of
relief and hope follows their discovery that there are
other gay people. Because of suppression and persecution, most of us have no knowledge of the part gay
people have played in world history. Scholars are
beginning to painstakingly reclaim our history, although much of it has been destroyed or camouflaged.

How we view ourselves is crucial to a complete
understanding of our human nature. Both gay and
straight people are enriched when a history long hidden
is brought into the light.

**Today I will do my best to study and understand
those who have gone before me.**

Friendship should be desired, not for consideration of any worldly advantage, but from the dignity of its own nature. —ST. AELRED OF RIEVAULX

Many of us developed the habit of cultivating friendships based on who people were or what they could do for us. Friendships based on this self-centered perspective often were disappointing. In time we learn that friendship is intrinsically valuable and not to be sought for benefit or advantage.

We learn a new way of relating to people. Developing true friendship requires time and patience. Our relationships need to be cared for and nourished like a garden. Deeper connections result when we allow ourselves to be vulnerable, trusting and open to emotional risks.

Friendship enriches and strengthens us. We see our own reflection in our friends. Sometimes a friend will voice a truth we cannot articulate. In recovery our circle of friends grows as we learn to listen, share, reach out and trust others.

Today I will be thankful for my friendships. I will conduct myself in a friendly manner to all those around me.

**This is the day the Lord has made; let us rejoice and
be glad in it.** —PSALMS 118:24

Yesterday may have been filled with difficulties, but
today is a new beginning. This day is the stage our
life is played upon, and we have a choice now about
how it is to be acted out. Embracing this day with
enthusiasm and grace will make us the star of the show.
Negative thoughts and pessimism will cast us in a
narrow, small role with little chance of ever expressing
our full selves.

Let us look at today as an opportunity to fulfill our
dreams. If we do not waste our time with anger,
resentment, fear or pettiness, we have a good chance
for happiness. Great delight can come from enjoying
the things at hand. When caught in a traffic jam, we
can use the time meditating and praying rather than
stewing or letting off steam. Whenever we have the
chance, we can praise those around us. We honor
ourselves by taking the time to perform the least significant act with care and thoughtfulness.

When faced with a challenge, we can view it as an
opportunity to use our intelligence and skills. We can
cultivate our abilities and talents. Let us claim our
divine inheritance as growing, evolving spiritual beings.
Today we celebrate the marvelous gift of life.

**This is a special day. I will take all the wonder
and good that life has to offer.**

May 4

It is never wise to try to appear more clever than you are. It is sometimes wise to appear slightly less so.
—WILLIAM WHITELAW

By being know-it-alls we close ourselves off from new experience and information. Often egotistical and conceited behavior masks a poor self-image. Because we suffer from low self-esteem, we crave attention, but boasting of our knowledge and skills is a poor way to get it. Such behavior only repels others.

Sometimes we show off and glorify ourselves so that others will have a high opinion of us. This usually backfires because people can see right through such blustering. They may be too polite to tell us, but no one cares for a braggart.

The Big Book defines humility as being "right-sized." We should not confuse humility with humiliation. Humiliation causes us shame. When we are humble, we are submitting to the will of our Higher Power. Taking an inventory teaches us humility and gives us self-knowledge. We know who we are, what our assets are and which areas in ourselves we need to improve.

If we are modest and unassuming, others will feel comfortable around us. Our good points will reveal themselves. We need not proclaim them. True humility will bring us contentment.

Today I will humbly ask my Higher Power to guide me in all things.

**The meaning of good and bad, of better and worse, is
simply helping or hurting.**   —RALPH WALDO EMERSON

As we go about our day, we might ask ourselves,
Am I moving toward or away from my addiction?
If we are in doubt about taking an action, we ask,
Where will this take me? When in doubt we can consult
with a friend or a sponsor before making a decision.
Some people can drink safely. There are those who can
eat foods that might be off-limits to us. Some behavior
that is appropriate for others might lead us right back
to our old compulsive behavior.

In the past much of what we did was hurtful to us.
Now we take actions to help ourselves in every way
possible. We judge a situation by its effect upon us.
This program is a practical guide to better living.
People, places and things that do not enhance our
sobriety should be avoided.

This is not a program about good or evil but about
what works. Once we have admitted our powerlessness,
we do whatever is necessary to stay sober.

**Grant me the willingness to take whatever
actions will strengthen my sobriety.**

Almost without exception, alcoholics are tortured by loneliness. Even before our drinking got bad and people began to cut us off, nearly all of us suffered the feeling that we did not quite belong.
— TWELVE STEPS AND TWELVE TRADITIONS

Alcoholics, addicts and those who suffer from compulsive behavior disorders all reveal that from earliest childhood they had a feeling of being on the outside looking in. For gay men, this feeling was doubly compounded. In high school we watched with fear and sadness as others went through the rituals of adolescence. We never felt we were full members of anything, and our addictions helped to ease the pain brought about by this feeling of exclusion.

When we come into the fellowship, we know we belong. At first our feelings are tentative, but as we hear more people tell their stories, our sense of identification with the group grows. Making a commitment to service and socializing with other recovering people is a sign of renewal and health.

Because we are extremely sensitive people, some might even say touchy, we have to guard against perceived slights and hurts. It will take time to learn to be comfortable and vulnerable with a wide range of people. We can take comfort in knowing that everyone else feels the same, no matter what their outer appearance may be.

Today I will be grateful for the fellowship and the newfound friends I have made in recovery.

Intuition is a spiritual faculty and does not explain, but simply points the way. —FLORENCE SCOVIL SHINN

One of the promises in *The Big Book* is "We will intuitively know how to handle situations that used to baffle us." As a result of being sober and working the Steps, we are no longer shrouded in a debilitating fog of confusion, depression, anger and resentment. Our minds are clear, and we can get in touch with our inner faculties. We refuse to let negative thoughts rob us of our spiritual birthright of love and abundance.

In the past our actions were guided by fear, and we were blind to the will of our Higher Power. Today when we are in doubt, we turn to prayer and meditation for guidance. If we are troubled or anxious, we remind ourselves that we are under the care of a power greater than ourselves. We ask that a way be opened for us in accordance with the divine will. The more we cultivate a spiritual outlook, the sooner we receive direct inspiration.

The answers to our questions begin to come through intuition or a hunch. A share by someone at a meeting or an article in the newspaper might be just the lead we need to set us on the right path. Following the principles of this program, we fearlessly trust that we will be taken care of in everything we do. We learn to have faith in our intuition and make decisions quickly.

Help me to establish divine order in my mind, my body and in all my affairs.

Insofar as you have problems with feeling good about being gay, no matter how subtle, they will show up in your same-sex intimate partnerships.

—DR. BETTY BERZON

How we feel about our sexual identity colors the way we act toward those we love. If we cannot accept ourselves for who we are, we will have a difficult time accepting someone else. If we inhibit or deny our gayness, we limit the possibility of growth.

Feeling bad about being gay can take many forms in a relationship. We cut off our feelings and are unable to be affectionate or spontaneous. We threaten to leave our lover as soon as the emotional involvement becomes too demanding. We never really commit ourselves and miss out on a fully loving partnership. Perhaps we denigrate gay organizations and the gay community and isolate in the relationship.

We have to continue to grow and explore our sexual identity. We may think of ourselves as fully out but still maintain certain reservations and harbor feelings of shame. Sometimes we might need professional help to deal with this problem. We certainly should open ourselves up at meetings and explore these issues. If we are to grow as a couple, we need to grow as individuals.

Today I ask my Higher Power to help me treat myself and those I love with respect and kindness.

When you are offended at anyone's fault, turn to yourself and study your own failings. By attending to them, you will forget your anger and learn to live wisely.
— MARCUS AURELIUS

Sometimes we get caught up in criticizing others for their shortcomings and failings. We might find ourselves excessively annoyed by someone chewing gum or speaking in a loud and raucous manner. Perhaps we are resentful because of an unkind remark directed at us, or we disapprove of a friend who is always late for appointments.

Much time can be wasted if we let ourselves stew and fume over such things. It is not easy to detach from the faults of others. But we need to concentrate on the things that are our concern. It is not our job to interfere with or monitor anyone else's behavior.

Minding other people's business is one way we distract ourselves from our own duties and responsibilities. We will never find serenity if we constantly dwell on others' errors and the disappointments we have suffered. An honest self-appraisal will highlight the many areas where we can improve our own behavior. By keeping the focus on ourselves we *Let Go and Let God* take care of the affairs of others.

Practicing detachment from what is troubling me often improves a situation. Today I will accept that things cannot always go the way I want.

May 10

In our era the road to holiness necessarily passes through the world of action. —DAG HAMMARSKJÖLD

S ome parents say to their children, "Don't do as I do but do as I say." What an exercise in futility. We all believe what people do over what they say. When we are given a good example, we have a positive model to follow. If we see someone behaving poorly, we often take that as permission to do likewise.

We have all dozed off during a sermon. Most of us find it easy to preach but more difficult to put our words into action. We earn no halos when we sit in judgment of others. All of our good intentions accomplish little. We accomplish more by doing the dishes than by telling someone else what to do.

We promote harmony when we visit the sick or imprisoned, feed the hungry or take the time to be present for someone in need. Positive action improves our character and makes the course of life smoother for ourselves and others.

Today let me do everything I can to be a force for good in the world.

For some of us, sex may be the only way we learned to connect with people. Our sexuality may not be connected to the rest of us; sex may not be connected to love—for ourselves or others. —MELODY BEATTIE

Multiple sexual partners and anonymous sex consumed many of us in the past. We engaged in behavior that left us feeling empty and alone. Sex became the way we communicated, and we used it as a vehicle for approval from others. Because sex was not the complete answer to our craving, we rarely found satisfaction and vainly repeated our search.

As recovering men we have learned what it means to respect ourselves and to attend to our true needs. We let go of our defenses and become vulnerable. This is a frightening step, but we don't have to do this alone. We begin by asking our Higher Power for help in establishing intimate connections and loving interaction with others. We share our fears and anxieties with the group to help us get a clearer understanding of ourselves. Sometimes we might need to seek professional help.

When we stop relating to people as objects and show respect for their humanity, we are released from our compulsions and find ourselves on the road to real relief for our underlying problems.

Today I ask for help to face who I am so that I may bring all of myself to a loving and respectful relationship.

My crown is in my heart, not on my head; not decked with diamonds and Indian stones, nor to be seen: my crown is called content; a crown it is that seldom kings enjoy. —WILLIAM SHAKESPEARE

D o we depend on material things or other people to make us happy? Are our expectations realistic or do we cling to unattainable fantasies? Perhaps we obsess over what might have been, or maybe we focus on our problems to the exclusion of anything else. If we constantly compare ourselves to others, we are following a sure recipe for unhappiness.

As we get to know ourselves, we set our own standards. We understand that happiness comes from within, and we become less dependent on the opinion or approval of others. A sense of well-being fills us when we practice the Twelve Steps, for we know we are doing the best we can to be true to ourselves. We begin to enjoy life and become comfortable with our feelings. As we continue along the road of recovery, we find that an inner peace replaces our former anxiety and indecision.

Saying the Serenity Prayer helps me to keep the events of the day in perspective and grounds me in reality.

As the breath slows, the thought-making process slows down and the mind becomes calm.

—SWAMI SATCHIDANANDA

Meditation can take many forms. Here is one we might want to try.

Repair to a quiet place. Sit or lie down in a comfortable position. Make sure your spine is straight. Now relax and begin breathing slowly and deeply. Ask yourself: What am I feeling? What energy inhabits my body? How am I doing today? Be calm and watch your thoughts flow by.

As you breathe out, picture letting go of everything negative: anger, frustration, anxiety, depression, tiredness or whatever is bothering you.

As you inhale, see yourself bringing in positive energy: good health, love, prosperity, happiness or anything you need to realize your full self.

Breathe in and out. Expel the negative. Inhale the positive.

Count backward from five to one. Relax more deeply into yourself. Imagine yourself floating through space. Let yourself be taken up into the arms of a loving Higher Power. Stay there and continue breathing gently.

After about ten minutes, slowly count from one to five and bring yourself back to the everyday world.

◇

I will set aside a portion of each day to enjoy a quiet and refreshing moment of meditation.

Every society has a tendency to reduce its opponents to caricatures. —FRIEDRICH WILHELM NIETZSCHE

Folklore and the media have presented the stereotypes of the bitchy, mincing queen and the stone-cold butch lesbian to the public. When straight people find out someone they know and admire is gay, they often wonder why that person does not fit the stereotype.

Do we hold stereotypical ideas about a particular group of people? Do we judge people as members of a class rather than as individuals? Perhaps we think of ourselves as unique, but of others as representative of a class. It is wise to remember there are too many exceptions for any generalization about people to hold true.

Society and our family condition the way we view the world. We tend to interpret things as they have been pointed out to us. If we see others as different from us, it is much easier to consider them as lesser beings and not worthy of respect. Let us use our powers of observation, look at each person as an individual and draw our own conclusions.

Each of us deserves respect and consideration. None of us wants to be treated in a particular way because of the actions of others. Let us extend the benefit of the doubt to all we meet, reserving judgment, until we have some actual experience upon which to base an opinion.

Today I will practice being open-minded and tolerant. I will treat others as I would wish to be treated.

The mark of the immature man is that he wants to die nobly for a cause, while the mark of the mature man is that he wants to live humbly for one.

—WILHELM STEKEL

When young we struggled with our identity and searched for a sense of purpose. For most of us our early youth was clouded by addiction. Today as our minds clear, our chance of maturing into responsible adults is greatly improved. Recovery allows us to grow in wisdom and vitality.

In recovery we will assess ourselves. No longer naive and innocent, we learn to accept life on its own terms. We base our decisions more on reason and less on impulse. We fulfill our responsibilities in a timely fashion and take whatever practical actions are required. We begin to act and think for ourselves.

We come to terms with the dark side of life—death, illness and misfortune. Spiritual imperatives guide us as we let go of our egos.

We accept our responsibility to pass on what we know to the next generation. We volunteer at a gay youth organization or share our organizational skills with a new group. We continue to socialize with people of all ages.

Today help me be of service while I share my experience, strength and hope with others.

The value of compassion can not be overemphasized. No greater burden can be borne by an individual than to know no one cares or understands.
—ARTHUR H. STAINBACK

There have been times in our lives when we were indifferent to the suffering of others. We were consumed by our own troubles and oblivious to anyone else's needs. In our isolation we became cynical and bitter. Perhaps we were not there when someone needed us.

Recovery thaws us and opens us to our kinship with all humanity. We no longer are indifferent. We learn to give of ourselves. When someone is troubled, we know the most important thing we can do is listen and try to understand what they are feeling. A person who is ill feels cut off from the world of the healthy. By hugging and touching, we show that we care. Being there emotionally for another lets that person know he has not been abandoned.

Offering understanding and support can take many forms. We might volunteer as an AIDS buddy, take care of an elderly relative or friend, invite a lonely person to lunch or sponsor a newcomer. Being sympathetic and conscious of another's distress, consoling a grieving person and writing to a jailed inmate are some of the ways we can show an understanding heart.

Help me to be a healing force wherever I am needed. Today I will remember that the gift is in the giving and the reward is in the doing.

May 17

Prayer is the key of the morning and the bolt of the evening. —MAHATMA GANDHI

Before we came into this program, very few of us bothered to pray. When we did pray, it was more in the nature of a bargain. Perhaps we said, "Oh God, if you get me out of this situation, I will do such and such" or "If you give me this, I will do that." Today we pray differently. We ask for knowledge of God's will and the power to carry it out. If we do petition for something, we are careful to qualify our request with the phrase "If it be thy will." For too long we operated on our willpower alone and it got us nowhere.

There are many ways to pray. We can praise our Higher Power or give thanks for blessings received. Some of us find that quiet communion with the divine is the best way to begin our day. It centers us and prepares us for anything we might come across. We also find it is helpful during the day to stop occasionally and thank our Higher Power for the gift of life. At the end of the day we put everything aside, quiet ourselves, review our day and pray. We cultivate an "attitude of gratitude" for the simple pleasures of life and the beauty that surrounds us.

Today I will cooperate with my Higher Power by setting time aside for prayer and meditation.

A talebearer revealeth secrets, but he that is of faithful spirit concealeth the matter. —PROVERBS

Learning to keep a secret is new to many of us. In the past we delighted in quickly revealing secrets. We found it was almost impossible to keep quiet about anything we overheard or were told in private. Our sense of boundaries was limited, and we didn't know how to mind our own business.

We have a responsibility in the rooms to keep secret what other members of the group reveal about themselves. If someone shares a confidence with us, they have every right to expect that we will tell no one else. By the same token, we want to know that what we share at meetings or tell another person is not going to be the subject of gossip.

We keep in mind that this program is a success because of the principle of anonymity. As we grow in emotional sobriety, we learn discretion and take pride in the fact that we are people who can be trusted to keep a secret.

Help me be responsible to the group by putting the common welfare first.

I have an increasing sense that the coming-out process of lesbians and gay men contains a spiritual element—that it is an aspect of a quest for what theologians might call "the authentic self." —BOB BERNSTEIN

Many of us had so much guilt and shame we felt that we did not deserve to stand up for our true selves. As we use the tools of this program—prayer, meditation, inventories, sharing—our integrity grows, and we learn to accept ourselves as we are. We discover that being honest is the easiest way to live our lives. When we hid important parts of ourselves, we became lonely and isolated. Once we have fully accepted that we are gay, we move into life and travel a road that leads to further self-knowledge.

We know we are loved by our Higher Power, and we learn to claim our rights as human beings. We look inside ourselves for guidance. No longer ruled by fear, we rejoice in the knowledge that we have worth. As time passes, we explore deeper levels of coming out and learn to live life for ourselves.

Today I accept myself and thank my Higher Power for the gift of being gay.

May 20

There are two times when you can never tell what is going to happen. One is when a man takes his first drink; and the other is when a woman takes her latest.
—O. HENRY

It is said in this program that the first drink gets a person drunk. This applies to any substance or behavior over which we are powerless. We are fooling ourselves if we think we can indulge in just a little cocaine or an occasional food binge. There might have been a time when we had some control over our addictions, but eventually we became unable to predict the outcome of our indulgences.

Once we admit that we are powerless, we abandon any reservations regarding our commitment to this program. For this reason we avoid people, places and things that might be a temptation. At first it is difficult for us to imagine doing without the things or people that we so depended upon. Yet we find that the more sobriety we have the better we feel, and we are grateful to be free of our obsessions.

Today I will be honest with myself and avoid playing games that might lead me back to self-destructive behavior.

May 21

Neither cast ye your pearls before swine, lest they trample them under their feet, and turn again and rend you.   —MATTHEW 7:6

Before we came into this program, we were slaves to our addictions. We had lost the power of choice and our willpower was nonexistent. Today we choose to use the tools of this program to gain a new freedom.

How we use our energy and spend our time is important. This program cautions us to be careful about the people, places and things in our lives. It is counterproductive to spend much time with old acquaintances who are still active and have no respect for our sobriety. People who are active don't like to see others getting well—it reminds them of their own problem and makes them uncomfortable.

By choosing healthy and healing environments, we let go of old habits that lead to self-destructive behavior. The choices we make have repercussions. If we aim low, the results will be disappointing. By pursuing a standard of excellence in all our endeavors, we have a good chance of gaining the high ground.

Today I recognize that my recovery is a miracle that I will not take for granted.

Such dreadful wallpaper, one of us must go.
                                        —OSCAR WILDE

T he above remark was said to have been made by Oscar Wilde as he lay dying in a cheap hotel in Paris. This ability to be humorous in the darkest moments is a great gift. Laughter serves us well in times of sorrow or oppression. Because gay men have been cast in the role of the outsider, some of us have developed the ability to discover and express the ludicrous and the absurd. We cherish the eccentric and the singular. Being able to laugh in the face of disaster is often what keeps us afloat.

At meetings we hear people laughing at the most horrendous tales. There is a healing in this laughter. We are able to listen to war stories and tales of desperation as landmarks on our journey toward recovery.

Today our greatest temptation may be to sink into depression. Without a mood-altering substance or compulsive behavior to shield us from reality, we find life difficult. Whenever we feel down, we try to take ourselves less seriously. At times like these, it is best to seek the company of good friends and rejoice in the divine comedy of life.

Let me raise my spirits by embracing humor. I will wear the world as a loose garment.

**Don't go around saying the world owes you a living;
the world owes you nothing; it was here first.**
—MARK TWAIN

Do we sometimes feel entitled to a free ride because of all the abuse we have suffered? Do we have a martyr complex, always blaming others for our troubles? Do we expect to be carried by our friends and family? Are we clinging to our lover, hoping he will provide all of our needs?

If we depend on others to take care of us, whether emotionally or financially, we will be disappointed. If we cultivate the air of a victim, we might gain some sympathy, but we will have a hard time standing as an equal in the company of others. If we are always crying out for special attention, we might attract more abuse.

This program teaches us self-respect. We do not have to grovel before anyone. It is important to learn the difference between asking for help and expecting it as our due. As we go along in this program, we have the capability of developing an independence of body, mind and spirit.

**Today I can free myself from any unhealthy
dependence I may have on people,
places and things.**

**Time is a flowing river. Happy those who allow them-
selves to be carried, unresisting with the current. They
float through easy days. They live, unquestioning in
the moment.** —CHRISTOPHER MORLEY

We may have regrets for time we feel we wasted
during our active days. Yet, we have come to
learn that all our experience has value and each past
chapter of our story has its lessons and rewards.

Sometimes we do not think our time is of value
unless we are doing something useful. However, we are
human "beings" as well as humans "doing." We remember that sometimes fast, sometimes slow, life moves to
the beat of an unseen drummer.

Time heals all hurt and pain. When we are in trouble,
we try to bear in mind that all things pass. Sometimes
simply waiting is the answer to our problems. In recovery we trust to the process, knowing we have been
taken care of up to now. Our Higher Power is not
likely to abandon us.

Nature shows us that morning follows night. Time
teaches us perspective, and we learn to hope for the
best. We cherish each period as we travel from youth
to old age. We bring the fullest expression of life to
each moment.

**Let us dedicate ourselves today to enjoying the
moment and going with the flow of life.**

Adversity is the first path to truth. —LORD BYRON

Some of the most lasting lessons we learn are born out of pain and struggle. When things are going smoothly, we tend to take the good for granted. When we are challenged by adversity and loss, we most often listen and learn. The anguish and despair we experienced when we bottomed out on our disease prepared us for the moment of truth when we were ready to embrace a new way of life.

The terrible tragedy of AIDS has changed the way we view this world. Despite all the horror, we see stunning examples of personal heroism and bravery. Our community has learned to compassionately care for others, and the bonds of brotherhood have been strengthened. In the depths of the dark valleys, we learn to treasure each moment of life and commit ourselves to living in the present. Because we have seen the worst, we appreciate the gifts we have been given and share them with others.

As individuals and as a community, we have matured by facing personal and communal tragedies. Our faith has been tempered in the fires of private hells. As survivors our spirits have been enriched at great cost. Because of our common woes, we are now able to bond and identify more compassionately with our fellow travelers on the road of life.

Today I will look to the mountaintop, knowing that all troubles pass in time.

The willingness to take risks is our grasp of faith.
—GEORGE E. WOODBERRY

Who has not faltered and been afraid of taking a risk? Very few of us! As recovering people we might err on the side of caution, when we think of some of our foolish past behavior. Yet the risks we took were often based on faulty judgment, guided by our desire for instant gratification. Today we take a different approach. Before embarking on a new venture or making a serious change, we consult with our sponsors and other people who are familiar with our situation. After reasoned consideration we make our decision based on the best information available. We then take action and turn the results over to our Higher Power.

Perhaps we are afraid to love again after a loss, or we fear to invest our time and energy and risk failure. Yet, we cannot win life's prizes without sometimes taking a gamble. If we must be certain of an outcome before we try something new, then we will never grow. We may fail, but we can learn to accept defeat without losing heart. We can not banish danger, but we can banish fear. Our newfound faith can help us survive anything.

It's okay to be afraid, as long as I don't let fear rule my life. I will remember that risks sweeten the game of life.

May 27

Wisdom is ofttimes nearer when we stoop than when we soar.   —WILLIAM WORDSWORTH

When we first came across slogans in recovery, some of us thought they were clichéd or hackneyed phrases that did not apply to us. They did not seem sophisticated or grand enough to be of any use. But we learned differently.

These slogans express valuable truths. They are genuine tools that serve us well. Whether we have one day or ten years, the phrase *Easy Does It* is a reminder to pace ourselves and guard against becoming frantic and unbalanced. *First Things First* counsels us to get our priorities straight so that we may continue to enjoy recovery. *One Day at a Time* helps us to keep the focus on the present and the possible. *Keep It Simple* cautions us not to overburden ourselves unrealistically. *Let Go and Let God* reminds us that we are not writing the script and that it is easier when we go with the flow of life. When we *Live and Let Live,* our relations with other people are made smoother and more pleasant. *But for the Grace of God* prompts us to be grateful that we have found recovery and have been introduced to a whole new way of life.

**Today I will choose a slogan and incorporate it
into my daily life.**

May 28

A life spent in constant labor is a life wasted, save a man be such a fool as to regard a fulsome obituary notice as ample reward. —GEORGE JEAN NATHAN

Many of us find it difficult to know when we are overworking ourselves. As men we have been taught that our worth and identity come from our profession. When away from our work life, we often feel vulnerable and adrift. Perhaps we use intense activity and a frantic pace to keep from looking inward. When we are consumed by schedules and deadlines and with making lists of things to do, we neglect the relationships in our life and suffer emotionally.

When we are too tired, our minds become muddled and we make poor decisions. If our minds are racing, we are unable to hear the messages that are good for us.

Learning to keep work in proper balance is a challenge we need to take seriously. At the end of our workday, we set aside time to unwind and loosen up. A warm bath, meditation or a tape of our favorite music will help us to slow down, relax and set our priorities.

We remember that *Easy Does It* is a good prescription. Breathing deeply, we focus on the present and feel the serenity that is our due.

Today I will resolve to relax when I find myself getting tense and out of balance.

The meeting of two personalities is like the contact of two chemical substances: if there is any reaction, both are transformed. —C. G. JUNG

The quality of our relationships with other people contributes to making our lives more interesting and enjoyable. We may meet someone who so impresses us that they become our mentor. Over time we absorb aspects of their personality that we admire.

Others become our friends, and we influence and enliven each other. Our sharing of mutual concerns, sorrow, joy and laughter supports us in both good and bad times.

Then there are those with whom we will be completely incompatible. We find it best to distance ourselves from these individuals to avoid becoming entangled in emotional turmoil.

All the people who cross our path will have some effect on us. We too will make an impression on those we meet. We need not compromise our basic principles or pretend we are someone we are not. However, we should be careful to show respect and kindness to everyone.

Today I will do my best to treat others as I expect to be treated myself.

Nothing on earth consumes a man more completely than the passion of resentment.

—FRIEDRICH NIETZSCHE

We have been told in this program that resentment is the number one killer. When we harbor grudges or have hostility toward others, we pay a great price. It is not possible to be at peace with ourselves when we are filled with rancor and hatred. Resentment clutters our mind, and we become its victim.

Too often our pride has led us to take offense when none is intended. When we compared ourselves to others, we became disappointed and full of envy. We based our happiness on the actions or approval of others and then were upset when they did not live up to our expectations. We now look at our own motives and evaluate our own actions. We stop judging others. We avoid retaliation.

If we resent our lot in life or some bad luck, we recognize this as a waste of time and energy. The best antidote to resentment is gratitude. We refuse to concentrate on the things that annoy us and instead direct our energy toward positive thoughts and actions. We are working toward becoming better people. We protect ourselves from the consequences of resentment and move away from wasteful emotions.

Today I will put my energy to the best possible use and discover why I react the way I do.

**There are none more abusive to others than they that
lie most open to it themselves.**   —SENECA

Many of us come from abusive backgrounds. Some
of us may have been beaten or verbally ha-
rangued by members of our family. Others suffered
abuse from teachers or peers. Because we learned a
pattern of abuse when growing up, we seemed doomed
to repeat this behavior as adults. Are we physically or
emotionally abusive to our lover? Do we engage in
verbal sarcasm and barbs directed at our friends and
acquaintances? Are we rude to strangers or intolerant
of those different from us?

In this program we learn that everyone, including
ourselves, deserves respect. Discovering our own
worth, we awaken to the worth of others. We shy away
from the catty remark or the impulse to lash out at
others whom we do not agree with or like. We refrain
from any behavior that harms or hurts someone. In
recovery we have the opportunity to repair the damage
that was done to us and to make amends for the harm
we have inflicted on others.

**Today I will show respect to my fellow man and
to myself.**

June 1

If we can bless warships, supermarkets, fox hounds and baseball stadiums why then can't we bless two homosexual people who want God to be a part of their relationship and commit themselves in faith and integrity to each other? —BISHOP JOHN SHELBY SPONG

When we make a commitment to recovery, we discover what it means to stick by our decisions and be faithful to those who mean the most to us. Our spiritual recovery teaches us how to build relationships. We learn to work through conflict. We build a sense of trust that lets us know our partner intimately. As addicts and codependents, we tried to avoid the difficulties of commitment to another human being. Now we have the courage to face what is necessary. We build an enduring relationship with another person by being present in a trustworthy and reliable way. We affirm what enhances our union and avoid whatever threatens it.

We make our Higher Power a partner. We ask for help in expressing our love. Perhaps we invite friends and family to be witnesses as we dedicate ourselves to each other. We attune ourselves to the rhythm of life by channeling our most positive energies into our union.

**Today I take actions to strengthen my
commitment to the one I love.**

Zest is the secret of all beauty. There is no beauty that is attractive without zest. —CHRISTIAN DIOR

A person who is enthusiastic about something can ignite a spark of interest in others. When we see someone who works the program in a willing and spirited manner, we are inspired to follow suit.

Bringing ardor to any endeavor quickens our gait and gives us a surge of energy. A zestful approach enhances our enjoyment. We can produce nothing great without zeal and devotion.

We bring this excitement into our lives first, by accepting where we are today. We resolve to look at our everyday actions in a positive way. If we clean houses for a living, we go a little further and really make things shine. If we have several employees under us, we make a special effort to consider their feelings and opinions. No matter what we do, we enliven our environment by performing our tasks cheerfully.

Recovery gives us a hunger for life. Suddenly we have more things to do, more friends to see and more places to go than ever before. We are regenerated by following the precepts of the program closely. Having bottomed out, we know what darkness and despair are. Now we can relish and savor life in all its manifest glory.

Today I ask my Higher Power to lighten my heart so that I may embrace life with passion and a sparkle in my eye.

June 3

When we are really honest with ourselves we must admit that our lives are all that really belongs to us. So it is how we use our lives that determines the kind of men we are. —CESAR CHAVEZ

In the past we lived lives of escape using our codependent relationships and our addictions. We lacked a sense of purpose and evaded our responsibilities by an unnatural dependence on people and things. Our behavior did little to enhance our sense of self-worth. By the time we came into the program, we were at a spiritual dead end.

Recovery challenges us to do better. It becomes apparent that selfish behavior won't work for us anymore. We realize that we are a part of a whole and begin to live our lives so as to make a contribution. As a result of our spiritual awakening, we are willing to give service.

How we behave tells a lot about us. Do our actions help to improve the environment? Are we the kind of people that others want to get close to? Are we willing to give our time, energies and money to worthy causes? Do we fulfill our roles as lovers, family members, friends and coworkers with love and kindness?

Our thoughts and actions mold our characters. When we live lives guided by ideals and principles, we are rewarded with the gifts of wisdom and growth.

Today I will bring my best effort to everything I do.

As a body everyone is single, as a soul never.
— HERMANN HESSE

As young adults we left home for our own apartment, college, a job, another town or a big city. This transition from the familiar environment of the family was often difficult. The initial thrill of being on our own might have been followed by feelings of loneliness and isolation. We then began to search for other people to whom we could relate.

As gay men we often found our earliest sense of community in bars. Although this experience was limited, we had few other choices. Afraid to be out at our jobs or in the larger social world, we compartmentalized our lives, which led to feelings of fragmentation and alienation. Our problem was compounded by the fact that we did not marry and as a result certain doors of opportunity were closed to us.

Today there are many new ways of meeting people. The growth of gay social, political and spiritual organizations offers gay men a wider choice of involvement. Let us look for ways we can contribute to the development of these groups. Developing a solid sense of community enhances our spiritual and mental health.

**Today I will open new doors and enlarge
my world.**

It is certainly not then—not in dreams—but when one is wide awake, at moments of robust joy and achievement, on the highest terrace of consciousness, that mortality has a chance to peer beyond its own limits, from the mast, from the past and its castle tower.　　　　　　　　　　—VLADIMIR NABOKOV

What a precious gift recovery is. It gives us the freedom to live our lives fully. We no longer are chained by our addictions to diminished horizons and lowered expectations. The irony is that we are living lives of joy because of self-restraint and abstinence. There was a time when we thought the solution was more—more of whatever we craved—thinking that would fill up all the empty spaces within us.

Life no longer frightens us. We enthusiastically embrace it. We are grateful for the opportunity to clearly face the world around us.

We now see the larger picture. We are more than the sum of our parts. We discover the spirit that is the glue holding us together. Where there had been emotional blindness, physical dependency and soul-sickness there is now clear-sightedness, independence and healing.

Our former self-centeredness fades as we take an interest in other people. Saying thank you is the prayer that most readily springs from our lips.

Today I will keep the focus on the Twelve Steps so that I may experience the joy of living.

A blow with a word strikes deeper than a blow with a sword. —ROBERT BURTON

The power of words is great, and by our words we are deemed either wise or foolish. In recovery we exercise great caution in the words we use. We may think of what we say as a joke yet hurt another deeply. Perhaps we were raised in an environment where certain racial or ethnic epithets were common. Because we were used to these words, we thought there was nothing wrong with them and never considered the harm they could do. As gay men we know that it is hurtful when a straight person uses the terms "faggot" or "queer" in a derisive way. Today we try to be equally sensitive to the feelings of others.

In our relationships we avoid cold or harsh language. Sarcasm and criticism can cut like a razor. Vulgarity lowers the level of conversation and cheapens us. We speak to people in the same way we would like to be spoken to. We take special care to use a courteous and kind tone of voice. This behavior goes a long way in softening our dealings with everyone.

We are also careful about what we say to ourselves. If we are in the habit of putting ourselves down, we reverse this trait by affirming our good qualities.

Today let me remember that a word once spoken is impossible to withdraw.

Saying No can be the ultimate self-care.

—CLAUDIA BLACK

As recovering men we learn that "No" is a complete sentence. Once we let go of "people pleasing," we realize that we need not explain ourselves. Formerly we might have said yes because we were afraid of making someone angry. Today if we are asked to do something that we do not want to do, we can simply refuse. There need be no excuses, lies or apologies. This applies whether someone asks to borrow money from us, to do something we know to be wrong or to do anything we find uncomfortable.

We also discover that we can say "No" to ourselves as well as others. We no longer have to surrender to our compulsions. If we keep the principles of this program in mind and are working the Steps, we find it becomes much easier to say "No" to the food that is not in our plan, the drink or the drug that tempts us, the bet we might want to place or the lure of an anonymous sexual encounter.

Once we thought our pleasure lay in getting more of certain things than we needed. Now we know that restraint and simplicity keep us on a path of harmony and give us peace of mind.

Today I am taking care of myself in ways that lead to health and happiness.

June 8

Nothing gives me the jitters like a bar room full of queers. —WILLIAM BURROUGHS

All of our insecurities come up when we walk into a room full of other gay men. How do I look? Will they reject me? When we were active, we needed a drink or a drug to fortify our nerves, to loosen us up and to help us feel relaxed. Learning new ways of socializing and relating is one of the biggest challenges in recovery.

The first thing we recognize is that everyone, to a certain extent, feels anxious about how they will measure up in the eyes of others. To hide this anxiety we often put on a suit of emotional armor that keeps people away from us.

A good exercise in making friends is to talk to someone to whom we are not sexually attracted and try to discover what we have in common. When we stop being judgmental, we leave ourselves open to meet new people. Letting go of prejudices, helping others and being available as a listener are some ways we can overcome our fears.

I pray for help today in overcoming shyness. I will do what I need to develop healthy relationships.

The true work of art is but a shadow of the divine perfection.
—MICHELANGELO

Sometimes, as we work hard to earn a living, we concentrate on the material and the rational. But to be well rounded we need to expose ourselves to a multitude of experiences. On occasion it is healthy to invite the irrational, the nonverbal and the beautiful into our lives. Visiting a museum or a gallery, touring a sculpture garden or taking an architectural tour are some of the ways we can expand our view of the world around us.

As we feed our body, so we need to feed our spirit. The contemplation of art opens us up to revelation and inspiration. A beautifully executed dance movement, a soaring aria or brilliant essay can be the gateway to another dimension of feeling and thought. When we keep an open mind about art, we are bound to learn something outside our usual experience of life.

Today I will treat my environment as a blank canvas awaiting my individual artistic expression.

June 10

The essential thing is to put oneself in a state of mind that is close to that of prayer. —HENRI MATISSE

In this program we aim to establish conscious contact with the God of our understanding. Prayer is the means by which we enter the presence of the divine. It has been said that prayer is the key to the morning and the lock to the night. Our feelings of brotherhood increase when we pray together at the end of a meeting.

A prayer can be as simple as the "Help!" we called out when we hit our bottom. Our lives are changed when we pray. Our burdens are lifted, and we are refreshed. Prayer brings us closer to our Higher Power and gives us the assurance that we are loved and cared for. If we are having difficulty praying, we can imagine we are conversing with a dear friend. We open up our heart and soul and share our deepest feelings.

We can bring a prayerful attitude to whatever task is before us. Prayer aligns our hearts and minds with something greater than ourselves, and we receive direction on how to live a better life.

Today I ask for knowledge of God's will and the power to carry it out.

The gay movement will be successful when a young man or woman can acknowledge his or her homosexuality to family, friends and co-workers without any sense of shame and without feeling in any way second class.   —DENNIS ALTMAN

Groups and individuals make social progress slowly. It is up to us as individuals to determine how we can each advance the cause of gay civil rights and our own status as gay people in society.

One member relates how while visiting his family, his mother noticed he was moody and asked him "What is the matter?" He replied "It hurts me that you never ask me how my lover of the past eight years is doing." He went on to say that his family expected him to have an interest in their affairs but no one expressed interest in his personal life. He then told his mother that he didn't feel comfortable with this situation and expected her to respect his relationship and take an interest in it. The next time they spoke on the phone she asked how his lover was doing, and ever since then has taken a more active interest in his life.

Because he stood up for himself and affirmed his relationship, there was a change in the way his family treated him. We can each take positive steps that will help break down whatever barriers exist in our relationships.

Today I will increase the circle of those who recognize me as a gay person of worth.

True Life is lived when tiny changes occur.
> —LEO TOLSTOY

Often in our anxiety to make something happen quickly, we ruin it. Today we are learning about process and what it means. To achieve a particular result we realize that change is gradual. We take baby steps when we are new and only tackle what we can comfortably do in one day. We accept that it is better to do one thing well than to do a dozen things sloppily.

We cannot rush our recovery. Where we are today is where we are meant to be. Mistakes become opportunities to grow rather than whips to beat ourselves up with.

When we have a goal, we make a list of all the things that may be blocking our progress. Then we tackle each obstacle one by one until we eliminate them all. The energy we expend working toward our goal energizes the other areas of our life. Remember it was the tortoise and not the hare that won the race.

Today I will explore the opportunities available for exciting new possibilities in my life.

June 13

Integrity is so perishable in the summer months of success.
—VANESSA REDGRAVE

This program provides us with a set of principles that we can practice in all of our affairs. Are we just "talking the talk" rather than "walking the walk"? It is easy to speak about the Steps but more difficult to apply them to our lives.

We developed a lot of bad habits when active in our addictions. Do we keep our promises—to ourselves and others? Are we trustworthy, or do we tell the truth only when it is convenient? Do we gossip under the guise of constructive criticism?

When people at work or in our families make anti-gay jokes, do we speak up or laugh along with the crowd? Are our beliefs like a set of clothes—to be changed when no longer advantageous? Are we faithful to old friends when our fortunes improve suddenly?

Being a person of integrity is not easy. It means standing up for what we believe in and being true to our values. If we want to maintain our self-respect or the respect of others, we keep to our word and have the courage to stick to our principles.

Today help me to be true to myself and others.

June 14

Man is a political animal. —ARISTOTLE

Our addictions isolated us. We rarely had a sense of community. We placed personal gratification first. Recovery opens us up to many new experiences. Some of us become politically active for the first time. Often our involvement is motivated by anger at the social injustice around us. It takes a while to learn to balance ourselves emotionally and channel our anger into social change. Placing principles before personalities, learning patience and having a sense of humor help us to keep our eye on long-term goals.

By being politically active, we heighten our sense of identity and strengthen our bonds with the community. Our old isolation falls away as we learn new ways of relating to people. We are grateful for the many organizations in the gay community that free us of our old dependence on bars, baths and clubs. Today we have a wonderful opportunity to give back to others some of what was given to us by the pioneers of the Gay Liberation movement. By becoming active and doing volunteer work, we enlarge our horizons.

Today I will be grateful for my new sense of community and look for ways I can be of service.

June 15

Chains do not hold a marriage together. It is threads, hundreds of tiny threads, which sew people together through the years. —SIMONE SIGNORET

The institution of marriage amounts to far more than a religious blessing. It is a legal contract designed to support and encourage intimate relationships as well as protect property rights. There are over one hundred legal rights and many economic benefits denied to gay unions.

Our relationships are relegated to second class status because they are not recognized by society. To counteract this negation, we celebrate and proclaim to our friends and families and to the world at large the sanctity of our love for each other. If we believe we are being denied a basic human right, then we take whatever action is necessary to change the situation.

Our marriages do not have to be imitations of the rigid patriarchal unions. We can provide a model of two equals, coming together in a loving and respectful way, who honor each other's individuality.

However, let us take the precautions necessary to provide for our partner in case of death or emergency. Making a will, giving power of attorney, and keeping clear financial records all simplify matters. While we acknowledge that emotional commitment and love are the glue that keep a relationship intact, we recognize the need to take practical steps to safeguard our rights.

Today I will demand equality for my relationship.

Never doubt that a small group of committed people can change the world. Indeed, it is very often the only thing that does. —MARGARET MEADE

When we were active in our addictions, we thought that change was impossible. We imagined that we were caught forever in the grip of our obsessions and we felt hopeless. Now in recovery, as we become more sane, we know that change is not only possible but inevitable. What direction that change takes depends on our attitude and effort.

Our prospects brighten as we notice the changes in ourselves brought about by working the Steps and attending meetings. We begin to fulfill our potential. Perhaps our example inspires another person to seek recovery. Carrying the message is one of the ways our fellowship grows, and by giving service we strengthen our own program.

We learn to live our lives by a set of principles. These principles apply not only to our recovery but to any worthwhile endeavor. We become an asset to any group we belong to by bringing commitment, an understanding of process and steadfastness.

I believe today that I can be a real force for good in this world.

June 17

The mature person has developed attitudes in relation to himself and his environment which have lifted him above childishness in thought and behavior.
—L.A. CITY SCHOOL PAMPHLET "MORAL AND SPIRITUAL
VALUES IN EDUCATION"

In the fellowship we hear the phrase "His Majesty, the Baby" to describe our immature behavior. As we recover, we discover that our emotional development was stunted the moment we first began our addictive behavior. As gay men we are doubly handicapped by the lack of socialization with our peers in adolescence. Most of us did not have gay role models or mentors who could guide us. In our confusion and pain, we developed slowly.

This program helps us to mature and grow no matter what our age. We learn to accept criticism without being on the defensive. Self-pity slips away as we learn our basic worth. We do not pout when we cannot get our way. We stop lying and bragging and cultivate a sense of humility. When others achieve success, we applaud them. We do not always have to win, and we learn to accept defeat gracefully. We practice listening and are open to others' opinions. We let go of harsh judgments and are tolerant of difference.

I ask my Higher Power for help accepting the pain of growth. Each day is a new beginning on the wondrous journey of life.

There is a paradox in pride; it makes some men ridiculous but prevents others from becoming so.
— CHARLES C. COLTON

Pride has two sides. On the one hand, when it is excessive or misplaced, it is a defect. However, pride is a virtue when it is justified, and reasonable pride is justified.

Pride leads the list of the seven deadly sins. Haughty, insolent behavior is poisonous. An ostentatious display of our material goods is not an attractive trait. We harm ourselves and others when we are disdainful and overbearing. Pride leads us to expect too much of others and ourselves. It fools us into thinking that we are the only ones who deserve abundance.

Yet, when it is reasonable and deserved, pride is proper. If we do a job well, perform a good deed or work hard on a good cause, our self-respect increases. Gay Pride validates the essential rightness of our sexual orientation and acknowledges our values, worth as a group and way of life. Standing up for what is right strengthens our self-esteem.

Pride in our recovery is appropriate. It takes vigilance and effort to stay sober. This does not mean we should lord it over others who have not been given this gift. It means we know who we are, what we have accomplished and how we are today.

◇

Help me to realize that I am the equal of everyone. Let me show kindness, respect and graciousness to all I meet.

June 19

The first time I called my sponsor in the middle of the night, he came right on over to my house and sat with me and we talked and talked. The next time he said "Now pick up your *Big Book* and look at pages so-and-so, and you will get your answer." That was the best gift my sponsor could give me. —ANONYMOUS

A sponsor is someone who has gone before us in the program. He shares his experience, strength and hope with us. We benefit from having someone who lends a sympathetic ear and shares his wisdom. The sponsor is enriched by passing the program along to us.

We are careful not to choose a person to whom we are sexually attracted. Sometimes it is best for a gay man to have a woman as a sponsor.

There is no need to accept this person's word as gospel, but we gain when we are able to trust someone else's opinion on matters of recovery. No matter how long we have been sober, we need a sponsor who can serve as a sounding board and a confidant.

We may choose several sponsors for different reasons. Perhaps one understands some special need, such as our career or issues other than our primary addiction, and another leads us through the Steps.

My program will be stronger when I keep in touch with my sponsor. Help me to be ready to sponsor others, so I may pass this gift along.

June 20

Gay Liberation should not be a license to be a perpetual adolescent. If you deny yourself commitment then what can you do with your life? —HARVEY FIERSTEIN

As addicts and codependents we used our drinking, drugging, gambling, overeating, sex, work, money mismanagement and unhealthy caretaking of others as ways to avoid deeper commitments. Sometimes as gay men this urge to act out and escape was compounded by the fact that we felt cheated of our adolescence because we had to hide our true selves during that time of our life. As adults we were determined to have a good time at any cost. As we grew older, we paid a price for this attitude but found it difficult to change our habits.

In recovery our first commitment is to the fellowship and the program. As we heal from within, we stop blaming others for the pain we have suffered and are ready to take risks and trust other people. We let go of the past and accept ourselves as we are now. We begin to deal with life by having grown-up responses.

Now we are ready to trust the future. Making commitments to work, partners and friends no longer frightens us. In fact, a deepening sense of security develops as we discover the rewards of making a commitment and standing by our decisions.

Today I will accept my responsibilities as an adult and embrace my new life with enthusiasm and loyalty.

June 21

**I question not if thrushes sing,
If roses load the air;
beyond my heart I need not reach
When all is summer there.**
—JOHN VANCE CHENEY

Each season has its glories. For many of us summer means the beach, a place of freedom, where we can frolic across the sands and float in the water. It is a time of restoration and lightness. Others retreat to the country to be rejuvenated by communion with the meadows and the mountains.

No matter how we take the season's pleasures, it is a time of letting go of care—reveling in sheer existence with no need for meaning or purpose. This is when we truly are humans *being* rather than humans *doing*.

At this time of the year we wear light clothing which allows our bodies much more freedom of movement. This program enjoins us to *Wear the world like a loose garment.* When we are immersed in the sensuous delight of fine weather, there is little that can bother us. Let us bottle some of that attitude and put it aside for times when we are tempted to be cross, resentful or bitter.

Today my heart sings a song of delight as I experience the spirit of summertime.

June 22

If you don't learn to laugh at trouble you won't have anything to laugh at when you are old.

—ED HOWE

S ome of us were accustomed to looking at life with a somber, depressing gaze. We were so used to our gloomy view that we failed to see the humorous side of what was happening around us. Others of us only laughed derisively or at the expense of someone else.

This program teaches us to laugh at our dramas and escapades without judging. We begin to see the comic aspect of humanity and of ourselves. When we get too serious, we could benefit from a large dose of laughter. Then we begin to loosen up, relax and put our troubles out of our minds for a time. Hearty laughter chases the winter from the soul and lessens pain. We are never poor if we can still laugh. Why waste our time being grumpy and sour? We feel relieved when we can look on the light side and help others to find humor in life.

We lose a day when we do not laugh. Laughter is a healing force and a by-product of a healthy mind.

Today let me cultivate a sense of humor so that I can laugh joyfully and love.

True to a vision, steadfast to a dream.

—STEPHEN PHILLIPS

How often do we find ourselves wondering what is the best way to achieve a particular goal? In the past our lives were filled with false starts and sudden stops. In recovery we learn the meaning of process. We set our priorities. We make a list of short-term goals that will help us reach our long-term objectives. Then we take the actions necessary to put our plans into effect, doing the best we can each day.

This program has helped to sharpen our listening skills. When we listen, we seek to truly hear and understand others. We let other people have their full say and do not plan our remarks while they are speaking. We practice courtesy and let the speaker finish before we reply. Then we express ourselves in the clearest possible manner so that there are no misunderstandings.

We surround ourselves with those who are on the same path. We seek out people, places and things that will steer us in the right direction. Our antennas are up, and we see how things fit into our plan. A sure and steady course will take us *One Day at a Time* to the fulfillment of our dreams.

Let me remember that perseverance pays. Today I ask my Higher Power for the strength and inspiration to reach my goals.

**You see, I am a homosexual. I have fought it off for
months and maybe years, but it just grows truer.**
—A TEENAGE SON TO HIS MOTHER

Our homosexuality is an essential part of who we
are. It is a result of hormonal, environmental and
genetic factors. Most gay men tell of having sexual or
romantic feelings for other men from the earliest age.
Some of us acted on those feelings sooner than others.
Fear of censure or harassment kept most of us from
expressing our true feelings. For many their environment is still so repressive that to be truthful is very
dangerous. In that case we owe it to ourselves to find a
safe place where we can be open about our interest in
other men.

Critics say our sexuality is a preference, but it is
unlikely that most of us would choose to live a life that
opens us up to discrimination and violence. While we
do not have a choice about our sexual orientation, we
do have the choice to come out as a gay man. This
involves revealing to our family, friends and coworkers
the truth about our primary sexual orientation.

To live openly requires courage. One of the benefits
is that we do not have to fear exposure or blackmail.
This frees us to be the people we have always wanted
to be. By standing up and being counted, we assert that
we are not ashamed of who we are or whom we love.

**Today I will remember that being gay is a
beautiful part of my essence.**

Ideals are like the stars; we never reach them, but like the mariners of the sea, we chart our course by them.
—CARL SCHURZ

Many of us strive for perfection. As children we were the objects of our parents' wishes and expectations. Some of these expectations were unrealistic. In order to please our family, we tried to "look good" at all costs. This attitude drove us to seek the perfect relationship, house, car and clothes, to aim for perfection in all our endeavors. When we failed, we were disillusioned and turned to compulsive behavior or addictive substances to soothe our hurts.

Today let us accept that we will never be perfect and will not always succeed. We will have moments of high achievement and moments when we fall short of our goals. We relax knowing that we have done the best we can today. As we become less hard on ourselves, we stop being critical and judgmental of others.

The only thing we can do perfectly is the First Step. Everything else is an ideal that we work towards. It is okay to aim high, but we need to understand that even if we do not reach goals, we are learning as we go along *One Day at a Time*.

Today I will tend to my own feeling, wants and needs, knowing that I am doing the best I can.

June 26

Seek ye first the kingdom of God, and all these things shall be added unto you. —MATTHEW 6:33

The maintenance of a fit spiritual condition gives us a daily reprieve from our disease. If we falter in this area, the quality of our recovery will suffer. Sometimes we are distracted from our primary purpose. Stress and tiredness can make us doubt our Higher Power. The pursuit of material gain or fame can seem more important than anything else.

On our spiritual journey, we choose actions that lead us closer to our Higher Power. Daily prayer and meditation become a habit. We cultivate our inner life like a garden. We make a space for quiet reflection. Whenever possible we commune with nature and enjoy the uplift offered by a sunset, a walk on the beach or a long hike in the country.

Shared experience at meetings binds us closer to others and fills us with the spirit of love and understanding. As we grow in self-acceptance, we become more receptive to the healing offered by our Higher Power. Our new way of life is immensely practical. We are guided on a path that gives us new gifts and the strength to live fulfilling lives.

I will strive today to put first things first so that I may be closer to my Higher Power and open to all of the good around me.

Our grand business is not to see what lies dimly at a distance, but to do what lies clearly at hand.
—THOMAS CARLYLE

We sometimes waste much of our time in fantasies or reveries. We dream we are something other than we are. We wish we had this or that. We worry whether we will be secure in our old age. We squander our time planning vacations or imagining what happiness we will have when some distant goal is attained.

If we want to realize our hearts' desires, we start by locating ourselves in the present. Realizing that the process is as important as the goal will help us to enjoy life more fully. Every journey must begin with a single step. As long as we take no action, but daydream idly, we will never move forward. It is good to ascertain a direction, but once we have fixed our course, we should keep moving. If we are at a loss for what to do next, we energize ourselves by taking single steps, such as cleaning the house or helping someone less fortunate.

We are the product of our deeds. Thoughtful action combined with forward movement will keep us alert and invigorated.

I will remember that actions speak louder than words.

Once a woman has forgiven a man she must not reheat his sins for breakfast. —MARLENE DIETRICH

Are we having difficulty in letting go of old hurts? Do we constantly bring up injuries and insults suffered long ago? When we disagree with someone, do we badger them until they agree with us? Are we grouchy, peevish and nagging until we get our way?

If so, we would do ourselves a favor by freely letting go of these resentments and character defects. Otherwise they will eat away at us until we have no room left for positive thoughts. Making a list of everyone we resent or cannot control and then mentally forgiving them is a therapeutic exercise. Accepting that we cannot always have our way opens us up to new experiences. We learn respect by taking the time to listen to someone else's viewpoint.

Recovery helps us to outgrow the childish need to control everything. When we loosen our grip and relax, we free ourselves to really enjoy life.

Today I will stop wearing myself out rehashing the past and embrace the Now.

June 29

The weak can never forgive. Forgiveness is an attribute of the strong. —MAHATMA GANDHI

How do we keep negative thoughts and feelings from taking hold of our minds and hearts? How can we stop nurturing grudges and perceived slights? We do this by forgiving.

At the end of each day, we take an inventory. We ask ourselves if we are holding a resentment toward anyone. If we are, we send this person forgiveness through our prayers. We do this even if we think the other person is at fault. Through forgiveness we release anger, resentment and frustration. We free ourselves from the powerful forces of negativity.

If we are having difficulty forgiving someone, we ask our Higher Power for help. We seek to understand, forgive and forget. We remember that we are all human and make mistakes. We extend the same generous spirit of forgiveness that we would ask for ourselves.

Today let me be at peace with everyone and acknowledge that we are all children of God.

June 30

God is love, and he that dwelleth in love, dwelleth in God, and God in him. —LIFE STUDY FELLOWSHIP

We so often hear about the power of love that its meaning has become trivialized for many of us. Love is a word that is used loosely and often, but we must look closely to see its effects in action.

It is easy to show love to those we are in harmony with, but we have difficulty showing love to those we either hate or dislike. That is why this program suggests we pray for those whom we resent. Rather than spewing forth negativity, we emphasize the positive.

When we develop an unselfish and benevolent concern for the well-being of others, our lives are enriched immeasurably. Developing compassion and empathy brings an assurance of love into our lives.

My personal growth is enhanced as I learn to widen the circle of those I love.

July 1

God made homosexuals, so he must love them. I love them, too.
                                            —SOPHIA LOREN

We are all a part of creation, each of us worthy of respect and love. The negative messages we internalized about being gay often made us doubt our self-worth. We begin erasing those lies from our minds by affirming the truth: We are children of God and we are loved for who we are.

As we ask for love, we should be prepared to give it. Some of us have been scornful or critical of our gay brothers and sisters. Today we release these negative attitudes and strive for love, acceptance and tolerance.

Society places great emphasis on difference. By pigeonholing people we can control them. This makes us judgmental and competitive. As sober people we take a spiritual approach and refuse to participate. When someone makes a derogatory remark about a member of our group or another group, we can refuse to comment or offer some positive remark.

Today let me be a source of love to all I meet.

Some people regard discipline as a chore. For me, it is a kind of order that sets me free to fly.
—JULIE ANDREWS

A young man spent a year in India, studying with wise men and gurus. When it came time for him to return home, he asked one of his teachers, "If there is one thing I should know, what would that be?" The reply was "Get a routine and stick to it." This answer seemed very uninspired to the student, and it was years before he fully understood its implications.

In order to accomplish anything, we must have a framework. That framework is supported by discipline. The same principle applies to working our program. Each day should include a time set aside for prayer and meditation and a review of our daily schedule. We ask for the guidance and strength necessary to fulfill our daily obligations. Vigilance in this area will keep us spiritually centered and better able to meet life's daily challenges.

Many of us shy away from Fourth Step inventory-taking because we think it will be an unpleasant task. In reality, taking inventory keeps us on the path of recovery. The Twelve Steps free us to deal with the wreckage of the past, rebuild our lives and grow mentally and spiritually.

Help me to take actions that are good for me. Let me overcome laziness or lethargy.

It is sad to grow old but nice to ripen.

—BRIGITTE BARDOT

Our attitude toward aging determines how we live our lives. Some people feel old at thirty and fight the changes that are inevitable. Others, at age fifty or sixty, embrace life enthusiastically and look forward to new projects and greater accomplishments.

We must always be cautious about getting stuck in one place. Some people bask in the memory of a certain era in their lives, thinking nothing could ever be so good again. Perhaps we have an idea in our minds that only young people can have fun. We need to get rid of our mind-set if we hold any ideas about age that limit or inhibit us.

Each day is a new beginning. We have the opportunity to reinvent ourselves anytime we choose. Everything from our past is raw material for ongoing creativity. Today we might want to return to some unfinished business or reclaim an old skill. Perhaps we want to undertake something new, such as learning to use a computer or studying a foreign language. Life's possibilities are endless, and sobriety has given us the clarity and courage to go anywhere and do anything our hearts desire. Gratitude coupled with willingness will help us fulfill our potential and realize our dreams.

Today I will recognize that each season of life has its own rewards.

July 4

It is a great shock at the age of five or six to find that
in a world of Gary Coopers you are the Indian.
—JAMES BALDWIN

Most gay men tell of feeling sexually attracted to
other men as early as age five or six. They also
knew instinctively that it was dangerous to confide
these feelings to anyone. Many of us thought there
might be something wrong with us. No matter where
we looked, we failed to find a reflection of our desires.
Before long we had a sense of being different from
everyone else. Sometimes this feeling caused us to
withdraw into isolation or fostered desperate attempts
at being accepted. Very few of us escaped trauma, and
we bore heavy emotional scars.

This feeling of uniqueness was compounded by our
addictions. We sometimes felt we were on the outside
looking in—unable to be a part of anything. As a result
we often became belligerent and rebellious.

We are greatly relieved in recovery to find the
company of others who are like us. Having a gay
meeting to attend further enhances our sense of community. The warmth and acceptance we receive go a
long way toward lighting up our lives.

**Today I will show my gratitude for the group
through love and service.**

July 5

Lying to ourselves is more deeply ingrained than lying to others. —FYODOR DOSTOYEVSKY

When a monkey looks into a mirror, he sees a monkey. What do we see? There are so many ways we deceive ourselves. How often do we pretend we are not gay? Do we have a history of denial concerning addiction? Perhaps we eat that extra cookie, saying we are hungry, when in reality we are just indulging ourselves. It is easy to claim we have done our best work when we know we could have tried harder. Maybe we are fooling ourselves when we say we don't need love.

Matching our feelings to the facts is a challenge we face in recovery. For years we deluded ourselves. A Fourth Step inventory helps us identify behavior traits and patterns that block our road to a happy and fulfilling life. The more we strive to know ourselves, the more doors open to us. We face reality and allow ourselves to be honest.

Self-knowledge gives us choice. It permits us to let others know us. We can relax and be ourselves without putting on any false fronts or trying to impress others. When we understand ourselves, we understand others better. Life becomes so much easier when we accept the truth.

Today I will accept both the good and the bad about myself.

July 6

I find the pain of a little censure, even when it is unfounded, is more acute than the pleasure of much praise.

—THOMAS JEFFERSON

Most of us prefer compliments and flattery to sincere criticism. However the mark of a mature person is the ability to accept just criticism without being overly sensitive. How we receive these kinds of remarks depends on our attitudes. If we think that we are above reproach, it is likely we won't respond well. If we keep an open mind, though, constructive criticism can be an opportunity to learn.

As recovering people we take special care when criticizing others. It is easy to point out what is wrong but much more difficult to set things right. If we invest too much energy in fault-finding, negative emotions will consume us. When possible, it is preferable to note the good points of others rather than their shortcomings. A carping, censorious, hypercritical demeanor quickly turns a friend into a foe.

If someone asks our opinion of their work, behavior or ideas, we can offer it—but it is best to remember that truth should be tempered with kindness and consideration. There is an old Boston adage that says "A gentleman does not wear a yellow jacket, but he may not tell another man not to wear one."

Today I will choose my words carefully.

A good way to get "out from under" our daily problems is to stop *reacting* to everything that occurs. Some of us have a constant drive to do *something* about everything that happens to us.

—*ONE DAY AT A TIME IN AL-ANON*

When we react to every unpleasant thing that happens, we surrender control to others. If someone screams at us and we scream back at them, it is our peace of mind that is disturbed. When someone disagrees with or contradicts us, do we get angry? Perhaps we are frustrated because someone will not do something our way. At these times we can ask ourselves: Is it my problem? Does it really matter so much? How important is it?

We don't have to fix every situation. Keeping the focus on ourselves and minding our own business helps us to know what we want today. Through the Twelve Steps we realize the futility of trying to control anyone else's thinking or behavior. We need neither to reprimand nor to rescue anyone. If we can't detach with love, we detach with consideration.

Acceptance of our own imperfections goes a long way in helping us to understand the defects of others. When we stop obsessing over other people's behavior, we have time for an honest self-appraisal. In time we learn to let go and relax.

Today I pray for the tolerance to allow others to live their lives as they best see fit.

I like homosexuality where the lovers are friends all their lives, and there are many lovers and many friends.   —ALLEN GINSBERG

What first attracts us to a person? It might be their physical appearance, their personality or their energy level. On some occasions we might be drawn to someone because of their status or money and then learn that we are smitten with them in ways we did not imagine.

Sometimes we grow apart sexually but remain close in other ways. We can continue to respect and enjoy the company of all those we have loved. Someone with whom we have formed a strong bond can remain in our affections even if we have parted. Perhaps they become a member of our "gay family" and our relationship continues on many levels.

As lovers and as friends we unite our minds and share amusement, excitement, troubles and all our moods. We support one another and readily give expression to affection and love.

I will appreciate all the wonderful people in my life.

July 9

Regret for the things we did can be tempered by time; it is regret for the things we did not do that is inconsolable. —SIDNEY J. HARRIS

All of us have done much that we wished we had never done. But more distressing are thoughts of the opportunities we have missed and the promises we have broken. These things can never be changed. This is the time when we need to practice acceptance. In recovery we put the past behind us and look at what is possible today.

Do we hesitate to pursue something we want because of fear? Do we think we are less than others and therefore not worthy of achieving our dreams? Do we torture ourselves by endlessly thinking about our unfulfilled hopes and plans and never acting?

We have to decide if we are going to live our lives fully. Is there a talent we have buried? Have we been postponing a project?

All we need to do is take action, no matter how small, and turn the results over to our Higher Power. As healthy, mature men we deal with our past and come to terms with it. Anything we want to achieve is possible one step and *One Day at a Time.*

Today I choose to set goals and take an action toward fulfilling my dreams.

July 10

The main reason we sleep is because the nobler part of the soul is united by abstraction to our higher nature and becomes a participant in the wisdom and foreknowledge of the gods. —DR. JOHN BIGELOW

While we sleep, all of our organs and senses remain active. The only thing that ceases is the activity of our conscious mind—the part of us that most needs rest. All day our mind races—planning and plotting, worrying and wondering—until it wears itself out. Sleep allows the conscious mind to withdraw from the world of things and commune silently with our subconscious, and we become both spiritually and physically recharged.

If we are deprived of sleep, we become irritable, moody and depressed. Most people need between six to eight hours of sleep, and if we think we can get along with less, we are fooling ourselves.

One of the reasons we pray just before we go to bed is that our subconscious mind is in a receptive state. We ask for the solutions to our problems, inspiration, counsel, healing and guidance. During our sleeping hours we unite with the universal life force. Our answers may come in our dreams. Upon awakening, we trust the hints we have received from our subconscious mind.

Help me to sleep in peace and wake in joy.

Some of the reasons that I am the way I am are precisely because of a negative history. Why would I erase that? Not that you have to act on it every day, but it is so much a part of your decision-making.
—JODIE FOSTER

A member of our group tells that during his drinking years his mother often apologized to him for the awful way he was treated as a child. He used to reply, "There is no need to apologize. I had a very happy childhood." Later he realized he was in denial and that indeed he had suffered much physical and emotional abuse as a child. After several years of meetings and therapy, he became aware of and accepted what happened to him as a child. He had been filled with resentment but was never quite sure of the cause of his troubled feelings. In time he forgave his parents.

As gay men we have suffered a great deal of oppression, individually and collectively. Recognizing how these forces have shaped us is an important step in self-discovery. Often we developed defense mechanisms in order to survive. Perhaps we developed a sharp tongue to combat hecklers or a cynical shell to repel harassment. Fear of rejection forced many of us into an emotional straitjacket; we became secretive and afraid to reveal ourselves. In time these mechanisms turned on us. In recovery we are given the awareness and the tools that help us discard this outmoded behavior.

Today I will not let old sorrows and hurts prevent me from living an open and loving life.

July 12

Life is a banquet and some people are starving.
                                                    —AUNTIE MAME

Are we shortchanging ourselves by not living up to our potential? Have we condemned ourselves to a dead-end corner because of imagined deficiencies? Does some old, nameless fear hold us back? Do we think that if we succeed at one thing then something else will be taken from us? Do we miss opportunities because we are afraid to dive into the river of life? Taking an inventory can uncover the root of our problem. We check our list for the patterns of self-doubt and low self-esteem that keep us from achieving. Eventually we reap the fruits of our words and thoughts, whether negative or positive.

The world is a place of abundance, yet we were blind to this. In the past we programmed ourselves for failure and disappointment. In recovery we learn to stop complaining. It is counterproductive. We stop voicing lack and limitation. We reprogram ourselves by focusing on positive mental pictures. We expect good things to happen. We are thankful for what we have and for what we are about to be given. We trust that we will be taken care of and place ourselves into the care of our Higher Power.

Today I will tap into the infinite abundance that is flowing through the universe.

July 13

Do something every day that you don't want to do. This is the golden rule for acquiring the habit of doing your duty without pain. —MARK TWAIN

Before we came into recovery, some of us were in a state of mental disorder and our lives had completely fallen apart. In the program we find it takes a while for this situation to change. We have all heard members of our group tell of not being able to clean house, pay bills, do a Fourth Step or fulfill other responsibilities. To a degree, none of us want to do anything that we feel would make us uncomfortable. We expend a lot of energy postponing important chores and other obligations.

A good exercise to help us take action is to make a list of things that need to be done. We then rate the things on the list in their order of difficulty. The first thing we choose to do is the most difficult thing on the list. Then we do the second most difficult thing, and so on. Finally we are left with the easiest tasks, and when we finish the list, we enjoy a sense of accomplishment. Eventually we take pride in dealing with difficult situations and willingly do our work.

I will jump into the stream of life with enthusiasm and diligence. Today I will enlarge the emotional, physical and spiritual territory I inhabit.

July 14

Truth and myth are one and the same thing—you have to simulate passion to feel it and therefore man is a creature of ceremony. —JEAN PAUL SARTRE

Mankind marks the important moments and stages of life with ritual. Ceremonies celebrate and consecrate the arrival of a new child. Symbolic gestures and words are used at weddings to cement the union of two people who love each other. Funerals are the place where we salute those who have died, give them a spiritual farewell and allow the living to grieve.

Every culture and society has rituals, symbols and holidays to express their basic beliefs. As gay people we have long been denied the opportunity to publicly display our affections, mourn our dead, praise our living heroes or celebrate the hallmarks of our lives.

Gay relationships can be supported and validated by special ceremonies. Pride parades and rallies afford opportunities to join with others and to feel a sense of worthiness and community. Giving a gift to a community or AIDS organization to commemorate a dead friend helps to keep his memory alive. Award dinners that extol gay accomplishments are a valuable way to commend those who have given greatly of themselves.

Our lives take on a deeper meaning when we observe with dignity and reverence the changing of the seasons, solemn personal and public moments and hallowed occasions.

I will imbue the significant moments of my life with an aura of respect and love.

July 15

There are moments in our lives, there are moments in a day when we seem to see beyond the usual. Such are the moments of our greatest wisdom and happiness.
—ROBERT HENRI

Sometimes we hold a grudge and then suddenly we recognize the futility of doing so and are released of our burden. Perhaps, while speaking to someone, we notice all the loveliness of their being and are grateful that we know them. A startling event or a close brush with danger can lift us out of the ordinary.

Often we get so caught up in our daily routines that life seems an endless round of repetition and drudgery. When this happens, we need to take time to stand back for a moment from the rush and whirl of our everyday world.

If we trust our intuition, we know that life has a deeper purpose, and we are a part of it. By keeping up an active dialogue with our Higher Power, we permit ourselves to experience life at its fullest.

Let me ponder all the wonder that is in this world and make an effort to appreciate the good in my life.

July 16

Kindness is a language that the dumb can speak and the deaf can hear and understand.
—CHRISTIAN NESTELL BOVEE

In the past we developed the bad habit of impulsively chastising or judging others. Recovery teaches us to deal gently with our fellow man. The world can be a rough and cruel place.

We show kindness by remembering the needs of others. We telephone someone who has been ill or is alone. We do not use force or compulsion. We seek to understand others and let go of self-will. Whenever we get an impulse to say or do something unkind, we quiet our mind and think before we speak. We avoid tirades and criticism. Today we can smile at a stranger or let someone ahead of us in a line.

We never regret being too kind. If we hurt others, we hurt ourselves. If we are kind to others, we receive kindness in return. Let us add to the store of good in this world by being loving and gentle.

May I be a gentle presence in this world.

July 17

Whatever crushes individuality is despotism, by whatever name it may be called. —JOHN STUART MILL

Society claims that gay men's difficulties with self-destructive behavior, low self-esteem and trouble with intimacy result from our sexual identity. The real cause of this behavior is the terrible oppression we experience growing up in a homophobic society. Being shunned and physically attacked, absorbing negative messages about our sexual identity and fear of exposure leave deep emotional scars. Our emotional development was stunted by growing up in such a terrible atmosphere without family or peer support for our sexual identity.

As adults we felt guilty about having loving and erotic feelings toward members of the same sex. We sought to escape through our addictive behavior. To end this cycle we need to understand that these behaviors were normal reactions to the stress and trauma we experienced. Recovery helps us to deal with our feelings and be released from self-blame. Healing comes from self-nurturing and building a supportive network of kindred souls. We learn to affirm that our sexuality is a gift, and we share it in loving and intimate ways.

Today I will acknowledge the pain of growing up in a homophobic society. I recognize that my self-destructive behavior was the result of the abuse I suffered.

Every form of addiction is bad, no matter whether the narcotic be alcohol or morphine or idealism.

—C. G. JUNG

One recovering alcoholic tells that when he stopped smoking cigarettes he pulled up a chair in front of his refrigerator and began to gorge himself on food. Psychologists say that unsatisfied needs in childhood cause us to seek fulfillment in a variety of ways, some healthy, others not. We may take a long time to find out why we are the way we are, or we may never know. We cannot wait until we know the answer to get better.

If we find ourselves acting compulsively in areas other than our primary addiction, we should use the same tools we used in early recovery. Before surrendering to an impulse, we think it through and imagine the consequences of our behavior. We avoid people, places and things that might be a temptation. Calling a program friend might just be the antidote to our craving. We apply the Steps to the problem.

The longer we are in recovery, the more we learn how to provide for ourselves in ways that are appropriate. We acquire a set of tools that permit us to live happy, joyous and free lives.

When I am bothered by cravings and compulsions, I will act as a beginner and use every tool at my disposal.

July 19

To be simple is to be great. —RALPH WALDO EMERSON

This is a simple program for complicated people. Some of us think that the more complex the answer, the better it is. However, time and experience have shown that a strong foundation based on the basic tools of recovery we learned as beginners will carry us a long way.

Let's take an inventory and see if we are working our program: Are we operating on the twenty-four-hour plan? How active are we in the fellowship? Do we remember to eat or drink something before we get too hungry? How often do we talk to other recovering people? Have we placed any conditions on our sobriety?

Have we cut down on meetings now that we are feeling better? Do we put ourselves into situations where our willpower is tested? Are we continuing to work the Steps and apply them to our daily life?

If we make a genuine effort at working this program, before long we see progress. Eventually great changes in our life take place. The small acts done on an hourly and daily basis culminate in the creation of a new person.

Today help me to keep it simple.

Sure, you can create your joy, but you have to over-come a lot of pain to get there. Many people just can't. There is nothing sadder than an old alcoholic dyke unless it's an old alcoholic queen. —RITA MAE BROWN

We have all seen older gay men perched on bar stools in what is sometimes known to the younger patrons as "the old queen's corner." There they sit: They have seen it all, they have done it all, and they have drunk it all. They're cynical and bitter, and alcohol has become their best friend. Too often, their life potential has been robbed from them by their addiction. They have become sad examples of compulsive behavior and a picture of hopelessness.

Thankfully, more and more people are becoming aware of this program. Gay men and women are being freed from the bondage of addiction and obsessive-compulsive behavior. It is not always easy, but the rewards are great.

In gratitude for our recovery let us reach out and carry the message to as many people as possible. Speaking at meetings, visiting gay men in prisons, taking a meeting to an AIDS hospice or volunteering to answer phones at the central office are some of the ways we can give back a part of what we have received.

Today I will take the time to give of myself. I will also remember that being a good example is an excellent way of carrying the message.

A healthy organization—whether a marriage, a family or a business corporation—is not one with an absence of problems, but one that is actively and effectively addressing or healing its problems. —M. SCOTT PECK

When we have a problem with someone, do we just walk away or do we try to work through our differences? Do we always try to be the person who has the last word? Are we in the habit of thinking our way is the only way to do something? Are we willing to compromise and look for solutions?

In every group we belong to or in every relationship, we will meet with difficulties. To face challenging situations honestly is the first step toward movement and renewal.

If we are to thrive, we need to learn to work in harmony with others. Patience and loving kindness, rather than harsh criticism and quick judgments, are the best tools to foster goodwill. Racism, sexism, homophobia and ageism divide people. To resolve conflict and promote harmony, we need to listen and be willing to understand other points of view. Obstacles can be positive hurdles where we come together and overcome differences. As we grow and learn in our relationships with others, we discover spiritual values that support us on our journey through life.

Let me work today to live a balanced life in harmony and accord with others.

**Ask and it shall be given you; seek and ye shall find;
knock, and it shall be opened unto you; for everyone
that asketh receiveth; and he that seeketh findeth, and
to him that knocketh it shall be opened.**

—MATTHEW 7:7,8

What is the source of lack? Some philosophers say it is in our attitude. Feelings of worthlessness and low self-esteem may prevent us from asking for what is due to us.

An empty pocket is just a need to be filled. If we find all the reasons it cannot be filled, it will remain empty. The universe is abundant, and our faith in a Higher Power will help us reap its rewards. These rewards are material, spiritual and emotional.

We ask our Higher Power for help. When what we lack is material, we ask for guidance in obtaining our share of this universe's abundant harvest. We remember that giving is the surest way to abundance. If we suffer from stress and anxiety, we petition our Higher Power for relief. The power of prayer has been demonstrated countless times. It has been said that the only ones who scoff are those who have not tried it.

Our Higher Power is the source of a mighty stream of substance. As channels of God's expression, we bless the world around us and know that ultimately all of our needs will be taken care of.

**I am a unique expression of the infinite and claim
my inheritance of abundance.**

July 23

There is no need for parents to fear homosexual teachers. Ninety-seven percent of child seduction is heterosexual. —DR. BENJAMIN SPOCK

Gay men have become the new bogeymen now that Communism has fallen. Societal fears of the unknown have been projected onto the gay community. We have become scapegoats and fund-raising tools for the Far Right. The ignorant have maligned us as child molesters and monsters out to undermine society. No distinction is made in the public mind between pederasty and homosexuality.

Every gay man has been exposed to heterosexual teachers, and yet this has not changed his sexual orientation. When we try to take care of our own youth we are accused of proselytizing. We must not let this deter us from creating organizations and institutions that guide and serve gay youth. Young gay men are bombarded with myriad negative messages that make self-acceptance difficult. There is a real need for positive gay role models and education among the young. This is an area of much controversy, change and challenge. Each of us has a responsibility to give serious thought to how we can help make a contribution to those who are following us. When we see a young person at a meeting, let us reach out in a respectful and caring way.

I will do all I can to create a loving and safe environment for young gay people.

Elegance is refusal. —DIANA VREELAND

When we were active, we had to have more and more of everything to satisfy our needs. Some of us ate to the point of gluttony or drank ourselves into oblivion. Many of us hid drugs, fearing our supply would run out. Others among us clung obsessively to the people in our lives. No matter how much of anything we had, it was never enough.

Learning to say no is not just an aphorism. When we eat a meal slowly, savoring every taste, we are adding an aesthetic element to a physical need. Surrendering our will and letting go of drugs and alcohol allow space for more refined and subtle pleasures, not only physical but mental and spiritual as well.

When we permit people the freedom to be themselves, we increase our own choices. When we choose carefully the people and things we want in our life, we show ourselves respect. In time, as we grow and discover our true needs, we gain a satisfaction unknown to us when we were in the grip of our addictions.

Today I will attempt to savor each moment for what it is and accept that as enough.

The behavior to which we've clung in order to prevent us from looking deeper into ourselves has lost its power to placate, erase, assuage. We've all felt the horror of thinking we were left with nothing.
—DAVID CRAWFORD

In the past we relied on chemicals, overeating, compulsive sex, dependent relationships, alcohol and other forms of self-destructive behavior to dull our senses and escape the pain we felt. We were caught in a vicious cycle. The more we consumed or acted out, the worse it became. Yet we kept repeating the same behavior, expecting different results. Our lives were in shambles, but we did not know where to turn or how to stop. We were spiritually bankrupt and had lost all hope. Nothing seemed to work for us anymore. By the time we sought help, we were usually in a state of despair.

Now that we have the program, we use the Steps and other tools to change our behavior and look deeply inside ourselves. When we see how others are recovering from their problems, we become hopeful that there is a way out for us as well. Where we once felt empty, we now sense the possibility of growth and change. The old demons that had us in their grip fade away, and we are given a vision of a new life.

◇

Let me be thankful today for the gift of hope.

July 26

Do not take life too seriously—you will never get out of it alive. —ELBERT HUBBARD

Do we feel we have to right every wrong? Are we always reacting to everything around us as though it were directed toward us personally? Do we feel with such an intensity that life takes on a tragic dimension? Are we walking around with a tortured and gloomy outlook? Everyone suffers and we all have troubles as we make our way through this life. But if we see everything as a problem, then our life will be only problems.

Sometimes it is useful to step back and ask ourselves, How important is this situation? Through practicing the Twelve Steps, we become willing to go with the flow and relax. We learn to sort out what pertains to us and what we should ignore. We learn to let go of our disturbances by practicing meditation and relaxation techniques.

Today's crisis can sometimes be tomorrow's comedy. A good sense of humor is our best fashion accessory and will make us welcome everywhere. Let us practice laughing and looking at the fun side of life.

Today instead of focusing on the negative, I will look on the light side of life.

For one human being to love another: that is perhaps the most difficult of all our tasks, the ultimate, the last test and proof, the work of which all other work is but preparation. —RAINER MARIA RILKE

Falling in love is easy, but staying in love requires discipline and patience. In any partnership conflicts will arise. How we resolve them is a test of our maturity. Our old inclination was to quit the relationship as soon as things became difficult, but now we know that nothing worthwhile comes easily.

Today we can put our old way of looking at love aside. We no longer take hostages. We share ourselves with our lover, but we respect his individuality.

Loving someone consists of more than sexual attraction or moonlight and music. Passion is only one part of the equation. Love is being present for someone whether they fall ill, make a mistake or fail to live up to our expectations. Thoughtful effort, frank communication and loving acceptance are tools that keep a relationship together. We listen carefully and show respect for our partner's opinions.

Showing our love is important. A hug, a kiss, a massage or a surprise gift are expressions of our deepest feelings. Little kindnesses and thoughtful acts strengthen our connection and help our love to grow.

Today I will treasure my love for my partner and do the best I can to cultivate it.

July 28

Negative action has one good quality; it can be purified.
                                                    —SOGYAL RIMPOCHE

When we did the Fourth Step, we identified patterns of negative behavior that were undermining us and destroying our peace of mind. We discovered in the Sixth and Seventh Steps that we needed to change our attitude, become humble and align ourselves with the will of our Higher Power.

Sometimes when we are at a meeting and hear a person reveal something awful they have done, we receive a shock of recognition. We know that we have behaved in similar ways. When we observe someone doing something wrong and we are offended, that person becomes a negative power of example, showing us how we do not want to be.

As our character defects drop away, we are given hope that we can become the person we always wanted to be. Recovery is allowing us to learn and grow. The extent of our willingness will determine our progress.

Today I will be more aware of those areas of my life that need improvement.

Nothing is really work unless you would rather be doing something else. —JOSEPH CONRAD

Our attitude toward work determines how we feel at the end of the day. If we see our job as drudgery, we will be exhausted and drained. However, if we make an effort to bring a cheerful and willing outlook to our appointed tasks, our work life will be rewarding.

Since our time at work takes up so much of our life, we need to make every effort to be involved with something that makes full use of our talents. Being fulfilled at work is part of our goal of leading a balanced life. Sometimes we stay at a job because of the security offered but we hate what we are doing, or perhaps we feel trapped in a dead-end job. If so, we should take the necessary steps to change our job. Until we do find something satisfying, we do the best we can in our present situation. Complaining and shirking our responsibilities does not make us happier. We take an inventory around work issues to help us establish priorities that are realistic and attentive to our inner needs.

Let me take a prayerful attitude toward the task at hand.

July 30

Slander slays three persons; the speaker, the spoken to, and the spoken of. —BABYLONIAN TALMUD

When we speak ill of, or tell lies about, another person, we are doing a grievous harm. First we pollute our own spirit. Then we drag the person we are speaking to into a poisonous, negative atmosphere. And finally we injure the person we are speaking about, possibly causing irreparable harm.

If we find ourselves slandering or gossiping about someone, we ask why we are acting this way. Are we seeking revenge? Are we harboring an old resentment? Do we want to make ourselves look better at the expense of this other person? Are we afraid?

We have come to realize that speaking about others in a cruel or unkind way reduces us in the eyes of others and harms our own self-esteem. We treat people with the same respect we would want. If we cannot say something positive, we refrain from speaking. If we are angry or have been hurt, we take a deep breath, count to ten and think through the consequences of speech. We have faith that our Higher Power will right all wrongs.

Today I will make a sincere effort to speak only kind and loving things.

He who is not sure of his memory should not undertake the trade of lying. —MONTAIGNE

L ying became such a habit for many of us that we could not distinguish between truth and falsehood. We retreated into a world of fantasy and lies. Some of this behavior was learned from our family, while the rest was a symptom of our addiction. Shame mixed with guilt drove us to cover up anything that did not match our imaginary reality.

Today we know that telling the truth makes life easier. Lying separates us from others and forces us to be always on guard. Facing up to facts gives us insight into how to proceed in our search for a fuller life. We are free to go forward without looking over our shoulders. Being honest binds us to others and gives us the capacity to grow. We build trust by sharing the true, intimate details of our life with our fellow recovering brothers and sisters.

Today I will give myself the gift of being truthful, knowing that it frees me from isolation.

August 1

**Why indeed must "God" be a noun? Why not a verb
. . . the most active and dynamic of all?**   —MARY DALY

This program places emphasis on action over theo-
rizing. It hardly matters what we believe if we do
not act in a principled and spiritual manner. The
person who does not practice what he preaches is an
all too familiar figure.

When we do unto others as we would have them do
unto us, we are practicing a simple but powerful spiritual precept. Loving our neighbor as ourselves brings
us into harmony with divine order. Doing good is the
best way of being good. Our noblest thoughts and
intentions mean nothing if we don't apply them. In our
loving, sharing, caring, helping and working, we can
make a difference.

When we take care of ourselves, help others and
contribute our energies to the common good, we reflect
the universal creative life force in action.

**Today I will strive to be an enthusiastic channel
for the spirit and actively use my talents for the
greater good.**

August 2

I believe that the masculine male homosexual is the ultimate symbol of human freedom, and that's why you have male homosexuality occurring at those great high points of culture such as classical Athens and Florence.
— CAMILLE PAGLIA

Because of the suppression of gay history, we grow up without knowledge of the great men who shared our sexual orientation. This suppression of the truth makes us feel weird and isolated. When we do learn that we are the continuation of a long line of free spirits, innovators, great thinkers and creative achievers, a burst of fresh air rushes into our lives. We no longer have to feel deficient. We can emulate some powerful examples of excellence and virtue.

As we go about our day, we reflect on what it means to be gay. Do we take it as a license to be self-indulgent, or do we cherish it as a freedom upon which we can base positive and meaningful lives? The principles of this program as embodied in the Twelve Steps have made us aware of our spiritual and social responsibilities to ourselves and others. Each day let us find the kernel of greatness within ourselves and nurture it. Let us not squander our heritage but strive to be people who make a difference, whether it be in our neighborhood or on the world stage.

Today I ask my Higher Power for the knowledge and inspiration necessary to fulfill my potential.

Joy is the most infallible sign of the presence of God.
—LEON BLOY

We are told in *The Twelve and Twelve* that the joy of living is the theme of the Twelfth Step. The key to obtaining that joy is action. By giving unselfishly of ourselves and practicing the Twelve Steps, we find emotional sobriety.

As a result of our spiritual awakening today, we are living a life of purpose and direction. We feel useful and needed. Our attitude toward other people is one of courtesy and fairness. We accept responsibility cheerfully. We realize that we are not alone and become constructive members of a community.

The small things in life take on new meaning and importance. A job well done, a favor granted, a pleasant conversation or a sudden understanding can give us deep satisfaction. Our new outlook on life is reflected in our laughter, the way we love and the peace of mind we enjoy.

Let me allow joy into my life so that I may be nourished.

August 4

Be thy own palace or the world's a jail.

—JOHN DUNNE

The most profound relationship we will ever have is with ourselves. If we look to someone else to affirm our existence, we will often be disappointed. We cannot expect anyone else to create the environment we want. Working the Steps and following the principles of this program assures us that we will have a measure of serenity.

Being a member of a minority is not always easy. We need to develop our confidence and self-esteem if we are to successfully face hostility. There are some who would make us feel unwelcome or who would do us harm because we are gay. We cannot ignore them, but at the same time we must be careful not to give our power away. We cannot allow their negativity to color our outlook.

We have the ability to take care of ourselves. The remedies for any problems we might have lie within us. The sooner we take responsibility for our lives, the more likely it is that we will feel at home wherever we go.

I will stop looking for others to fix me. Today I affirm that I am all right as I am.

It has long been an axiom of mine that the little things are infinitely the most important.

—ARTHUR CONAN DOYLE

Often little things affect our minds more strongly than big things. It is sometimes easier to cope with major calamities than with the incessant annoyance of minor disturbances—such as the constant ringing of the telephone, the pettiness of bureaucrats, a rude person or a roommate's untidiness. A friend may have an annoying habit, such as using the same catchphrase repeatedly, that drives us crazy.

We must be careful not to overreact and treat these events like disasters. It is necessary to keep a sense of proportion if we are to live comfortably. Small provocations may be like thorns in our side, but we must not let them overwhelm us. If we find ourselves unable to cope, we can take a quiet moment and ask ourselves, How important is it? When we get some distance from a situation, we can put it into perspective. Ultimately, we must accept that life is often filled with petty aggravations that must be borne with good grace if we are to keep our peace of mind.

Grant me the serenity to be able to meet any challenge—large or small.

August 6

Love yourself first and everything else falls into line. You really have to love yourself to get anything done in this world. —LUCILLE BALL

It is easy to love others. Loving ourselves is more difficult. We may harbor such exaggerated and unrealistic standards of perfection that we always fall short. We then judge ourselves as unfit and unworthy. Perhaps we believe the homophobic rhetoric we grew up hearing. Do we think we are less important than others because of economic or educational status? Were our parents cold and unloving?

Self-hate manifests itself in so many ways. Our former abuse of food, drugs, alcohol and relationships was a symptom of our lack of self-esteem. We did not believe ourselves lovable and found this intolerable. We avoided reality. In time, our unpleasant behavior drove people from us. We were paralyzed with fear and self-loathing and were unable to realize our ambitions.

Today in recovery we shed our old skin and practice self-respect, and we work on fulfilling our needs. We avoid those who do not give us the love and nourishment we need. We stop giving others permission to put us down. We refuse to compromise for the sake of pleasing others. We affirm ourselves daily as people worthy of love. We free ourselves to make the most of our lives and accomplish our wildest dreams.

I acknowledge that I am a person worthy of love and respect.

The more one pleases everybody the less one pleases profoundly.   —HENRI STENDAHL

One member tells that when he first came into the fellowship, he wanted everyone to like him. When his charms did not always work and he found that some people did not care for him, he was dismayed. He then realized that his desire to be liked by everyone was futile and that in reality there were many people whom he did not like. Learning to live with this fact was a turning point in his life.

Are we afraid to upset our parents by bringing our lover home? Do we change our minds when we find out that someone disagrees with us? Have we remained in the closet because we are afraid people will not like us if we are open about our sexuality? Are we hesitant to say no to someone because they will be angry with us?

We are all anxious for other people's approval. It is natural to want to be liked, but if we sacrifice our own needs to fulfill others' expectations, we are the losers. When we compromise too much and let someone else control our reactions, we severely limit ourselves. Learning how to be assertive is one of the gifts of sobriety. We no longer need to please everyone, because we now have a sense of our own worth. Our opinions and beliefs count, and we have the right to express them.

Today I will strive to be true to myself and do what is right for me.

August 8

In diving to the bottom of pleasure we bring up more gravel than pearls. —HONORÉ DE BALZAC

We often do things to excess, yet find no satisfaction. How many times have we repeated behavior only to be disappointed by the results? When we binge, our initial reaction might be elation, but this is quickly dissipated. Sometimes it seems that nothing can make us feel full, yet we continue to act out, using the same ineffective behavior. Our old habits tell us we need to gratify our desires immediately. We think that happiness will result from having everything we want when we want it.

Practicing this program and stopping our compulsive behavior teach us that happiness is the result of a process. Good things come to us in time as we make an effort to grow and learn. We learn the value of moderation and balance. Because we are compulsive people, we need always be on guard against our old ideas. Working the Twelve Steps will keep us centered in the present and enable us to enjoy what we have.

We eventually realize that overindulgence always backfires and dulls the senses. If we learn to savor our pleasures, our appreciation will be deeper and last longer.

Let me use reason and moderation in the pursuit of pleasure.

Our knowledge can only be finite, while our ignorance must necessarily be infinite. —SIR KARL POPPER

There is no end to new things to learn. Yet we sometimes fall into the false notion that we know it all, believing that our way is the only way. Ultimately this closed-mindedness produces stagnation. Do we refuse to recognize that someone younger than ourselves may know more on a certain subject? Perhaps we dismiss an opinion because we think the person expressing it is beneath us. Are we rigidly tied to a dogma or doctrine? If we become cynical and bitter, our vistas narrow and doors begin to close.

The principles of this program were foreign to most of us. The idea of powerlessness was at first difficult to swallow. Yet when we surrendered, a whole new world opened up. When we realized our old ways did not work, we developed a willingness to try another way. Admitting that we need help and that we have much to learn is the first step toward real growth.

Today I will make the most of my opportunities, knowing that whatever I should know will be revealed to me.

The most radical contribution the gay movement has made to society is the idea that pleasure justifies sexuality at least as much as reproduction.

—CHRIS BULL

Many of us have had difficulty expressing ourselves sexually because we did not feel that our sexual identity was valid. Perhaps we thought that being gay was not as good as being straight. We were fooled by the teachings of family and church into thinking there was something wrong with the way we loved. Some of us had to use drugs or alcohol before we could have sex with another man. This backfired and drove us deeper into isolation.

Now that we accept ourselves as we are, we can freely enjoy our sex lives. An awareness of our bodies, brought about by our increased self-respect, awakens us to subtle as well as passionate responses. Our pleasure is amplified because we no longer harbor feelings of guilt. As long as we do not harm anyone or ourselves, we are free to explore a wide range of sexual experiences. In seeking to become whole, happy people, we gladly pursue healthy sexual gratification.

I will be respectful of my body, incorporating an emotional and spiritual component into my pursuit of sexual pleasure.

Every creator painfully experiences the chasm between his inner vision and its ultimate expression.
—ISAAC BASHEVIS SINGER

There is usually a gap between our intentions and the outcome of any project. Whether we are painting a picture, writing a paper, doing a business deal or working on a relationship, things often do not turn out the way we envisioned them.

Perfect fulfillment of our goals is rarely possible. If we expect perfection, we will always fall short, and we may allow our disappointment to cause us to sink into despair.

Let us stop judging ourselves harshly and learn to be more flexible. Just because an outcome is different from what we imagined it would be, it is not necessarily wrong. We need to learn to work with our mistakes and build upon them.

Being creative requires a certain amount of struggle. If we try to control the results too closely, we stop the flow. The real reward is in the doing.

Today I will remember that I am an original expression of God's creation, and I will share myself with others.

Certainly, the best works and those of the greatest merit for the public, have proceeded from the unmarried or childless men. —FRANCIS BACON

Since most gay men are not parents, they are free of many responsibilities and financial burdens. The energy and time released by this independence opens up numerous choices. How we use these gifts determines the type of person we become. When we were active, we indulged in much selfish behavior. Because we were not fettered by family responsibility, we took that as a license to do whatever we wanted. Some of this behavior was self-destructive. More often than not, we thought only of ourselves and our own desires.

Recovery teaches us responsibility. We realize that we have received many blessings and it is our duty to give back some of what we have received. This responsibility can take many forms. Giving generously of our time and money to organizations and charities provides a rich spiritual reward. Doing the best we can at our jobs helps to improve the atmosphere for everybody around us. Sharing our ideas and energy with the community uplifts everyone. We also can reach out and help young gay people who have just come out. By sharing all our skills and talents, we enhance the quality of life for the family of man.

Today I will be grateful for all the good that I have received and will joyfully share my time and energies with others.

August 13

How important to find ways to eroticize "safe sex," how necessary not to allow AIDS to usher in a denial of the power and beauty of Eros.

—CHRISTINE DOWNING

As addictive and compulsive people, we became accustomed to instant gratification. We never learned process and always went for the quick fix. In our sex lives we gave little thought to anything but the pleasure of the moment.

In recovery some of us let the pendulum swing in the opposite direction and shut down sexually. Once again we let fear govern our lives. We practically threw "the baby out with the bathwater." Now that we are leading healthy lives, we have an opportunity to change and explore new and more subtle modes of expression. We challenge ourselves to find fresh ways of relating sexually. Most of us were used to having sex under the influence of drugs or alcohol. Learning to relate to someone as a sober person can be difficult.

Our gay sexuality can be expressed as passionately as we choose. Taking the time to educate ourselves about AIDS and other sexually transmitted diseases frees us of fear. We talk with our lovers and find out what turns them on. We develop negotiating skills and protect ourselves and our partners. Acting safely and responsibly does not keep us from celebrating our sexuality in an exciting and loving way.

Today I accept the responsibility of "safe sex" and relish the beauty and power of my sexuality.

August 14

The average man finds life very uninteresting as it is. And I think that the reason why . . . is that he is always waiting for something to happen to him instead of setting to work to make things happen.

—A. A. MILNE

All of us have idled away many hours daydreaming. Do we sit on counter stools waiting to be discovered rather than going to auditions? Do we hope that someone will see our true worth and take us away from our present life? Do we think that life will be more interesting when we retire?

Sometimes we feel we deserve better than what we have, but we can't seem to find a way to go about getting it. Our attitude is like that of a person who wants to win the lottery but never buys a ticket. We are disappointed when nothing happens, and sometimes we become bitter and cynical toward anyone who has accomplished something.

We do not have to be passive observers. We can shape our own lives. Find a passion and pursue it. If we are unhappy with a situation, we can stop complaining and find a remedy. We are the only ones who can change our lives. Taking personal responsibility frees us to be the person of our dreams.

Today help me to take positive actions toward a fuller life.

**Let yourself be silently drawn by the stronger pull of
what you really love.**   —RUMI

The forces of society and the committee in our
minds are constantly telling us what to do. Most
of us can think of dozens of reasons why we *cannot* do
something. Are we afraid of failure or ridicule? Are we
discontented but afraid to make a move?

Taking positive action to create change requires
courage and curiosity. What would we attempt to do if
we knew we would not fail? To help ourselves act, we
make a list of three things we would like to do. Under
each category we write the steps necessary to achieve
our dreams. Then each day we do one thing on the list
that moves us closer to our goals. This might mean
putting away a small amount of money each week to
start our own business or networking with someone
who can help us enter the field of our choice. If we are
diligent, before long we will have made definite strides
toward achieving our objectives.

To overcome obstacles we act despite our fears.
We take risks. Once we have made the leap of faith
necessary, we often wonder why we were so afraid.

**Today I will take positive actions toward making
my dreams come true.**

August 16

Homosexuality was illegal in my father's time, just as it was in Joe Orton's time, which wasn't very long ago . . . and we might see it becoming illegal again. People will live their own lives no matter what oppressive legislation is passed, but at what a great cost to them and society as well! We must do everything to make sure this doesn't happen.   —VANESSA REDGRAVE

It is difficult for some young people to realize how oppressive life was for gay people just twenty years ago. Police harassment on the streets and in bars was common—just standing on a street corner was an offense. The murder of a gay person meant nothing to the authorities. Being out, except in a very limited circle of people, brought social ostracism.

Much progress on the economic, legal and social levels has been made, but we cannot take this new freedom for granted. Our right to exist is constantly being challenged.

When we were active in our disease, we were often too self-absorbed to care about our human rights or the rights of others. This fellowship is a bridge back to life. In recovery we give some thought to how we can make a contribution to our community. Each one of us can pick an area that concerns us—perhaps domestic partnership rights, repeal of the sodomy laws or the world of gay sports—and give to it the gift of our time and energy.

Help me to do today what is right for myself and others.

Associate reverently, as much as you can, with your loftiest thoughts. —HENRY DAVID THOREAU

Each of us needs a sacred place. In times past people gathered in holy groves or other special natural places to connect with the divine. In our busy modern world our sacred place might be a space within ourselves where we are free from material bonds. Here we experience and bring forth our true self.

When we settle into a still, quiet space we calm our anxieties and fears. We detach from our daily concerns and compose ourselves. Through prayer and meditation we find ourselves the center of the universe. We recognize each moment as a moment in eternity. Aligning ourselves with our breath, we come upon that shining point where all lines intersect. In the quiet we see that the movement of time gives us our sense of life.

Meditation allows us to glimpse the plane of being behind the visible. We begin to understand that our body is a vehicle for consciousness and that the eternal within us does not die.

Knowing that the center of everything is right where I stand, I bless the universe and send out waves of love.

God's gifts put a man's best dream to shame.
— ELIZABETH BARRETT BROWNING

As addicted people we constantly undervalued ourselves. We asked for rhinestones instead of diamonds. The things we thought we needed often turned to ashes when we got them. Our fears and insecurity prompted us to think that vast wealth or great fame would be the answer to our dilemma. We were so busy wanting what was out of our reach that we overlooked those things of value that make life truly rewarding.

Today we are grateful for the gift of recovery and a new life. Sometimes it is easy to take these things for granted and think that we have accomplished everything by our unaided will. But it is only through the grace of our Higher Power that we have been rescued from a life of addiction and codependency.

Good things come to us when we turn our will and our lives over to our Higher Power. Having faith that our needs will be met gives us the ability to appreciate the good things in our life. We begin to see the value of lasting relationships, peace of mind, good health and the beauty and love that surrounds us. We make the most of what we have and open ourselves to an endless array of possibilities.

Today I will ask for the vision to see what is truly of worth in my life.

Pain makes man think. Thought makes man wise. Wisdom makes life endurable.　　　—JOHN PATRICK

How can we profit from all the pain that we have endured? Sometimes our experiences are overwhelming. A survey of our life reveals the cause of our suffering and helps us not to repeat our mistakes. As recovering men, we have the unique opportunity to participate in a community of people who are learning about themselves through self-examination, sharing, listening and service.

Change takes time. To develop a deep understanding of our situation and the ability to choose soundly, we need to have patience. Keeping company with other recovering men and women makes good sense. We seek advice when we have a problem and follow the good example of others. The accumulated wisdom of those who have gone before us helps in times of challenge and pain.

The wisdom that is within us emerges as we develop insight and discernment. Self-acceptance fosters balance. Our inner feelings begin to match our outer actions. Honesty and self-respect give us the courage to stand up for what we believe. Our compulsive actions are restrained by the capacity to choose wisely.

I pray for the wisdom to do what is right and to accept life on its own terms.

August 20

We are so fond of one another because our ailments are the same.   —JONATHAN SWIFT

One of the ways this program works is through identification. People tell their stories and we listen to them attentively because we know where they have been. When we hear something that is similar to our own experience, we often laugh, sigh, cry or nod in recognition. This helps to bond us to the speaker and the other people in the room. We share a common problem and together we are striving to overcome it. A sense of awe comes over us when we realize that we have survived the devastating effects of this disease that unites us.

Our character defects are symptoms of the disease. We empathize when we see someone struggling to overcome a particular shortcoming. Their struggle can illuminate our own journey toward physical, spiritual and mental health. We feel the pain that accompanies growth. Our sense of self-worth increases when we realize that we can be helpful to fellow members of the group.

As gay men getting sober together, our bond of brotherhood is further enhanced. We feel a closeness to other recovering men because we care for them and share the same feelings. We understand one another and have a genuine interest in one another's well-being.

Today I will be grateful for the brotherhood that unites me to everyone in this program.

August 21

Take what you can use and let the rest go by.
— KEN KESEY

We need to remember that those speaking from the podium or sharing from the floor at a meeting are only expressing their own opinion. They are telling us what worked for them. If we are touched by what they say or are moved to act, then we are grateful we have received a gift. If we disagree with what is said, we have the right to ignore it. If someone injects controversy or their personal dogma into a qualification, we can remind them of the tradition that states we have no opinion on outside issues.

Just because we are in recovery does not mean we surrender our reason. If we are uncomfortable with something said at a meeting and have doubts about its validity, we discuss it with our sponsor or a trusted friend. The Twelve Steps and all the slogans are but suggestions. They are derived from the wisdom and experience of members who have gone before us. Everyone goes at their own pace and progresses to the best of their ability. No one has a right to tell someone else how to work their program.

**I respect everyone's right to express themselves,
knowing that I do not always have to agree
with them.**

Many lesbians and gay men who are chemically dependent do not succeed in traditional treatment programs. Heterosexism and homophobia are magnified in many centers where lesbian and gay concerns are ignored, silenced or confronted with hostility. Even in centers that seek to be sensitive to the concerns of lesbians and gay persons, there are subtle barriers to honest disclosure of sexual orientation and lifestyles.

—DAVID A. DUBOIS

Some of us came into this program through treatment centers. If we were not in an environment where we could be completely honest about all aspects of our life, then our chances of recovery were diminished. A safe, supportive setting was crucial if we were to open up and share our deepest feelings and secrets. This same need holds true for meetings. If we do not feel supported or welcome at our present meetings, we keep searching until we find one where we do feel safe.

It is important to find a gay meeting to go to where we can unburden ourselves and communicate openly and honestly. Holding onto secrets keeps us stuck in the same old places. Sharing helps us to develop trust and move closer to others.

Today I will resolve to find a meeting where I feel safe and can openly share without fear of being betrayed or judged.

August 23

Follow your bliss. — JOSEPH CAMPBELL

Wouldn't it be sad to come to the end of our lives and feel that we never did what we wanted to do. Are we letting social and economic factors determine our actions? Do we always do what we feel our family requires of us? What good is life if we don't go where our body and soul want us to go? Rather than being caught up clinging to the wheel of fortune, wouldn't it be better to be in the center doing the spinning?

This program helps us let go of our fears. Through faith, trust and self-inventory we enter into a realm where we are free to make choices. We are given the courage to live the lives we were created to live.

For the moment let us imagine three things we would like to do if money were not a consideration. As an exercise we can close our eyes and visualize ourselves leading the lives of our wildest dreams. Today would be a good day to begin the pursuit of those dreams.

Today help me to uncover my source of joy and sing my own song.

Music is well said to be the speech of angels.
—THOMAS CARLYLE

Sometimes in recovery we are in a hurry to make up for lost time and wasted opportunities. Too often we do not set aside moments for relaxation. We forget to recharge our batteries. One of the most restorative gifts we can give ourselves is music.

Music relaxes us and puts us in touch with our inner self. Surrendering to the harmony and rhythm of music is a tonic that energizes and renews us. Listening to an old favorite can revive pleasant memories. Hearing a new piece of music often opens us up to new levels of communication and understanding. Feelings that have lain dormant become activated and enhanced. Our spirits are uplifted, and we come closer to our Higher Power. Listening to the music of different cultures broadens our outlook.

Music is the universal language of humankind. Like silence, music refreshes. It takes us out of a controlled and rational state and transports us to a higher plane.

Today I will set aside some time and allow myself to be lifted by the power of music.

I very clearly remember feeling isolated because I was the only one who was gay. I thought I would never have any friends. A black person would have other black friends, but gay kids can't even count on having other gay friends. —JASON CURRY

Gay people must hide the very essence of their being during the most sensitive and formative years of their lives. No other group of people grows up in such extreme isolation. We are without peers, counselors or role models to give us support. Because of ostracism and harassment, many gay youths commit suicide. Those who survive are testaments to the triumph of the human spirit over adversity.

Our youthful struggles leave their mark. We internalize society's message of hate and turn it upon ourselves. Our self-destructive behavior reflects inner conflicts that can often rip us apart. By the time we enter recovery we have endured much physical, mental and spiritual abuse—some self-inflicted and some imposed on us.

In this program we are learning to love ourselves. Our old isolation is dropping away as we make new friends and meet a wide variety of people. We are weaving a web of connection with kindred spirits. For once in our life we feel we belong to something larger than ourselves.

Today I am thankful for the love and support of my friends.

I don't know any parents who look into the eyes of a newborn baby and say "how can we screw this kid up?"
—RUSSELL BISHOP

Many of us grew up in dysfunctional families. As a result we lacked security and tenderness. Often we have a difficult time forgiving our parents for the harm they did to us.

It certainly makes sense and is mentally healthy to explore our family background and identify patterns of behavior that influenced us. Sometimes the truth that we uncover is horribly painful. However, we do what is necessary to process our feelings and then move on. Getting caught up in the "blame game" is counterproductive. As we grow, we learn to look at our role in the family and how we affected the other members.

We try to understand our parents in the same way we would ask others to understand us. No doubt they were passing on what they did or did not learn from their own parents. Most likely they tried to do the best they could. Besides raising us, they had other responsibilities and might have been overwhelmed by them.

We pray to forgive our parents' shortcomings so we can heal. We let go of resentments and take responsibility for our own lives by connecting to responsible, nurturing and caring adults in Twelve Step programs.

Today let me be grateful for that which I have received from my parents.

Men are often capable of greater things than they perform. They are sent into the world with bills of credit and seldom draw to their full extent.

—HORACE WALPOLE

In the past we wasted much time and energy on obsessive behavior. Our lack of self-respect prevented us from exercising our full range of abilities. Some of us felt excluded because we were gay and therefore isolated from much of life. Our inner conflicts caused us to neglect and deny many parts of ourselves. We were given to excess and often felt badly about every aspect of our lives.

Now we have the opportunity to heal by integrating the physical, emotional and spiritual parts of ourselves. Physically, we treat our bodies with respect by developing a program of exercise, getting plenty of fresh air and eating nutritious food. Emotionally, we reach out and do our best to establish meaningful, loving and sound relationships. We end our spiritual isolation by seeking to know our Higher Power's will for us.

In recovery we strive to become effective and well-integrated people. We take new actions, and if we don't succeed, we try again. We know the joy is in the journey. We end our separation by letting ourselves unfold and make full use of our potential.

I ask my Higher Power for help in balancing my inner and outer selves.

The only people who never fail are those who never try. —ILKA CHASE

Many of us have been afraid of success. Our poor self-image says we do not deserve to succeed. Perhaps we heard messages from our family that told us not to try. It is possible that we are afraid of surpassing our parents. Do we think that if we succeed, others will like us less? Fear of new places and new people can hold us back from achieving our goals.

Sometimes the problem is that we aim too low and do not challenge ourselves. Or perhaps we spend all of our time daydreaming and never take the necessary actions. One of our bad habits may be that we are constantly starting things and never finishing them.

To succeed we need to take risks and accept change. Taking a leap into the unknown is frightening, but we can reach out to friends and colleagues for support. By working this program, we increase our confidence. We stop feeling sorry for ourselves or blaming others for our shortcomings. We no longer work for others' approval but strive for inner satisfaction.

Today I will no longer let others make claims on me that keep me from achieving my full potential.

Don't let anyone live in your mind rent free.
—AL-ANON SAYING

Are we obsessing over someone else's behavior? Does someone else run our life? Is our happiness dependent on another? If so, we need to detach with love. This is never easy, but necessary if we are to attain emotional sobriety. Sometimes we are so deeply enmeshed in an unhealthy situation we think that by detaching we are being cruel. What we don't realize is the person we are being cruel to is ourselves.

How do we recognize when our attitudes are unhealthy? One sign is when we assume responsibility for someone else's feelings and behavior. Another is when we allow others' actions to determine how we respond and make decisions. Do we tiptoe around the truth, afraid that if we speak up we will be rejected? Do we put our own values aside to connect with another? Do we only feel good about ourselves when we know someone likes us?

This program teaches us to respect our own and other people's boundaries. We need to replace internalized negative messages from the past with positive messages of recovery. We do not have to sacrifice our individuality or integrity to receive the love and respect that is our due.

Today I acknowledge that I am whole and good.
I am not alone but am one with my Higher Power
and the Universe.

Character is not a fashionable concept. Now we think we act because our family situation was so, because our historical location is so, because we are sailing with the tide of history, or because it has abandoned us as reactionary deviants. Today all of our actions are really performed by our grandfathers; we take no responsibility, like the owners of umbrella stands in hotels. —MALCOLM BRADBURY

There is no denying that our family and place of birth had a great influence on us. It is also evident that we are part of a larger whole and are sometimes swept up by forces greater than ourselves. However, there is a trend today not to accept personal responsibility for our actions. Instead we get caught up in the "blame game." As gay men it is particularly easy to attribute all of our defects to oppression and exclusion.

We are not just pawns. We are creatures of will who have made many choices. This program teaches us we are responsible for our actions. Once we realize that our past was molded by addiction, we make a genuine effort to change our attitudes, find solutions and act as mature adults. This means admitting when we are wrong and trying to do the best we can in all our endeavors.

Today I refuse to blame others for my problems.

To keep oneself safe does not mean to bury oneself.

—SENECA

In the past we might have done many foolish and dangerous things. When we got sober, we sometimes overreacted and erred too much on the side of caution. Living a sober life does not have to be dull or limited. Only in growth and change can we find a true sense of security. If we cling to the status quo, life will pass us by, and before long we will be isolated and lonely.

This program is a bridge back to life, and we can cross it with enthusiasm and courage. If we have anxiety about changing jobs or moving to another town, we remember that we have placed ourselves under the care of a power greater than ourselves and need not waste our time worrying. When we are in doubt about which way to turn, we ask our Higher Power for guidance. Everything in the past prepared us for this present moment. We have the resources not just to survive but to prosper and bloom.

Every time we take a risk or try something new, we reveal more about ourselves to the world. Taking action requires courage, but if we trust divine guidance, we will know that we are being carried safely through every experience.

**Today I have the wisdom, strength and courage
to do whatever I need to do.**

September 1

I refused to go to gay groups because I did not want
to be identified as a homosexual. Because of this, and
not being able to let anyone really know me, I did not
make any progress in my first six months. Finally I
went to a gay group, got a sponsor and started on the
road to sobriety.   —AN A.A. MEMBER

I solation is one of the hallmarks of our disease.
We suffer from the delusion that we can solve our
problems without anyone else's help. Because of shame
we keep our deepest concerns secret.

Most groups welcome all people, but sometimes we
may feel uncomfortable sharing our sexual identity with
strangers. The support we need will be found only
if we can be open and honest about every aspect
of ourselves.

Recovery is difficult, and we bolster it in every way
we can. We seek out a gay group near to us and become
involved. We find a sponsor whose sobriety we admire
and establish a solid relationship. We need to be in
touch with someone who knows who we are and can
help point us in the right direction. We keep in regular
contact with members of the group. If there are no gay
groups in our area, we make plans to attend round-ups
where we will meet other kindred spirits. It is important
to feel a part of a fellowship where we can see a
reflection of ourselves.

**I am thankful for the love and support of gay
groups everywhere.**

September 2

We are the hero of our own story. —MARY McCARTHY

When we are at a meeting listening to someone tell their story, it is like being around a prehistoric camp fire, where hunters would gather at the end of the day and relate the adventures of the chase. Similarly, the person qualifying might speak of dangerous encounters, hilarious incidents or close brushes with death. We hear tales of horror, excitement, romance and desperate drama. The story ends when the hero hits his bottom and by some miraculous grace finds this program. We share this point with the qualifier. We have survived and are gathered together for mutual support.

Telling our story and listening to others is an important part of the program. It draws us closer to one another. Usually, at some point during a person's story, we experience a spark of recognition. Oh, I did that, or I felt the same way.

Sometimes it is easy to take recovery for granted. When we hear a newcomer, fresh from the battlefield of drunkenness, addiction, compulsive sexuality or binge eating, it keeps our story green for us. We were all on a quest—searching for something to fill us up. We took many wrong turns. Finally we have found something that fulfills our needs—a spiritual way of life that restores us to our true selves.

Help me never to forget the darkness and horror of my bottom. Today I will say a prayer of thanks for the renewal of my spirit and the gift of life.

September 3

If you want to make a difference, if you want to feel good about yourself, find a cause and lend your time and talents. Nothing is more rewarding.
—ELIZABETH TAYLOR

Love and service are the essence of this program. We have learned that in order to keep what we have we must give it away. Helping newcomers, being there for people returning from slips and reaching out to those who are troubled or in pain does more for us than for the person we are helping. Serving as a group officer, ordering the literature, being the treasurer or doing hospitality at a meeting are all necessary functions. Volunteering for one of those positions helps to keep the group running.

Doing service frees us from the bondage of self. Too often we are caught up with our own concerns and fail to see the world around us. Now that we are mature, responsible people, we welcome the opportunity to give of ourselves. Being a friend to someone who is sick, tutoring a child, stuffing envelopes for an organization we believe in or working at a food bank are just some of the ways we can make a positive contribution.

Today I will give the gift of myself to help make this a better world.

September 4

We live in an atmosphere of shame. We are ashamed of everything that is real about us; ashamed of ourselves, of our relatives, of our incomes, of our accents, of our opinions, of our experience, just as we are ashamed of our naked skins.   —GEORGE BERNARD SHAW

Most of our lives we have been angry and depressed as a result of the things we were ashamed of. The only time we ever felt relief was when we drank, drugged, overate or gave into some other compulsive disorder.

We find that when we get sober, we often switch addictions. The ex-smoker becomes the overeater, the drunk becomes a codependent or the sex addict turns to alcohol or drugs. Some people who give up substance abuse become workaholics or religious fanatics. These are all manifestations of the same problem.

To get rid of our shame we must get to its source. We stop denying the truth. We mourn the love we never received and grieve for our lost childhood. Sober, we experience for the first time the pain we tried to push away. We allow ourselves to feel our feelings and stop acting out. It takes a lot of hard work, but eventually we can be released from the bondage of compulsive behavior and enjoy the power of choice.

Today I will ignore the voices that tell me that I am flawed. Instead I affirm that I am a perfect example of God's creation.

We should pray for a sane mind in a sound body.
—JUVENAL

Mental, physical and spiritual health is our greatest treasure. Without it our lives become poor and narrow. If we do not pay attention to all of these areas, we will suffer from a lack of balance, making it easier to return to our old ways.

Our pasts are full of irrational acts. By the time we came into this program, we were insane in many ways. Who, in their right mind, would repeat the same destructive behavior over and over, knowing the damage it was inflicting? We have been left with many grave emotional scars. The Twelve Steps are a sound base for a restoration to sanity. If we continue to have problems, however, we seek professional help.

To keep as well as possible physically, we get plenty of fresh air, exercise and nutritious food. Periodically we see our doctor for a checkup. We become familiar with our bodies, inspecting ourselves regularly, alert to any unusual changes or disturbing symptoms.

A fit spiritual condition results from daily prayer and meditation, and service to others. We forgo resentment, ill will, hate and fear as unhealthy destroyers of the mind and body. We establish an intimate relationship with our Higher Power and give thanks and praise for our continuing recovery.

Today I will acknowledge myself as a perfect expression of the divine will.

September 6

The great enemy of the truth is very often not the lie—deliberate, contrived and dishonest—but the myth—persistent, persuasive and unrealistic.
—JOHN F. KENNEDY

M any myths about gay people are pure fiction, yet we often believe them ourselves.

We reject the idea that we choose our sexual orientation and affirm that our condition is a wonderful and natural part of the spectrum of human sexuality. We dismiss the notion that we are harmful to families and point out that gays and lesbians, like anyone else, have families they love and cherish.

Critics have said that gays are unable to sustain stable relationships. However, this notion is a homophobic fabrication. It is important to note that the number of lifelong gay and lesbian relationships is impressive, especially when you consider that society gives no support or endorsement to these unions.

Let us consider what we can do today to help deflate the myths that have been created about gay people. If we hear someone make an untrue remark about our community, we can point out the fallacy of their thinking and replace fiction with fact.

Today I will examine my thinking about gays and lesbians. Help me to be on the side of truth.

September 7

It's never too late to be the person you always wanted to become.
—GEORGE ELLIOT

How often do we say something like "I would like to be a lawyer but it takes four years and I'll be forty by then, so why bother?" The answer to that remark might be "Well, you'll be forty in four years anyway, so why not become a lawyer?" Recovery permits us to do the things that we left unfinished or missed doing because of our addictions.

There are many accounts of people fulfilling their dreams in sobriety. One man, a stockbroker for many years, quit his job and became a nurse working with AIDS patients. A waiter in his mid-thirties, who dropped out of college in his sophomore year, went back to school and got his degree with honors. An accountant, who worked for his family and hated it, became a travel agent who now leads tours all over the world. An actor became a friar, while another man quit the priesthood to become a filmmaker.

At some point in our lives we have imposed limits upon ourselves. Now is the time to break these constricting boundaries and dare to do what our hearts desire. In recovery we use the day at hand in a way that makes us feel worthwhile and happy.

Today I will make the best use of my talents and abilities. I ask for help to release my old fears so that my spirit can soar.

September 8

It is better to be hated for what one is than loved for what one is not.   —ANDRE GIDE

In the past many of us were always trying to please others. We pretended to be someone we were not. Perhaps we were ashamed of our sexuality. We lied about who we were and where we came from. Our biggest fear was that we would be rejected. We lied and deceived ourselves in order to be loved. The deeper we got into our addictions, the greater the deception became. Eventually, we lost touch with our true selves. Life became a masquerade. Constant comparison of ourselves to others made us feel unworthy.

In recovery we learn self-acceptance. We gain self-knowledge and self-respect by doing the Fourth and Fifth Steps. The Eighth and Ninth Steps put us on the best possible terms with other people.

As gay men we may have absorbed many negative messages. Our new way of life teaches that we are children of God and have every right to a full and happy life. Our feelings of inadequacy begin to fade. As we become comfortable with ourselves, we come to terms with the past and self-acceptance.

Today I will list my assets and make an honest effort to acknowledge my self-worth.

September 9

If all pulled in one direction, the world would keel over. —YIDDISH PROVERB

Sometimes we find it hard to settle our difficulties with others. We have trouble admitting that someone else might be right, or we feel we have to have the last word. We often argue past the point of reason. We feel that if we compromise, we lose. From pride we stubbornly cling to our position. Our serenity suffers, and in the end no one wins, because discord and dissent have prevailed.

Recovery teaches us a different approach. We listen patiently to others and let them explain their position. We carefully weigh and analyze what we have heard. We sort out what is important and recognize where we can be flexible. Placing principles before personalities is a helpful tool in any debate. Respect and courtesy for the other person go a long way toward finding a solution. As mature people we realize that we cannot always have everything our way. Learning to be relaxed and adaptable will bring us much peace of mind in the long run.

Today I will easily and effortlessly go with the flow of life.

Writing is nothing more than a guided dream.
—JORGE LUIS BORGES

Our self-image determines our life experience. We may be trapped acting out old mental pictures of who we are and what we think we should be doing. One way to break that cycle is to make an Image Book.

In this book we write down our dreams and aspirations. We note the things we want to have, to do and to become. By putting our strongest desires on paper, we give them a voice. Our self-concept becomes clearer, and we are able to map out a direction.

Some useful categories for an Image Book might be family, spiritual, self-improvement, health, career, financial, community and material desires. Under each category we write the steps we plan to take to achieve our goals.

By putting our dreams and desires on paper, we are committing ourselves to take direct action. We see what changes we need to make. We set goals for the next six months, the end of the year, and for the next five to ten years. We look at our book daily and review our progress. We reserve a page for any special problem areas.

**I affirm that good orderly direction will help me
make positive changes.**

September 11

Do not the most moving moments of our lives find us all without words?   —MARCEL MARCEAU

All kinds of sounds surround us in our daily lives. The endless chatter on radio and TV, the sounds of construction, the clamor of coworkers trying to make a point, the din of background noise and the roar of traffic are only some of the distractions we must endure. With all the noise that assaults us each day, it is often difficult to find our center.

At the end of a meeting, when everyone is holding hands and about to pray, the speaker frequently asks for a moment of silence, and a hush comes over the room. A powerful yet tranquil space is created where we all come together on a special level.

Setting aside a time each day to keep silent is a potent spiritual exercise. Silence helps to rid our minds of annoyances and superfluous thoughts and focuses our concentration on the essence of our beings. Long periods of quiet calm us and reward us with the precious gift of serenity.

In silence we receive strength, are given answers, find inspiration and begin to feel at one with the world around us. Silence is a habit that, when cultivated, benefits our mental, physical and spiritual health.

Today I will seek peace of mind in tranquil silence.

September 12

It's all right to have butterflies in your stomach. Just get them to fly in formation. —DR. ROB GILBERT

Fear often prevents us from doing the things we want to do. We say we will act once the fear has passed, but often we are too late. Our fear enslaves us and we become submissive victims.

Maybe we want to tell someone we are gay but dread their reaction. If we waited till we knew the outcome of everything, we would have a limited life. Are we afraid to ask someone out on a date because they might say no? Are we too shy to speak to someone new? Do we hesitate to go for the job we really want? There are no assurances in this world that we will not be hurt, but if we do not take risks no growth can take place.

We often waste a lot of energy procrastinating and let opportunities slip by. Recovery shows us that it is better to deal with the situation at hand and move forward. When we are afraid to do something, we swallow hard and take the action, doing the best we can and turning the results over to our Higher Power. We ask for the support of friends, draw on our faith and trust that no matter what happens we will survive.

Today I will face whatever I fear and do it anyway.

September 13

The only Zen you'll find on top of the mountain is the Zen you bring up there.　　　　—ROBERT M. PIRSIG

We do not have to be in a special place to get in touch with our Higher Power. That power is found within us. However, being in a clean, quiet space where we will not be distracted by extraneous influences does help. That is why, since ancient times, people have set aside special places for worship. The first temples were groves of trees that were considered sacred.

When we attend meetings, we are with people who have joined together for a common purpose. Inspired by the sharing and empathy, we often feel the presence of some spiritual force.

At other times we will want to retreat to a private place where we can enjoy a time of renewal unbroken by outside disturbances. Some of us set aside such a place somewhere in our house. Others find an outdoor spot where they feel comfortable.

No matter where we are, our attitude determines our spiritual state. To make a spiritual connection we need to create an inner calm. If we are harried or stressed, it is best to meditate before we approach our Higher Power. This helps to put us in a receptive space to receive the guidance and sustenance that we need.

Help me to remember that I will find the strength, joy and wisdom I need by looking deep within myself.

If gay sexuality is socially constructed, as our best and brightest continue to insist, gays should be capable of socially constructing it in such a way that it is compatible with health. —GABRIEL ROTELLO

The post-Stonewall ethic of sexual freedom gave rise to a period when many gay men engaged in unprotected sex with multiple partners. Often this behavior was accompanied by heavy alcohol and drug use. Gay men had been oppressed for so long that this sudden burst of sexual activity became a statement of gay liberation. The coming of the AIDS epidemic rang a death knell on this lifestyle. We courted death if we engaged in this high risk behavior.

In order to survive today we need to practice safer sex every time we make love to someone. Learning what is safe and what is not is crucial. There are many sexually transmitted diseases other than AIDS. Often the transition to safer sex is a difficult one to make—but one that is essential if we are to maintain our health.

For those in recovery this adjustment is similar to the one we made when we came into recovery. It means taking responsibility for our actions. Accepting that there are limits does not mean that we are anti-sex. Our sexuality is a beautiful gift, and as such we must use it wisely.

Today I will respect others and myself by learning how to practice safer sex.

September 15

You're allowed to be in despair for a few years in the middle of your life. And then all the things about which you were in despair cease to matter, and you start all over again. —QUENTIN CRISP

We all experience times when we are filled with regret and remorse over things not done or unattained. Perhaps we never reached a career goal or we still mourn a lost love. It is natural to feel sorrow over loss or failure but at some point we have to put the past behind us and move on. As adults we recognize that we will not always get what we want. If we morbidly obsess over what could have been but is not, we stagnate and choke our creative growth. When we look back on what was important five years ago, we are often amused at how insignificant those problems seem now.

Learning to embrace where we are in life right now is a spiritual challenge. Sometimes the prospect of change or loss can be frightening. Recovery gives us hope for a better tomorrow. Once we accept that we cannot change the past and that life goes on, we gain a new strength to go forward with enthusiasm. As we work the steps, we will not regret the past nor wish to shut the door on it.

I will be grateful for every experience that has brought me to this point in life. Let me use what is best from the past as a foundation for a fuller today.

September 16

The most beautiful thing we can experience is the mysterious.
—ALBERT EINSTEIN

Even in recovery, sometimes our lives seem humdrum and pointless. When they do, we take the time to stop and contemplate our place in the universe. There is an ultimate reality that is not apparent to the senses and cannot be grasped by intelligence alone. Through prayer and meditation we can commune with this reality and sharpen our insight and intuition. The mysteries of life and death are beyond our rational powers, but a glimpse of our true nature is given to us when we enter the silence and center ourselves.

When we get too caught up in consumption or become stubbornly attached to our worldly identity, we become easily jaded and dissatisfied. Our physical wants and needs are only part of our total requirements. Our souls need to be stirred by the ineffable if we are to keep a sense of excitement, wonder, curiosity and surprise.

We find it healthy to set a part of each day aside to attend to our spiritual needs. A period of quiet, a walk in the park, reading a philosophical book or creating a private altar of objects we find meaningful can do much to refresh us.

Today I will cooperate with my Higher Self by getting in touch with some part of the divine expression of the life force.

Simplicity is making the journey of this life with just enough baggage. —CHARLES DUDLEY WARNER

We are asked in this program to *Keep It Simple*. This advice will serve us well in any situation. The more we complicate our lives the greater the chance that we will become stressed and confused. As addicted people we were accustomed to lying. Now that we tell the truth, everything is easier because we don't have to remember the lies we have told. In our desire to be supermen we often took on too many tasks and ended up performing them all poorly or giving up. By doing one thing well, we are building a foundation for further accomplishment.

If we keep the focus on ourselves, we do not have to waste our energy trying to write the script for everyone else. We lighten our burden by living *One Day at a Time*. Accepting things as they are helps us to relieve tension and function more efficiently.

When we keep things simple, we stay centered and see where we are going in life. As we pare down we develop the ability to discover what is important and what is only a distraction.

May I find ways today to distinguish between the essential and the unimportant.

September 18

They threw me out and now I am basking in the fierce
white light that beats upon the thrown.
—ALEXANDER WOOLLCOTT

As members of a minority we are often excluded
from certain aspects of society. This has forced us
to look at ourselves and ask: Who am I? Why me?
What's going on here? In response to a painful situation
we gay men have become analytical and detached from
the larger society we live in. Our powers of observation
have been sharpened as a protective measure. We
become quite adept at taking other people's inventory.

In recovery we take this talent for observation and
fearlessly turn it upon ourselves. If we are thorough in
this process, we become better men and more comfortable with our sexual identity.

The gay community has been the object of great
scrutiny in the press and other media. Much has been
revealed that was once secret. Straight people are
getting a better idea of who we are, and we are learning
that we are everywhere. Bringing our lives into the
light of day will go a long way toward healing the
many wounds we have suffered, both as individuals and
as members of a group.

Help me to cultivate a keen sense of introspection
so that I may know the many parts of myself and
celebrate them all.

September 19

Confession of our faults is the next thing to innocence.
—PUBLILIUS SYRUS

No one likes to clean a stove. We usually put it off until the dirt is too thick to tolerate. While we are cleaning, we sometimes scrape our knuckles and curse the task. However, when we have finished, we are glad we took the time to do the job right.

Some of us approach doing the Fourth and Fifth Step in the same manner. We are filled with dread and postpone what is necessary. But if we want to stay sober, we do not skip these vital Steps.

After we have taken our written inventory, we look for someone to share it with. We choose carefully, finding a person we can trust to keep a confidence. This may be our sponsor, a therapist, a clergyman or a close confidant.

Sharing our inventories is a humbling experience. It is not the criminal but the ridiculous and shameful things we have done that are hardest to acknowledge. All of our lives we have kept up a public facade. We presented this view to the world while we hid our shortcomings.

By telling our life story to another, without any reservations, we take the first step toward an honest life. We swallow our pride and reveal every detail. When we are finished, our fear and anxiety slip away, and we move into an entirely new phase of our lives.

I will unburden myself of all my secrets so that I may move into the light of the day.

September 20

Tis a gift to be simple, Tis a gift to be free
Tis a gift to come round where we want to be.
—OLD SHAKER SONG

Are we in the habit of complicating our lives? Sometimes this is the result of being unfocused. Setting priorities and goals helps us to avoid being swamped by unnecessary details. Concentrating on the basics simplifies our lives. Learning to take short inventories when we are confused or anxious is an excellent tool for putting *First Things First*.

Our new freedom makes life go more smoothly. We can let go of old, useless baggage and drop our guard. There is no longer a need to be a know-it-all. Saying "I don't know" can be a big relief.

Gratitude for the gift of sobriety directs our attention to what is important in life. Now that we are unfettered by the bondage of addiction, we can put our energies into becoming the kind of person we always wanted to be. Our understanding deepens as we move toward a connection with our true self.

As I go about today's activities, I will be grateful
for the gifts I have received.

September 21

Season of mists and mellow fruitfulness,
Close bosom friend of the maturing sun;
Conspiring with him how to load and bless
With fruit around the vines that round the thatch-
eaves run.
To bend with apples the moss'd cottage-trees,
And fill all fruit with ripeness to the core.

—JOHN KEATS

This ode to autumn is a striking reminder of the abundance of the season. A walk down a country lane, contemplation of a meadow or a picnic at a scenic overlook are wonderful antidotes to the stress and strain of daily life. Perhaps we will be surprised by the sound of an animal scuttling through dead leaves or feel a twinge of sorrow at the passing beauty.

This is also a good time to go on a retreat and enjoy an undisturbed period of prayer and meditation. Some of us will want to take our annual inventories, noting the blessings we have received as well as our short-comings.

**I will take the time to be silent and contemplate
the wonder and beauty of this earth.**

September 22

Pain has a thousand teeth.   —WILLIAM WATSON

While we are experiencing pain, we think it will last forever. It is difficult to believe that all things pass away in time. We need help to endure, and we reach out to our sponsor and friends in the fellowship for comfort and solace. The pain we experience after the death of a loved one or the end of a relationship will pass. Time will help us heal. Meanwhile, we practice the principles of this program and call on the resources of our inner spirit for strength and patience.

Sometimes to avoid pain we cut ourselves off from people and new experiences. This never works. All people suffer. The cycle of growth and learning includes some pain. Growing up gay was painful for many of us, and we sought relief with harmful substances and unhealthy behavior. In this program we learn that running away from pain doesn't bring solutions. With the help of our Higher Power and the support of our friends, we realize we will survive.

**I ask for the faith and courage to endure
whatever comes my way.**

The most gentle people in the world are macho males, people who are confident in their masculinity and have a feeling of well-being in themselves. They don't have to kick in doors, mistreat women or make fun of gays.
                                          —CLINT EASTWOOD

Our society has exaggerated the toughness and resiliency of men and slighted men's ability to be sensitive. Gay men, as well as straight men, can have a distorted idea of what it means to be a "real man." Most men are always comparing themselves to other men—who has the most money, the largest sexual organ, the most power? Who is the most attractive or the smartest? Often this takes the form of abusing others, putting them down or acting superior. Thinking like this leads to isolation, insecurity and loneliness.

Learning to be mature men involves letting go of the fear that others will dominate us or take something away from us. Self-confidence grows when we see our similarities and connections with others. Rather than comparing and contrasting, we seek to identify and bond. We try to let go of the need to establish our identity at the expense of someone else. When we successfully paint a whole and healthy picture of what it means to be a man, we can go on to lead fulfilling and happy lives.

**Today I will do my best to discard any
stereotypes I may have internalized
about myself.**

September 24

There is only one corner of the universe you can be
certain of improving, and that's your own self.
—ALDOUS HUXLEY

On certain days the world can seem like a dismal
place. People act the way we don't want them to
and we are frustrated. The evening news is filled with
horror and bloodshed. Politicians appear to be corrupt.
Prejudice and intolerance are everywhere. No matter
how much we bemoan these situations, we are powerless to control them, and trying to leads to frustration
and disappointment.

We need to remember that we are not responsible
for other people's actions or feelings. Everyone is fulfilling their own destiny. Let's take the focus off others
and take care of ourselves. We create our own happiness. When we stop overreacting to other people's
behavior we can tend our own garden.

If we want to effect real change, we begin with
ourselves. The longer we are in recovery, the more we
become a powerful example. When others see the
changes in us, they are often inspired to improve their
own lives.

**Today I will refuse to allow other people to set
my agenda.**

September 25

An addiction—any addiction—takes on the qualities of a primary relationship, but a destructive, not a productive one. —JOSEPH NOWINSKI

Addiction consumed our lives. Over time we needed more of the substance or engaged in more of the destructive behavior. Satisfaction escaped us. We were powerless and out of control.

The program helps us to overcome our primary addiction and stay sober *One Day at a Time*. We work the Twelve Steps, with the support of the group, adopting a spiritual way of life. But sometimes, much to our surprise, we begin to substitute one destructive behavior for another. This has been described as "changing seats on the *Titanic*." Emotional desperation, more than physical craving, can lead us to relapse. We are still uncomfortable with reality. We can in time overcome this state of mind and learn to lead whole and productive lives. To get at the root causes of our addictive behavior, we may need additional help in the form of group or individual therapy.

Today let me find the courage and strength to look deeply inside myself so that I may learn to love myself and be comfortable in my own body.

I'm not afraid of storms for I'm learning how to sail my ship.
—LOUISA MAY ALCOTT

L ife is a great adventure. There will be terrifying moments, times of uncertainty and strange terrains to explore. If we never leave our home port, mentally or physically, we will lead very narrow lives. A log needs to be turned to make the flame grow brighter. Similarly, we need to change our course every so often to prevent stagnation. As students of life, we open ourselves to a wide variety of new learning experiences.

Letting go of our addictions was a frightening experience for many of us. We did not know what would happen to us. We labored under the illusion that our lives had been exciting and glamorous when often they were nothing more than stressful and deluded. However, we hesitated to make a change. We were afraid we would fall into an abyss. We could not imagine what our life would be without our props and disguises.

What a relief to discover that we made a wise choice when we chose sobriety. Life is not the dull affair we imagined it would be. Instead we find ourselves on an adventure that brings exciting and fulfilling change.

Help me to meet all challenges with enthusiasm and curiosity.

September 27

The stellar universe is not so difficult of comprehension as the real actions of other people.
— MARCEL PROUST

We may think we know the motives of another person. Yet we are not mind readers and must be slow to judge others. Perhaps we have been hurt by someone who we felt was intentionally malicious toward us. It is possible that this person's action was due to indifference, self-centeredness, ignorance or carelessness rather than a deliberate wish to hurt us. If we retaliate, we may regret it.

Some of us are burdened by the memories of our childhood. We hold resentments toward our parents. Acknowledging their humanity and imagining what we would have done in their place can help us have compassion and forgive any hurts or wrongdoing.

We may feel injured by a former boyfriend or lover or disappointed by an old friend. Having the wisdom to realize that everyone makes mistakes softens our hearts and allows us to extend the same sympathy we would desire from others.

There are many actions taken by other people that we will never understand. There are as many opinions and viewpoints as there are individuals. Learning to relax and to be flexible and open in our outlook makes us more generous people.

Help me not to judge any man until I have walked in his shoes.

There is such a buildup of crud in my oven that there is only room to bake a single cupcake. —PHYLLIS DILLER

Some people live in clutter and chaos so they don't have to face themselves. Others depend on disorder to give themselves the illusion that their lives are full. In the most extreme cases we hoard garbage as though it were a treasure.

Do we create such frantic activity in our lives that we never take a moment to sit silently and meditate? Some of us like noise and distraction. It makes us feel busy so we never have to listen to that still, small voice within.

Let us remember that outer appearances often reflect inner states of mind. Today we look for ways to simplify our lives so that we can have peace of mind. We make an effort to find what is truly important and then focus on that.

Today I ask for the courage to take a good look at myself.

Style is the perfection of a point of view.
> —RICHARD EBERHARDT

We each have our own style shaped by our temperament and reflected in the way we dress, talk, move and act. Style is an outward signifier of inner feelings. It is a mirror. We express it in many ways. How we set a table, write a letter, do a favor or act toward a stranger reveals something about ourselves.

Someone who is sloppy and unkempt signals to the world that they are disorganized or indifferent. A person who is excessively formal in dress and movement places a barrier between himself and the world. Someone who assiduously pursues the latest fashions displays a certain amount of insecurity.

Style and fashion are not the same. Fashion is the mode of the moment. Style is an expression of our individual character and is refined over time as we grow and change.

We might disapprove of a person's style, but that does not make them wrong. We must be careful not to think that our way is the only way.

When we make our spiritual condition our top priority, that becomes part of our style. Loving and helpful acts toward others shine as our most beautiful stylistic ornaments.

Let me take a careful look at how I present myself to the world. Today I cultivate qualities that reveal my Higher Self.

All our resolves and decisions are made in a mood or frame of mind which is certain to change.

—MARCEL PROUST

In the past we tended to make decisions impulsively. Today, we step back and consider carefully before taking any action. If we are angry, upset, resentful or tired, we postpone decisions and wait till our mind is clear. In a time of crisis, we consult our sponsor or a trusted friend before we take any action that might have permanent results and cause later regrets.

Whenever we are faced with a decision, we temper our actions with kindness, courtesy and love. A generous spirit, which gives everyone the benefit of the doubt, will keep us on an even keel.

Knowing that all things pass in time, we practice patience. We exercise caution and restraint in our dealings with others. If we are unsure of which way to proceed, we wait until we have had time to pray and meditate upon the situation. Before acting, we consult our inner voice and choose to act in an emotionally sober manner.

I will ask for the guidance to know when to say yes and when to say no.

October 1

The struggle for sexual self-definition is a struggle for control over our own bodies. —JEFFREY WEEKS

One of the reasons gay men are oppressed is that they are seen as a threat to the existing social order. What this point of view overlooks is that gays are everywhere and are an essential part of the social system. Being honest about ourselves makes us better people and able to contribute more to the world around us. Those groups that seek to control us do so not for the common good but to maintain their own power.

Recovery allows us to no longer repress our instincts. We are free to express a wide range of feelings and behavior. As healthy recovering people, we can choose to define ourselves with confidence and pride. We begin to take responsibility for our actions. Our community is one of diversity, and we learn to appreciate one another. We treat people with the same respect that we ask for ourselves. We accept difference and grow in tolerance. Moving beyond mere survival as gay men, we become assertive and self-affirming.

Today I am free to explore all the possibilities contained within me and to act on them in a responsible manner.

No pessimist ever discovered the secret of the stars, or sailed to an uncharted land, or opened a new heaven to the human spirit. —HELEN KELLER

An ingrained, deep pessimism haunts many of us. There is a part of all of us that wishes to retreat from the world and avoid any responsibility. When we were active, many of us used sleep as an escape. Seeing no reason to get up, we lay lethargically under the covers. Our bed became a retreat in which we hid.

Even in sobriety we often cannot think of a reason to get out of bed. It is only hours after we have gotten up that we think of all the things that we could have done if we had not stayed in bed so long. Indecision grips us, and we lose many opportunities.

No matter what causes this attitude, it robs us of experiencing a full life. An antidote for our pessimism is the practice of the Eleventh Step. As we develop a conscious contact with a power greater than ourselves, it becomes easier to choose the positive and reject the negative. We keep ourselves in fit physical condition—recognizing that our mental outlook is affected by exercise, nutrition and proper rest.

**Today I make a commitment to embrace life
with enthusiasm.**

October 3

The trouble with unemployment is that the minute you wake up in the morning you're on the job.
—SLAPPY WHITE

One of the facts of life is that most of us have to work for a living. Recovery qualifies us to do a better job. In the past many of us were either too distracted or hung over to fulfill our career potential. Today we have been given a chance to start our work life anew.

In early recovery some of us take part-time or "get well" jobs that do not create too much stress. We might want to seek retraining or job counseling. A new job might be in order if the demands of our present job interfere with our sobriety.

We learn to pace ourselves and to do one task at a time. Accepting less responsibility helps to reduce pressure. Remembering that we are human and therefore not perfect helps us to keep a realistic perspective on our lives.

Exercising, eating properly and getting the right amount of sleep prepare us to do the best job we can. If things get frantic on the job at any time of the day, we seek a quiet corner where we can meditate and take a few deep breaths. Going to a meeting during lunch hour also revives us.

I will bring my best creative efforts to the task at hand.

October 4

Down in their hearts, wise men know this truth: the only way to help yourself is to help others.

—ELBERT HUBBARD

We have been given the gift of sobriety. The only way to keep it is to pass it on. We often become so consumed with our problems that we reach a dead end. The way out is to help someone else. Even if we only have a few weeks in the program, we can help others. We help a confused and hurting newcomer by letting him know we have been in the same place and that things do get better. Often we are amazed to realize how much we have learned and how helpful we can be.

When we make ourselves available for families, friends and neighbors, we affirm our common humanity. Our self-esteem grows with the knowledge that we have something to offer. Sharing our experience, strength and hope connects us with others.

It is easy to complain about the awful things that happen. But there is very little we can change except ourselves. In recovery we look for opportunities to be helpful. A good deed, such as running an errand, offering a gift of money or giving an encouraging word, goes far toward lighting up our corner of the world.

Today I ask my Higher Power to reveal to me the way of service so I may clearly see the blessings in my life.

Lack of confidence is not the result of difficulty; the difficulty comes from the lack of confidence. —SENECA

To have confidence means to have faith in one's self. As compulsive people we never thought we were enough. We tried to do everything perfectly, and when we failed we withdrew into our cocoons. Then fear began to govern us. We became afraid to express our own ideas and stand up for what we believed. Sometimes we were not even sure what we did believe and looked to others for direction. We neglected our own needs and hesitated to do anything unless we were sure we were right.

Recovery teaches us to trust our intuition and listen to our own messages. Our self-confidence grows as our self-esteem increases. We are on a journey and need not wait for others to tell us what to do. The process of growth is slow. The rooms provide a safe, warm space in which to open up and express our true feelings. Not everyone will agree with us, but we have the right to be ourselves. Working the Twelve Steps frees us to be independent and make our own choices. Our horizons expand as we take risks. We make choices and stick by them. As we lose our fears, our difficulties begin to fade away.

I ask my Higher Power for help in overcoming my fears and establishing self-confidence.

Money, it turned out, was exactly like sex. You thought of nothing else if you didn't have it and thought of other things if you did. —JAMES BALDWIN

The desire for sex and money is common to us all. When we lack either, it is easy to become fixated upon these subjects and slight other important areas.

Some of us have money problems because we are underearning, spending beyond our means or constantly incurring debt. Did we grow up in poverty and never learn how to handle money? Is it because we received mixed messages and think that "money is dirty"? Whatever the cause of our financial difficulties, a thorough inventory will reveal the areas where we need to improve. It is very difficult to be a whole person when plagued by money worries and a feeling of deprivation.

When our sexual needs are not being fulfilled, we need to take action. We communicate our needs if we are not being satisfied. If we compulsively have sex and still do not feel fulfilled, we seek help. Putting our sex and money issues into proper perspective gives us a chance at living a well-rounded life.

Help me to live a balanced and fulfilling life.

Surely both personal growth and political growth involve a balance between listening to the inner voice and speaking out, between withdrawing to grow strong and going out into the world to spend this strength.
—BETSY PETERSEN

When we first get sober, we need time to rest both our bodies and our minds. In recovery from any disease there is a recuperation period when we go slow and treat ourselves gently.

Recovery is a bridge back to life. Once we have established a solid foundation within this program, we apply the principles we have learned in every area of our life. This might mean standing up for ourselves at work, volunteering in a political campaign or asserting ourselves in a relationship. At other times we might need to look inside ourselves and reflect on the state of our being.

If we are at a crossroads and are unsure what action to take, we consult with our sponsor or a close friend. In all events we turn to our Higher Power and ask for guidance and the strength to do what is required.

Our fear of speaking out for what we feel is right no longer paralyzes us. We might still have the fear, but we act through it. As invigorated, spiritually renewed people, we are free to choose how to best use our energy.

◊

Today let me take the time to reflect upon what is right and find the strength to act on it.

Solitude vivifies; isolation kills.   —JOSEPH ROUX

Cultivating solitude gives us time to be alone with ourselves and look inward. Our conscious contact with a power greater than ourselves is strengthened when we are alone in silence. We listen to that small, quiet voice within. Communion with the center of our being allows us to build a base for healing and regeneration. Many of us never practiced quiet reflection when we were active. We were afraid of the stillness and lost ourselves in frantic activity and noisy endeavors, or dulled ourselves with harmful substances. Recovery teaches us to uncover the truth that is revealed in solitude. We take the time necessary to get to know ourselves.

Our addictive behavior separated us from people, and we suffered from loneliness. We break this cage of isolation by using the tools of recovery. We reach out to other members of the group and share our true feelings. We derive nourishment from our new healthy relationships. We work at being on the best possible terms with our family, friends and lovers.

Ultimately, everyone is alone. Acceptance of this goes a long way toward alleviating some of the pain. Making intimate contact with others can help us to know that we are alone but do not have to be lonely.

◇

I open myself to the quiet voice within.

October 9

If you read widely on the subject of death—in the literature of grief and consolation, for instance—you realize that the subject isn't death at all; it's survival.

—VERLYN KLINKENBORG

When we are young, we feel we are invincible and immortal. Our experience of death is limited, and the thought that we will die is remote. As time passes, death touches us more closely. We are reminded of our own inevitable organic decay. This can be chilling, and care must be taken not to morbidly obsess over this fact.

Funerals and memorials are as much for the living as for the dead. They provide closure and a chance to express our deepest emotions. Mourning is a process. The anniversary of the death of someone close to us can stir up painful memories. Acceptance of death, our own or someone else's, is not easy. We should stay close to our support group.

Sometimes after a death we find it difficult to do anything. This is natural, but eventually we will find the strength to go on with our lives. We each have our time on this earth. Letting go of the dead frees us to fulfill our own destiny to its fullest.

Today I will mourn the dead with all my heart and soul and embrace the life around me.

October 10

Pray to God but continue to row to the shore.
—RUSSIAN PROVERB

As addicts we fell into the bad habit of expecting something for nothing. False feelings of entitlement made us lazy and indifferent. Our level of desire was high, but our willingness to take action never matched our wants and needs.

In sobriety we sometimes continue to whine and complain when we do not get what we want immediately. It is easy to forget that we must do our part if our needs are to be met.

During prayer we unburden ourselves and communicate with our Higher Power. We ask for guidance. Praying clarifies our thoughts and aligns us with God's will. In times of need or confusion, prayer sets us on the right track. It is a powerful tool that can help move us closer to our goals. However, no amount of prayer or wishful thinking will accomplish what we want unless we take appropriate action.

The truism "God helps those who help themselves" teaches us that very little good will come our way until we take positive actions. We concentrate on the quality of our performance and turn the results over to our Higher Power.

Today I will ask my Higher Power for the help to do what I can to live a full and happy life.

Straight people must come to accept gay people the way they accept people who have blue eyes or those who are left-handed. . . . This can be reached only if everybody comes out and stays with the cause.

—DR. MATHILDE KRIM

S tudies show that those most prejudiced against gay people say they do not know anyone who is gay. By being out, we give these people an opportunity to face their fears and learn the truth. Coming out requires an act of courage. Often we need support before we reveal ourselves. If we live in a rural or isolated situation, we may want to communicate by mail with other gay people before we let those close to us know the facts. If we live in a more urban setting, we can more easily be involved with gay organizations and find congenial social groups.

By letting our family or coworkers know, we allow them to see that someone they love and respect is gay. This helps them to grow and expand their horizons. We must not assume that because someone is straight they are going to automatically reject us because we are gay. There is more tolerance and love than we might imagine, and by coming out we give people a chance to show it. By our being open and honest about every aspect of our life, our recovery is enhanced.

I will strive to be open and honest about my sexual identity.

Never speak loudly to one another unless the house is on fire. —H. W. THOMPSON

We can choose today to change the way we treat other people. In the past we might have thought we could get our way if we screamed or bullied others. Sometimes we even resorted to violence to impose our will or show our displeasure. These tactics never won us any friends and in fact alienated anyone we treated this way.

Practice of the Twelve Steps helps us change the way we relate to people. Before recovery we lived life as though each moment were a crisis—and indeed many of us went from one disaster to another. Our inner and outer lives were filled with turmoil, and as a result the importance of every incident was exaggerated.

In recovery we learn to appreciate a calm manner. When we speak in a soft and thoughtful fashion, our listeners take us seriously. Those we are speaking to can concentrate on what we are saying rather than how we are saying it. We show respect to others by treating them in a dignified and gracious manner.

Our pleasures become more subtle. We value our quiet moments and gain great energy from silence. Now that we are on a spiritual path, we no longer need to fill up our lives with noise and chaos.

Today I will open myself to the quiet side of life.

October 13

There are two ways of spreading light; to be the candle or the mirror that reflects it. —EDITH WHARTON

It is so easy to complain about what is wrong with the world. Sometimes we have an investment in only seeing the dark side of life. Then we can say that things are so awful nothing can be done, and we absolve ourselves of responsibility.

We cannot change the world, but we can change ourselves. We embrace the good and the positive. One way we can do this is by being less critical. Rather than finding fault, we look for what is interesting and uplifting.

As recovering people we are powerful examples of the strength of the program. When people see the changes in us, they know that there is hope. Our growth inspires those around us. We carry the message of recovery to those who still are active and suffering. When we treat others with love and tolerance, we make this world a brighter place.

Today I will think of three ways I can help to make the world a better place.

The big lie about lesbians and gay men is that we do not exist. —VITO RUSSO

When asked in a survey "Who do you think are some good role models for gay men?" a group of recovering men cited very few well-known people. One man said that people do not have to be famous or materially successful to be good role models. For the most part the respondents said they admired men who had long-term recovery. They praised as good examples gay men who told their stories and shared at meetings. These men were viewed as powerful, truthful, understanding and compassionate channels that create an uplifting, purifying and healing energy.

Others who were appreciated were those active in helping the community in political and AIDS work. One respondent said he was grateful for any gay man "who through his creative expression added buoyancy and understanding to how being gay is today." People who express individuality and freedom are viewed as valuable assets to the community.

Most said that "any gay man who is sober" was someone to admire, especially considering the odds he is up against. Self-esteem was evident in those who replied "me."

All of us who stay sober, show up and keep talking about it are helping others in the best way possible.

October 15

An affirmation is a strong, positive statement that something is already so. —SHAKTI GAWAIN

We may find it is easy to beat ourselves up with negativity but be embarrassed to affirm the positive. How often do we say things like "I can't," "I'm not good enough," "Who do you think you are?," "I can't because I'm gay." Do we waste time and energy criticizing those who have achieved more than we have? Are we filled with jealousy and resentment?

Let us eliminate this self-doubt from our lives. When we make an affirmation, we are removing the blockages that inhibit our spiritual and emotional growth. We stop reinforcing the negative and quit condemning ourselves. We find it helpful to write down every negative thought that comes to mind about ourselves and reverse it by turning it into an affirmation. As we get into the habit of making positive affirmations, we begin to see great changes in our lives. In time we become accustomed to these statements of belief and begin trusting enough to enjoy our new freedom.

Today I will stop putting myself down and accept all the things that make me a wonderful person.

Morality is simply the attitude we adopt toward people whom we personally dislike. —OSCAR WILDE

We need to be careful about taking other people's inventories. A defect that we forgive in someone we like seems especially glaring in someone we dislike. It is easy to sit in judgment of people who offend us. Perhaps we condemn one person for being loud and boisterous but excuse a friend whom we call high-spirited. We might forgive a slight or injury from someone we love but hold a grudge for a long time against a perceived enemy.

If we harbor a dislike for a particular ethnic or social group, we often find fault with their behavior and accuse them of moral weakness. A coworker who does not do things our way is seen as a bad person. Those who do not agree with us are thought to be flawed.

Instead of being quick to judge, we should pause. Often we reproach others for the very defects that we struggle with ourselves in recovery. We try to exercise fairness and show compassion to everyone.

Today help me to be less harsh in my judgments of those I dislike. Let me grow in understanding and empathy.

October 17

Happy he who learns to bear what he can not change!
—JOHANN FRIEDRICH VON SCHILLER

This program asks us to pray for those who offend us. In doing so, we practice nonresistance. Rather than squandering our energies on a fight, we summon up positive forces. If someone displeases or angers us, we will torment ourselves if we plot how to get even with them. A more constructive approach is to bless our enemies, robbing them of ammunition. No one will be able to walk over us if we use nonresistance wisely. We do not have to be doormats.

When troubled or perplexed, we accomplish more by relaxing and getting in touch with our Higher Power than by moaning and bewailing our fate. So long as we resist a situation, it remains with us. If we run away, the situation follows us. Much of the disharmony in our lives comes from our attitude. When we change our attitude, life flows more smoothly. In recovery we stop battling the world. If we are under attack, we pray to remain calm and poised. We do not give our power away.

We let go of the past, for it blocks our future good. We turn the future over to the care of God. We live fully in the present, accepting everything that happens as part of the divine plan.

Help me to remain calm in times of trial so that
I may affirm the power of divine guidance.

October 18

Just try the program for ninety days, and if you don't like it we will always refund your misery.

—ANONYMOUS

The risk of a relapse is greatest in the first few months of our sobriety. However, it is something we must be ever vigilant about. Most people who slip say that they stopped going to meetings. But meetings are our medicine. There we hear the message that keeps us sober.

We prevent relapsing by building a strong foundation. It is never too soon to get a sponsor or to start working the Steps. We also help ourselves, even after a few weeks in recovery, by helping newcomers.

We should not be so arrogant as to think that we can easily return from a slip. Whether our behavior is controlled or uncontrolled, when we return to our old ways there is a chance that we might never make it back to the program. However, some, after having a slip, find themselves committed to the program in a way they never were before.

Avoiding slippery people, places and things can help prevent a slip. Because we have a disease, we must never let our guard down. If we are willing to work at it, we can have a happy and productive life in recovery—free from relapse and the horrors we left behind.

I will make every effort today to strengthen my program. Helping others will insure that I remain grateful for my sobriety.

October 19

Good company and good discourse are the very sinews of virtue.
                                              —ISAAK WALTON

It is not necessary to attend a gay group to get sober. The important thing is to identify with the feelings expressed at a meeting and focus on what we have in common with other recovering people. However, we may feel more comfortable in a gay group, especially when discussing certain topics. Most big cities have a number of gay groups, but in the suburbs or rural areas there are few or none. If there is no gay group near us, we might want to start our own group. We do whatever is necessary to stay sober.

Starting a meeting is a big commitment but one that is very rewarding. It is a real service to gays and lesbians in our area and might be the deciding factor in our sobriety. Such a group creates a sense of community and a strong support network for its members.

To get the word out, let the local Intergroup office know about the new meeting and place a notice in the area gay paper. If you are comfortable with it, you can announce it at local meetings. In some areas the members will want assurance of anonymity about their sexual identity as well as their addictive status.

**Today I am grateful to my Higher Power
for the support and love I receive from all
recovering people.**

Cheer up, the worst is yet to come.

—PHILANDER JOHNSON

Do we walk through life with a sense of impending doom? So many of us are still comfortable with failure and negativity. We find it easier than dealing with success. If we succeed at something, we might have to continue to produce results, and we panic at that prospect.

Today we take care not to reinforce old negative beliefs. Perhaps one of our parents always said "Why bother?" or "What's the use?" When we hear an internal voice telling us that something is impossible or urging us to give up, we ask ourselves where the message comes from. Does it reflect today's reality or is it something from the past that we need to sweep away?

The grace of our Higher Power has brought us to this program. In recovery we learn to change our attitudes. Instead of focusing on all the bad that could happen to us, we direct our energies toward building a rich and fulfilling life. As an exercise, let us go one week without complaining about anything.

◊

Today I banish all negative thoughts and go forward with faith and cheerfulness.

October 21

The game of life is a game of boomerangs. Man's thoughts, deeds and words return to him sooner or later, with astounding accuracy.
—FLORENCE SCOVIL SHINN

Where we find ourselves today is the result of all that has come before. As addicts and codependents we made many choices that we later regretted. Our priorities were skewed and our behavior was often reprehensible. In recovery we have to deal with the consequences of our past actions.

Today we work the Steps and practice the principles of this program. We do our best to put right any past failings and resolve to do better in the future. We guard against behavior that would lead us back to our old ways.

We avoid self-pity and negative thinking. It only leads to despair. Just as we program a computer, we program ourselves to approach life with a positive outlook. As we grow, we are careful not to say hurtful or untrue things. We examine our motives and think before we act. We remember that what we do affects others.

Today I resolve to be a loving and helpful person and add to the world's store of good.

God gives us relatives, thank God we can choose our friends. —ADDISON MIZNER

As gay men we often feel excluded from our birth families. Perhaps we have been rejected outright because of religious beliefs or homophobic prejudice. Our family and relatives may accept us but not our partners or friends.

For some of us, the deepest experience of family happens with those with whom we have established bonds of mutual interest, shared commitments and affection. Our gay families can include lovers, former lovers, coworkers, sex partners, mentors and a diverse collection of friends. We look to these people to provide support and comfort in times of difficulty. We share our joys and successes with them. Through mutual reliance, we give one another strength and encouragement.

People come and go. Some die and others move away, yet shared experience still binds us. Sometimes this experience can be so intense that it lasts a lifetime no matter how separated we are by distance. In some instances, we may come together with someone, burn brightly together for a while and then grow apart. Over a lifetime, many people will join us on our journey. Each one adds to the meaning and understanding of life, and for this we treasure them all.

I am thankful for the love and friendship of the people in my life.

A misty morning does not signify a cloudy day.
—OLD PROVERB

When we came into this program, our outlook was bleak. Our own efforts had failed us. Hope came as we learned to rely on a power greater than ourselves.

Still sometimes we are impatient. It seems that for every step forward we go back two. At times we think that others are recovering faster than we are. We want results quickly, and when they don't come at the pace we demand, we get discouraged. We avoid surrendering to despair, knowing it can lead us back to our old ways.

The example of other recovering people can be a source of strength for us. When we hear others' stories and see how far they have come, we find solutions to our common problems. Eventually our own signs of progress give us hope, and soon our faith lets us trust that we are healing and growing. Slowly but surely we see that time brings positive change.

Today my newfound hope lets me believe in the endless possibilities that life has to offer.

October 24

Worry is interest paid on trouble before it is due.
                    —WILLIAM RALPH INGE

If we added up all the time we spent on worry, we would find we suffered more from fear of what might happen than from any real trouble. Worry is a thief. It robs us of our sleep, our appetite and our peace of mind. Worrying accomplishes nothing and actually gets in the way of solutions. Things that seem trouble-some from a distance often shrink to nothing up close.

Living in the present is a good antidote to worry. We cross our bridges when we come to them and don't put up an umbrella till it rains. Very little is worth the anxiety and stress caused by fretting.

Worry shows a lack of faith. It is a destructive habit. We free ourselves by sharing our concerns with others, keeping busy and turning to our Higher Power when we feel anxiety or have misgivings.

Today I will trust that my Higher Power is with me at all times.

Love does not just sit there, like a stone, it has to be made, like bread; re-made all the time, made new.

—URSULA K. LE GUIN

Have we gotten into the habit of taking those we love for granted? Do we forget to say "I love you"? Or do we show our love by our actions? Perhaps we think that sex and love are the same. If so, we need to reshape our thinking and work on ways to strengthen the bonds of love in our lives.

There are many ways to show love. If we are in a committed relationship, we should always show respect to our partner by listening thoughtfully to whatever he has to say. Being there in times of illness as well as health is a sign of true devotion, as is showing support in difficult times. Love has its moments of passion, and we should enjoy them. However, much of the time spent with our lover will be routine, and that is when our affections will be tested.

If our relationship becomes static, it will wither. To allow our love to grow, we must think of ways to keep it fresh. Small acts of kindness and consideration will lighten our lover's day. Being flexible and open to suggestions helps to keep things new. Showing patience and acceptance deepens our connection. Treating our partner as an equal increases our regard for each other.

I will remember that the richest love submits itself to the test of time.

October 26

We define genius as the capacity for productive reaction against one's training. —BERNARD BERENSON

If we come from a dysfunctional family, we were programmed to think in certain negative ways. We were taught to deny our problems, to keep secrets and to feel ashamed of ourselves. We assumed unrealistic roles that were demanded by our families. Our individual needs were never met, and our sense of self disappeared into an unhealthy family system.

All of this gave us a distorted view of the world, and as adults we had difficulty coping. If we are to function properly, we need to start taking care of ourselves. This means detaching from old patterns of self-defeating behavior and developing a new viewpoint. In recovery we no longer allow people to control our feelings or to make unwarranted emotional claims on us. We assert ourselves and set boundaries when necessary. We choose how we will lead our lives and stick by our decisions.

Breaking free from the poisonous effects of our childhood is frightening. In our prayers we ask for the courage to separate ourselves from the past. Our inventories show us what we need to discard. If necessary we remove ourselves from our families until we feel comfortable.

Today I will ignore the old voices of negativity and explore ways I can open up to health and happiness.

Some of your hurts you have cured,
And the sharpest you have even survived,
But what torments of grief you've endured,
From evils which never arrived.
—RALPH WALDO EMERSON

Too often, we tortured ourselves with worry about what would happen in the future. We fretted and lived in needless dread about what tomorrow would bring. When we were active, our lives were fear-driven and filled with apprehension. Being off balance, we felt guilty, and we awaited punishment from an unseen source. We were often paralyzed and could not take any decisive action.

Today we are learning that constant worry is stressful and unproductive. We place our trust in a power greater than ourselves. Over time we see that our new way of life gives us a strength and courage that we did not know we had. When a challenging situation arises, we intuitively know how to handle it. We stop dreading life and embrace it fully. Taking risks may stir some fear, but we have faith that we will be taken care of no matter what happens.

**I will keep myself in the present moment so that
I can discover more of the world around me.**

October 28

In the factory we make cosmetics. In the store we sell hope.
— CHARLES REVSON

I t is easy for us to get trapped by illusion. On all sides we are bombarded with advertisements for alcohol and cigarettes and food aiming to create a mood of glamour. The model puffing on a cigarette implies pleasure—nothing is said about lung cancer. The people at a cocktail party in a poster look totally in control of their lives—the hangovers and blackouts are not mentioned. We are urged to eat sweets and other unhealthy foods, and the consequences are ignored.

Today we assume responsibility for ourselves. If we have a problem, we think it through or call a friend for help before we succumb to temptation.

As adults we recognize that no particular clothing or product is a solution to feelings of inadequacy. Only through honesty and self-knowledge can we hope to have the beginnings of peace of mind and self-assurance. With practice we learn to distinguish between desire and our real needs.

Help me to pierce the veil of illusion and center myself in reality.

As for money, enough is enough; no man can enjoy more. —ROBERT SOUTHEY

We wasted a lot of money on alcohol, drugs, gambling or unsound business ventures before we got sober. Many times we used money to show off and bolster our egos. Some of us were fearful and miserly and refused to spend what was necessary for a well-rounded life. Distorted and diseased attitudes toward money made us forget that it is a tool and not an end in itself.

If we find ourselves constantly in debt, it may be due to the idea that we cannot take care of ourselves. Perhaps we grew up poor and did not learn the proper skills for handling money. In recovery we affirm that we deserve material, emotional and spiritual wealth.

Those of us accustomed to having lots of money often took it for granted. When we found ourselves on our own, we were at a loss as to how to act financially responsible. Even when we had a great deal of money, it never seemed to be enough. We could reverse this outlook by being grateful for the gifts we have received.

Let us create a vision of what money can do to make our lives fuller and more expansive. When we are generous to others, our money becomes seeds to sow an abundant harvest. Money is put into its proper perspective as a tool and not as an end in itself.

I will remember to enjoy what I have and ask for the wisdom to use it properly.

October 30

There isn't any formula or method. You learn to love by loving—by paying attention and doing what one thereby discovers has to be done.　—ALDOUS HUXLEY

Did our past relationships founder because we brought unrealistic expectations to the partnership? Perhaps we thought that all of our problems would be solved by being in love, or were we afraid of being alone? Did we need another person to make us feel whole? Were we attracted to someone solely because of his appearance or status? In recovery we discover that to be successful a relationship must go deeper if it is to last.

Growing up gay, we rarely had positive relationships we could emulate. Distorted myths told us that gay people could not love and were condemned to live lonely, sad lives. Because we absorbed these messages, some of us made them self-fulfilling prophecies.

We need to learn to be in a relationship in the same way we would take driving lessons if we had never driven before. Problems should be identified and dealt with as soon as possible. There are many books for gay men on the subject. Taking the time to read and learn from them will eliminate much trial and error. We honor our commitment by making an honest effort to understand the other person and give fully of ourselves.

I will express my love for my partner in a trusting, honest and generous spirit.

The closing years of life are like the end of a masquerade party, when the masks are dropped.
—ARTHUR SCHOPENHAUER

During our lifetime we all play many roles. As brothers, sons, lovers and coworkers, we are expected to play prescribed parts. Subconsciously we adopt the particular manners associated with our role in life. When we stray too far from these predetermined conceptions people think we are "acting funny" or misbehaving.

Ideally, the longer we are in recovery the freer we feel to be true to ourselves. Our self-worth does not depend on what others think of us. We feel less compelled to perform for others. We become more flexible.

Our understanding of our common humanity lets us tolerate and accept a wider range of people. We let go of judging others based on their appearance or status. In time we come to accept ambivalence and apparent contradictions in ourselves and in others. We learn that we are more than the sum of our parts.

Today I pray to be true to myself and open with others.

Who except the gods can live forever through time without any pain? —AESCHYLUS

No one is exempt from suffering. However, as addicts and alcoholics we wanted to escape all pain. We had sex, medicated ourselves, drank, lost ourselves in others or overate until we deadened our feelings. Finally we were sick and tired of being sick and tired, and we surrendered.

This program teaches us acceptance. One of the things we need to accept is the reality of pain. When a friend or family member dies, we feel great emotional pain. Denying this feeling will not make it go away. We only postpone confronting it. The pain we feel when physically injured is a sign that we need treatment. In times of deep emotional stress, the pain we feel can seem unbearable, and we should not hesitate to seek solace from friends or professional counselors.

In the midst of pain it is difficult to realize that all things pass. But the longer we are in recovery, the more we understand that we have survived much and are stronger than we realized.

Perhaps the worst pain comes from spiritual bankruptcy. We feel hopeless and desolate. Life has no meaning. Constant attention to our spiritual needs can reverse this condition, nourish and warm our souls and restore our lives.

When I am in pain, help me to remember that it will pass.

November 2

What would happen to all of our life without negative emotions? What would happen to what we call art, to the theater, to drama, to most novels?

—**P. D. OUSPENSKY**

We dream of a world without conflict. Anger, jealousy, greed and other negative emotions often frighten us, and we wish to be rid of them. However, strong emotions are a natural part of the human condition. The important question is how we react to these powerful forces. Do we try to suppress and deny them? If so, we will have to smother all the good feelings as well as the bad ones, because our control is limited and capricious.

When an unpleasant emotion surfaces, we find it helpful to detach ourselves and seek to understand the emotion's origin. Underneath most of our rotten feelings is self-centered fear. Fear that others will get more than we have—fear that others will take what we have or fear that we will not get what we deserve. Over time, through taking inventories and sharing our feelings at meetings, the intensity of our reactions will subside, and we will begin to see things clearly.

Today I will do my best to accept the world as it is, knowing that it is my attitude that determines how I feel.

That which makes people dissatisfied with their condition is the chimerical idea they form of other people's happiness. —JAMES THOMSON

We can never know what is really going on inside someone else. On the surface things may appear to be wonderful, and yet that other person may be carrying a burden that we would find insufferable. Have we wasted time thinking that our life would be so much better if we were like someone else? Or if we had what they had? How many times have we envied someone else only to find out their life was not as ideal as we imagined?

We often look at someone's externals and think we are less than they are because we do not match up to their outside appearance. This is a sure setup for disappointment. We gain more benefit when we identify rather than compare ourselves with others.

Each one of us is given different challenges. How we deal with those challenges shapes our destiny. The measure of true happiness is inner satisfaction. Let us ask ourselves what unites us with others rather than focusing on seeming differences.

Today I will be thankful for what I have and practice compassion toward others.

To love without roles, without power plays, is revolution.
—RITA MAE BROWN

When two gay men come together in a loving situation, each is sometimes unsure of the role he is expected play. What determines our status in a relationship? Does one partner have to be "masculine" and the other one "feminine?" Is it easier if one assumes the role of "husband" and the other of "wife"? Should we imitate what society considers normal?

The answers to these questions are culturally determined. Gay people reflect the societies they live in. Our culture relies heavily on role-playing between the sexes to maintain the social order. Gay people mimic the dominant pattern as a protective device and in order to fit in.

As gay men grow in self-acceptance and realize that their sexual identity is natural and valid, they can come together as equals. This means that roles need not be rigidly defined and may change over time.

A loving relationship is not an arena for a power struggle. To function in a psychologically and spiritually healthy manner, we need to create our own safe paces. If a lover tries to assign a role to us that makes us uncomfortable, we speak to him about our dissatisfaction. We can satisfy our lover's needs without playing a role that does not fit us.

Help me to be open and honest about who I am and respect the integrity of my partner.

November 5

Self-restraint may be alien to the human temperament, but humanity without restraint will dig its own grave.
                                                    —MARYA MANNES

We often justify an action by merely saying "I want to do that" and ignore the consequences. The results of this kind of thinking can be seen in overpopulation, polluted waters, lowered quality of life in our cities and diminished resources.

Sadly, in our individual lives, we often take the same attitude. We overeat and wonder why we gain weight. We spend money without a thought to our future needs and go from one financial crisis to another. We thoughtlessly say hurtful things, unmindful of the effect on others. We toy with others' emotions, not caring if we hurt them.

Ours is a society that encourages instant gratification. We are encouraged to take what we want when we want it and ignore the outcome. We are ruled by our whims and desires and often take a short-term view of life.

We are learning that to live happy, sober lives we must practice self-control. There are many indulgences other than our primary addiction that can derail us. Learning to live in moderation and balance is the key to healthy living.

Today I will apply the proper use of willpower. I do not need to surrender to unhealthy urges or craving.

November 6

Life could not continue without throwing the past into the past, liberating the present from its burden.
—PAUL TILLICH

As we go about our day in recovery, we strive to be present for everything we do. Whatever we are engaged in—whether exercising, typing, making something or eating—we concentrate on the moment. But sometimes thoughts of the past so absorb our minds that they interfere with our ability to concentrate on the task at hand. To get a fresh approach, we can take a few moments to meditate and clear away the clamor.

Our old ways did not work, so when challenged to do something new, we make an effort not to be constrained by old habits and hidebound ways of thinking. Willingness to listen to other people's opinions is a hallmark of emotional maturity. Sometimes the greatest inspirations come from the most unlikely sources. We will never make any headway if we persist in thinking our way is the only way to do something.

We learn a new way of life in recovery. Humility, keeping an open mind and willingness to try something different are guarantees that we will make progress.

Today I resolve to let go of anything that prevents me from focusing on the present.

November 7

When animals do something that we like, we call it "natural." When they do something that we don't like, we call it "animalistic."　　　—JAMES D. WEINRICH

The poet Goethe once wrote that homosexuality is as old as humanity itself and can therefore be considered natural. There are those who believe that whatever is found in this world is natural. Homosexual behavior is also found in many other animal species. However, certain societies have suppressed this behavior and called it unnatural. On the other hand, some societies accept or condone homoerotic behavior. Such cultures appreciate the complexities of human sexuality.

We may have felt some shame or embarrassment about being gay. Many of us shaped our world view based on negative social attitudes. This often led to addictive or self-destructive behavior that made us feel out of synch with the world around us.

In recovery we receive many gifts, and one of those is self-acceptance. We realize that social and religious attitudes toward homosexuality are not universal but conditioned by time and place. We come to learn that our sexual behavior is part of the flow of life and very much a part of the natural order. We reject the prejudiced notion that we are acting in an unclean or animalistic way. As members of the human family, we have every right to express our sexuality.

Today we celebrate our place in the universe and give voice to our way of loving.

November 8

> I am large,
> I contradict myself.
> I contain multitudes.
>
> —WALT WHITMAN

The greatest joy of recovery is discovering who we are. In the past we may have seen the world in terms of either/or. Now we see that we are both good and bad, fearful and brave, selfish and altruistic, stubborn yet willing, and a host of other complex contradictions of our self.

We can let go of self-images that limit us. Perhaps we thought if we were in business we could not be artistic or that as gay men we could not be athletic. Learning that we are capable of much more than we assumed releases great reserves of energy. Opening our minds to infinite possibilities can lead us to fulfill dreams that we dared not articulate.

Gaining self-knowledge is a process. With each new piece of information we add another stroke to our self-portraits. We shine as lovers, brothers, workers, caretakers, proud gay men, citizens, adventurers or anything we dare to be.

Like a garden in spring I am capable of producing many flowers.

Question with boldness even the existence of God; because if there be one, he must more approve of the homage of reason, than that of blindfolded fear.
— THOMAS JEFFERSON

Even though this program speaks of "God as we understand Him," some recovering people have a definite idea of who or what God is and wish to impose that idea on others. Certain religious traditions visualize God as an omnipotent father. This image is offensive to some people who hold other beliefs or who do not believe in a personal God.

We must be careful to honor the wisdom of this program's founders by being tolerant of the diversity around us. Any prayer said at a meeting that reinforces one creed over another should be avoided. Our program's message is a universal one. Anyone should be able to walk into a meeting anywhere in the world and feel at home. When we succumb to denominational practices, there is a good chance we might turn away someone who needs our help desperately.

Some people do not hold any particular notion of God and make the group their Higher Power. We must be careful not to mistakenly think that what we believe is the answer for everyone.

Today I will study the Traditions to keep in mind that the survival and unity of this program depends on tolerance and open-mindedness.

November 10

If an outbreak of cholera might be caused either by an infected water supply or by the blasphemies of an infidel mayor, medical research would be in confusion.
—W. R. INGE

Some politicians and religious fanatics have claimed that AIDS is a punishment from God upon homosexuals. This idea is full of holes because it does not explain cases of AIDS in the heterosexual, hemophiliac and infant populations or its relative scarcity among lesbians. Medical science disagrees with this homophobic claim and states that the cause of the disease is exposure to a virus.

Most of us were raised with the idea of a punishing God. We had guilt and shame drilled into us by a society that projected its shortcomings onto its conception of God. As we grow in wisdom, we realize that this is a primitive notion that reflects the social structure of ancient times. This program assures us that we are under the care of a loving God. Getting in touch with that Higher Power means learning to listen to the still, small voice within us that tells us when something is right or wrong.

This does not mean that we are not responsible for our behavior. Besides AIDS there are many other sexually transmitted diseases. Taking the proper precautions protects our partner as well as ourselves. Responsible behavior is loving behavior.

**Acting responsibly today will improve
my self-respect.**

The greatest assassin of life is haste, the desire to reach things before the right time which means over-reaching them. —JUAN RAMON JIMINEZ

At an anniversary meeting a newcomer admitted that he wished he was celebrating his fifth anniversary. An old-timer replied that the newcomer should focus on enjoying the process of getting sober and that that process includes both ups and downs. He said there are the peaks, where we relish our achievements, and the valleys, where we learn many lessons. He then wished the newcomer a long, slow recovery.

Our addictive thinking sometimes leads us to want the appearance of recovery rather than the real thing. However, when we learn to drop all pretense, become honest and do the work required for real sobriety, we feel a great sense of relief. We shortchange ourselves when we try to skip the necessary steps it takes to move forward.

There is no point in hurrying anything. When learning a language, we first study the basics of grammar and syntax. Then we add to our vocabulary and practice pronunciation. If we overlook any aspect, our command of the language will be poor. However, if we studiously devote some time each day to improving our skill, we will eventually learn to speak the language well. This principle applies to everything we do.

Today I will remember that haste makes waste.

There is no limit on how complicated things can get, on account of one thing always leading to another.

—E. B. WHITE

Too often we forget that every action has a reaction. Rudeness will probably be repaid in kind. An enraged tirade will elicit an angry response. Violence will be met with violence. If our work performance is poor, we will most likely lose our job.

We need to be aware of the effect we have on other people. If we act in an unprincipled fashion or neglect our responsibilities, this behavior will come back to us in time. As recovering people we try to harm no one. We make amends to those we hurt in the past and try to keep the slate clean.

Sometimes we are unable to make amends, because we cannot find the person to whom they are due or because that person is dead. In this situation we make amends by doing service.

As adults we accept the consequences of our actions. If we want to have peace of mind and to be on good terms with others, we will incorporate the Steps into our daily life.

Today I will be mindful of my effect on the world around me.

Every child should be taught that useful work is worship and that intelligent labor is the highest form of prayer. —R. G. INGERSOLL

Sometimes we have to perform tasks that are not pleasant. Putting them off only makes it worse. Our greatest weariness comes from work that we fear doing but have not yet done. Doing the difficult first is often the best use of our energies. Instead of wasting our time fretting about it, we just roll up our sleeves and finish the job. No matter what kind of work we do, we bring our best efforts to it.

Since we spend so much of our day at work, we strive to fulfill our potential and achieve a sense of accomplishment and satisfaction in what we do. An inventory of our talents, professional counseling and studious research can reveal the vocation most suited to us.

Keeping active and interested in our work helps to ward off depression and is a cure for many maladies. Our attitude has an impact on our coworkers. Courtesy and cheerfulness lift everyone above routine and drudgery. The rewards of work are many, but we do not expect work to meet all our emotional needs. We remember to provide time for leisure and repose so that we are refreshed and able to do what is required of us.

Today I will remember that there are many interesting things that remain to be done in this world. Let my work add flavor to my life.

November 14

The holiest of all holidays are those kept by ourselves in silence and apart; the secret anniversaries of the heart. —HENRY WADSWORTH LONGFELLOW

Holidays can be a time of anxiety and intense pressure. We are often exposed to people, places and things that challenge our recovery. Friends and families make demands that can be emotionally upsetting.

It is possible to enjoy the holidays if we take them *One Day at a Time* and even moment by moment if necessary. We will want to go to extra meetings, and if we are traveling, we find out where meetings are held before we leave. Holidays are also a good time to reach out to newcomers or do volunteer work at a hospital or shelter.

We make plans so we do not find ourselves suddenly alone during the holidays. This is a good time to invite a friend to join us in seeing movies, museum shows and plays. Or we host a party for friends in the fellowship.

If we go to an office party, we take a friend and leave early. We skip any occasion we are nervous about. We keep the telephone numbers of recovering friends handy.

We remember that this is a time of spiritual renewal and a celebration of life. We focus on what is good about this time of the year and enjoy the true beauty of the holidays.

I will relax and give the gift of love to everyone I meet.

Live your own life for you will die your own death.
—A LATIN PROVERB

Too often we live our lives guided by the voices of others. Perhaps we were fed negative messages as a child and have been guided by fear ever since. Sometimes we are afraid to stray too far away from our family's example, and we fail to follow our own vision. Do we echo the opinion of the majority lest we be ridiculed or ostracized?

When we were indulging in our addictions, it was difficult to be true to ourselves. We engaged in deception and subterfuge to satisfy our cravings. Because our minds were dulled, we never took the time to discover our true feelings or to get to know our real selves.

In recovery we face ourselves squarely and look at reality for the first time. As our self-esteem grows, we get to know and like ourselves. We see where we need to change, while acknowledging our assets. Becoming our own person is one of the great gifts of recovery. May we live today so that when we die we will feel that nothing has been left undone.

**Today I will reflect on who I am and what
I believe.**

The best way to cheer yourself is to try to cheer someone else up. —MARK TWAIN

When we feel down in the dumps, we tend to isolate and get lost in ourselves. The deeper we get into self-pity and depression, the more discouraged we feel. The best way to pull ourselves out of this negativity is to help someone else.

If someone is ill, we can run an errand for them or make a meal. A grieving person might appreciate a telephone call or an invitation to dinner. Someone going through difficulties would benefit greatly if we shared our experience with them. A senior citizen would welcome company for an afternoon at the movies or a walk in the park.

When we reach out to others, we draw on our inner resources. Our recovery frees us to be loving and helpful. When we show support and concern for someone else, we are amazed at how quickly we forget our own problems. We cannot fix others, but we can offer compassion and understanding. Listening, sharing, and giving of ourselves is the best antidote to depression. Being with others breaks our isolation and opens the door for the spirit to enter.

Today let me take the time to help at least one person who is suffering or alone.

When the head aches, all the members partake of the pain.   —MIGUEL DE CERVANTES

How fortunate we are in this fellowship to have the support of a group of fellow sufferers—people who have trod the same path and who understand us. We do not have to explain ourselves. We share the language of recovery.

Having a supportive place to go where they can share their joys and sorrows is not something most people have. At work we have to be on guard and at home we fear judgment. Our friends can rarely understand us unless they too have this disease.

The members of our group are there when we share important aspects of our lives. If a lover or friend dies, we have someone to comfort us. When we lose a job or make a mistake, we find understanding listeners. If we act foolishly or repeat some old inappropriate behavior, we can find relief and inspiration through unburdening ourselves at a meeting. When we share our troubles or our pain, some of the weight is removed from us and taken on by the group.

When we first come into this program we take a risk and open up to complete strangers. We expose our deepest fears and longings. The other members of the group share our vulnerability and relate to us. We become a part of a community. Our isolation is ended.

Today I will focus on the similarities between members of the group and myself.

November 18

There is really nothing more to say except why. But since why is difficult to handle, one must take refuge in how.   —TONI MORRISON

When we were active, we would cry out, "Why me?" Life seemed unfair, and we did not understand why we had to suffer. We were always searching for the root of our problems, but our minds were so fogged with disordered thinking that the answers never came to us. We saw no way out of our dilemma.

This program concerns itself with "how," not so much with "why." We do not know why we are compulsive-obsessive people, alcoholics, or addicts, but we do know how to recover *One Day at a Time.* Chapter Five of *The Big Book,* "How It Works," tells us we will not fail if we thoroughly follow the path suggested. That path is the Twelve Steps. Countless people have followed them, with sometimes miraculous results.

When we concentrate on "how" rather than "why," we have the key to changing our compulsive behavior. In the past we had to know why before we changed. The program urges us to change our behavior first, assuring us the "why" of things will gradually become revealed. It is said that if we bring the body, the mind will follow. By staying sober and following the program suggestions, we slowly begin to change.

Grant me the willingness to take the necessary steps to strengthen my recovery.

Small groups nurture our self-esteem, at least in small ways, because the other people in the group take us seriously. —ROBERT WUTHNOW

Before we came into recovery, we suffered alone with our feelings of uniqueness. Now we know the value of group support. We have the gift of a place to go to share our fears and joy. The other members of our group understand us because they share our common problem. They listen to us and share the same goal: freedom from addiction and emotional sobriety.

Healing occurs when we participate in the group. Our sharing is met with a sympathetic ear and words of encouragement. Attendance at meetings renews our energies and gives us the strength to stay sober for one more day. Often when we are with the group, a feeling of closeness to our Higher Power comes over us.

Having received so much from the group, it is only natural we would want to give something back. We find satisfaction serving as an officer, making coffee, setting up chairs or greeting newcomers. Our newfound sense of community helps us to grow spiritually and provides us with a safe harbor in a stormy world.

Today I will promote the common welfare and unity of my group by performing service so that it will be there for me and others who need it.

November 20

As children we were told to be "seen but not heard." The message was that what we had to say was not worth hearing. As gay men we had to hide an important part of ourselves if we were to survive. As alcoholics, drug addicts and sufferers of other compulsive-obsessive disorders, we lived lives of shame and secrecy.

In recovery we do not remain silent. We share our secrets, our hopes, our fears and dreams. No longer do we hide those aches that gnaw deep inside us.

It takes courage to express our true feelings. There are many situations where we would rather not say anything but where by remaining quiet we damage our self-esteem. Perhaps we speak up at the office if we hear an anti-gay joke or write a letter to a newspaper in response to a homophobic article. We can choose to be counted on Gay Pride Day and join rallies and marches at other times of the year.

Being out and open and a good example is the best way we can let our voices be heard.

Today I will refuse to allow fear to silence me.

That it will never come again is what makes life so sweet.
— EMILY DICKINSON

Once a moment is gone, we can never regain it. None of us knows for certain what the future will bring or if there is life after death. We can only hope and have faith that life continues in one form or another. Recognizing this truth makes us even more aware of the importance of each day.

Are we wasting our lives by indulging in excessive anger, self-pity, fruitless resentments or compulsive behavior? Do we postpone taking actions that could lead to contentment because we focus on what we lack rather than what we have? Are we sincerely trying to work the Steps so that we may have the happy, joyous and free life that has been promised to us?

Today we are able to reach out to others. A smile, a handshake or a kind word will brighten someone else's day as well as our own. Let us look for ways we can enjoy the present. We bring our best efforts to whatever tasks are at hand. We find contact with our Higher Power most often comes through communion with other people.

If we are having a bad day, we are free to stop, take a deep breath and begin the day anew. We build a good life one moment at a time.

Today let me look around and see what makes life worthwhile.

The process of coming out does not automatically inform gay people about how our bodies function, nor does it eradicate shame. When we talk loosely about "the gay community" we are referring to a group of people with a variety of erotic tastes, drives and fantasies.
—PAT CALIFIA

Most gay men never had anyone explain "the facts of life" as they pertained to gay men. As a result we came into adulthood with myths and misinformation that retarded our ability to be fully functioning sexual beings.

Some of us grew up in environments where any talk about the body was shameful. Perhaps we were scolded when we touched our private parts or were punished when caught masturbating or experimenting sexually. This inhibited us, and often we regarded anything to do with sexuality as "unclean." Learning that sexuality is one of our God-given gifts helps us to put this aspect of our life into perspective.

Sex education is something we owe ourselves if we are to stay safe and healthy.

We may have sexual tastes that do not conform to the mainstream idea of what is correct. As long as we do no physical or emotional harm to ourselves or our partners, no one has the right to judge or condemn us.

I choose today to express my sexuality in a loving and respectful manner.

Think of your fellow men and women as holy people who were put here by the Great Spirit. Think of being related to all beings.
                                                —ED MCGAA

Growing up, we were taught to look down on those who were different from us. We were dismissive of people who spoke differently or dressed in a way we considered tasteless. People from another class or race were ridiculed. The basis of our behavior was fear. We were afraid of being overwhelmed or tainted. Our fixed expectations of others became a source of conflict and a barrier to communication.

In recovery we are exposed to a wide variety of types of people, and we see we can learn from their experience. If we get locked into a clique, we close ourselves off from discovering that there are "many mansions in our father's house." It is not possible to like or befriend everyone, but we should not limit ourselves by shutting the door on someone just because of their outward appearance.

Underneath the skin we are all remarkably similar. In time we come to see that all of creation is an expression of the divine.

Let me move closer to others so that I may find a balanced and meaningful life.

Gratitude is not only the greatest of virtues, but the parent of all others. —CICERO

A good way to start and end the day is by saying thank you for all the abundance in our lives. We are grateful for our recovery and the guidance of our Higher Power. We give thanks for those who are traveling on life's journey with us. With their help and companionship we are sustained and nurtured and continue to grow.

As recovering people we are able to see the goodness of life more clearly than when our minds were clouded by addiction and codependency. We realize that there is a divine order that underlies everything and are grateful for the opportunity to be in harmony with all creation.

We are thankful for the material and spiritual gifts we have received. Knowing that we have been and will continue to be taken care of lets us appreciate how loved we are.

Whenever we are troubled we make a Gratitude List. When we see in writing all the blessings we have received, it is difficult to continue being depressed or upset. We are particularly grateful to be free of our obsessive and self-destructive behavior.

Today I will set aside some time to quietly express my gratitude.

November 25

Fall seven times, stand up eight. —JAPANESE PROVERB

Even after we come into recovery, we often have to bottom out on things other than our primary addiction before we can surrender completely to this program. Sometimes we feel discouraged and wonder where to find the courage to go on.

Reliance on our Higher Power is our best insurance against despair. Through practice of the Twelve Steps, prayer and meditation, we learn patience and persistence. When faced with a challenge, we accept it and take an inventory of our present situation. We ask for advice and help from others. We draw on the inner resources we have built up through working this program.

A change of attitude, time and detachment can remove most obstacles. If we are confronted aggressively, we wait till our opponent calms down before taking action. If our surroundings are depressing us, we make plans to go elsewhere. If a particular defect is constantly surfacing, we trust that the Sixth and Seventh Steps will supply the help we need.

Today I will take whatever steps are necessary to remove obstacles to my happiness and growth.

You can do the most wonderful things when you are really close. It is hard to take showers with only one of the five men you're dating. —CHER

What causes some of us to flee once a relationship gets too close? Psychologists say the origin of this behavior is rooted in the family. A mother or father who is physically or emotionally distant toward a child gives out negative messages regarding intimacy. If there is constant quarreling, divorce or several marriages, the child grows up feeling doomed to repeat his parents' mistakes. Adults with such a background find it difficult to trust anyone and often lack the self-esteem necessary to fully open up to another person.

By refusing to commit ourselves to one person, we deny emotional depth to our relationships. There is nothing wrong with dating widely, but once we have fallen in love with someone, we should give the relationship a chance to flourish. This can not happen if we are only partly there for the other person.

Opening up to someone else involves taking a risk. We are perhaps afraid to be hurt, but if we do not reveal ourselves, there is little chance of establishing an intimate connection. Holding hands, cuddling without having sex and talking about one's family history are good ways to begin disclosing ourselves to each other.

Grant me the patience and courage necessary to expose my heart and soul to the one I love.

In making amends, we should be sensible, tactful, considerate, and humble without being servile or scraping. As God's people, we stand on our own feet; we don't crawl before anyone. —BILL WILSON

We make amends to repair the damage we have done others, to change things for the better and to safeguard against repeating our mistakes. Before approaching the person, we consult our sponsor and review the situation. We take a few moments to meditate and ask our Higher Power for the necessary strength and willingness.

There are three parts to an amend. First, we say we are *sorry* for our actions when we acted deliberately. We *apologize* if our action was a mistake. We *express regret* if the situation was due to circumstances beyond our control.

Second, offer restitution. This might involve repaying money we owe or attempting to right the wrong we committed.

Third, we resolve that, God willing, these actions will not be repeated.

Finally, we let go and turn the results over to our Higher Power.

To the best of my ability I will try to repair the harm I have done and resolve to do better in the future.

November 28

Emotion turning back on itself, and not leading on to thought or action, is the element of madness.
—JOHN STERLING

In this program we are encouraged to "feel our feelings," and for many of us this is a new experience. When active we often repressed our emotions and became humorless and rigid. Now we are learning how to identify our feelings and to deal with them. This is a good and necessary thing for continued recovery. However, there is a danger that we might wallow in such feelings as self-pity, anger, depression, selfishness and ungratefulness. If we let these negative emotions rule us, there is always the possibility that they will consume us and we will return to our addictive behavior.

When we do a Fourth Step inventory, we identify patterns of behavior. We take note of both positive and negative character traits. If we find that we are given to an excess of emotionalism, we try to achieve balance by giving more weight to our rational side. We ask what is the cost and the effect of giving into these negative emotions. We pray to our Higher Power for help in using our resources wisely.

As I feel my feelings today, let me rely on reason to be my guide.

Procrastination is really sloth in five syllables.
—BILL WILSON

When active we may have found our behavior unacceptable, but we kept postponing doing something about it. Only when the pain became unbearable did we seek help. Now that we are in recovery, we do not have to wait till matters reach a crisis point before we take action. Happily we have learned that taking one step at a time moves us toward our goal.

We have many bad habits to break. Laziness is one of them. If we are having difficulty in a particular area, we ask our Higher Power to show us the way out. We set daily goals and try to work a little bit each day on moving forward.

Similarly, we do our best to begin working the Steps as soon as possible. We must guard against complacency. If we do not move forward, we will slide backward. We make a commitment to this program and find new meaning and purpose in life.

Help me to avoid self-satisfaction as I work toward changing and growing.

The garden was perhaps the one place where the men in my family could be in touch with the nurturing and caring sides of themselves. . . . A garden is a very personal expression of the relationship of the goddess within.
                                                    —JOSEF VENKER

Society places limits on everyone. Some of these are reasonable and others are not. The patriarchal structure that is presently dominant had its uses when people were hunter-gatherers. Many today find it lopsided and restrictive.

Do we find ourselves clinging to unworkable notions of what it means to be a man? Do we freeze up when someone touches us? Do we hold back our tears for fear of censure? Are we afraid someone will think of us as effeminate? Let us examine the underpinnings of our world outlook and try to enlarge our viewpoint. By recognizing the eternal feminine that resides within us, we are reclaiming the fullness of our humanity.

In a garden we reawaken our relationship to nature. As gay men we can look to a long spiritual tradition that has been hidden. By exploring the legends of the past, we see our kinship with the sacred. By recognizing the goddess within, we link ourselves with the powers of growth and place ourselves in the loving care of the divine maternal.

Today I will express the gentle part of my nature.

December 1

There is the illusion that homosexuals have sex and heterosexuals fall in love. That is completely untrue. Everybody wants to be loved. —BOY GEORGE

Perhaps the real clue to our sexual orientation lies in our romantic feelings rather than in our sexual feelings. Being gay means being able to fall in love with a man as well as having sex with him. When we were active in our addiction, we had difficulty with feelings of intimacy. We longed to be loved but did not permit ourselves to be vulnerable and trusting. Everything was put on the physical level. We allowed our fear of rejection to govern us and so revealed very little of our real feelings. In recovery we let our guard down and opened ourselves up to a wide range of emotional experience.

As we grow in freedom through the practice of the Twelve Steps, we come to love ourselves. We are then ready to love someone else. We act in a loving way, and this attracts people to us.

Our growth allows us to accept our lovers as friends as well as sexual partners. We find a reflection of God's creation in our lovers and treat them accordingly.

Let me remember to make a special effort today to be loving to all those around me.

December 2

Self-pity in its early stages is as snug as a feather mattress. Only when it hardens does it become uncomfortable. —MAYA ANGELOU

A member of the fellowship lost a job he liked very much. For the next two months he stayed at home, feeling sorry for himself and bemoaning his fate. Then he heard that a friend had suddenly died of a brain tumor. The shock of this news made him realize he had been wasting time feeling sorry for himself—in truth he discovered he rather liked wallowing in self-pity. The payoff for his self-pity was the permission not to take action. Spurred on by this realization, he was able to free himself from this habit and to accomplish things that his former job had prevented.

Do we feel sorry for ourselves because we were not born rich or healthy? Do we think life would have been better if we had not been gay? There are so many things in ourselves and the world we can find fault in. If we let these things overwhelm us, we will never accomplish anything. Self-pity becomes a trap that consumes all of our energy.

Rather than looking at the negative, let us focus on the positive. We begin by making a list of everything good about ourselves. We then take actions that will enhance our self-esteem. There will always be people with more than us and others with less. We work with what we have been given and make the best of it.

Today I am grateful to be alive and for the opportunity to fulfill my potential.

December 3

At age fifty, every man has the face he deserves.
—GEORGE ORWELL

I f we survey people in a room, we will notice many different expressions on their faces. One may seem gloomy, pinched and worried, while another will seem cheerful and happy.

How do we present ourselves to other people? Do we carry the weight of the world on our shoulders? Is our brow furrowed with worry lines? Do we frighten people because we are so angry? When asked how we are, do we always unload a litany of complaints?

Some of us are trapped in the habit of thinking and acting negatively. Everyone has bad days. If we need help, we should ask for it. Sometimes we get so caught up in negative thoughts that we forget that we are part of a group. We are afraid to look at life positively because we think no one will pay attention to our problems.

We can take care of our emotional needs without appearing to live under a dark cloud. A cheerful countenance, a sympathetic response to the concerns of others and a willingness to lighten up will help us be the kind of person who attracts good things.

Today I make an effort to let go of self-centered fear. I take an inventory of all the good things in my life and choose to be grateful for them.

Most things come and go, however good to watch; a few things stay and matter to the end, rain for instance. —REYNOLDS PRICE

Things happen. People get sick and die. Friends move away. Relationships end. We win the lottery or lose a job. Very little in life is permanent. No matter what happens to us, our sobriety needs to take first place. Without it our lives would be on a downward spiral.

In recovery we are careful to guard against both elation and depression. When things are going very well, we get excited and are reminded of past highs. At such moments we may be tempted to revert to our old behavior. If we are downhearted or upset over something, we might feel that drinking, drugging, overeating or compulsive sex will banish our uncomfortable feelings.

By sticking close to the program, we build a strong foundation for long-term recovery. Developing a deep relationship with our Higher Power, going to meetings and establishing a strong support network are good insurance against being overwhelmed by the winds of change.

I willingly accept change and ask for the strength to handle anything that comes my way.

December 5

We are not trying to imitate women.

—TENNESSEE WILLIAMS

Since we are taught that only women may love men in a romantic way, many of us become confused about our true nature. Must we act like women to attract men? If we assume a passive sexual role or our gestures and mannerisms do not conform to conventional male imagery, does this mean that we are not real men? Answering yes to these questions has caused a great deal of self-loathing in our community.

Today these old stereotypes are being dissolved as more and more openly gay men in sports, business and other traditionally male preserves come out. Two men can come together as equals and form loving, lasting partnerships. More and more, the distinctions among transsexuals, transvestites and gay men are becoming known. Each group has valid concerns and the right of self-affirmation.

The psychologist Carl Jung taught that everyone has both a masculine and feminine spirit residing within their psyche. Many gay men are in touch with the anima or feminine spirit. This does not make them any less men. In fact, this heightened awareness of the duality of our natures permits us to move toward a fuller integration of our spiritual and emotional components.

Today I ask for the courage to be true to myself.

December 6

The world is large, but in us it is as deep as the sea.
—RAINER MARIA RILKE

Mystics and spiritual teachers have proclaimed many times that everything found in the universe is reflected within ourselves. This awe-inspiring thought affirms that there is no separation between us and all other existing matter. We carry the laws of divine order within us.

When we feel out of balance, the most effective remedy is to be quiet and go within. There we find the *God of our understanding* that the founders of this program relied upon. Developing a rich interior life will give us the strength and nourishment that are required to face the rigors of daily life.

Prayer and meditation open us up to a joyous and more fulfilling life. They are like a spaceship that carries us to the source of that which is profound. When we enter inner space, we embark upon a great adventure of self-discovery.

Dependence on externals slips away. We begin to see what is really important and to let go of distractions that impede our spiritual growth.

Help me to accept myself as a perfect expression of the creative force.

December 7

The understanding now is that some form of HIV will be around as long as there are humans on the planet. All of a sudden gay men have to learn to change the way they relate to one another permanently.

—DAVID L. KIRP

A newly sober twenty-eight-year-old man shared that when he first moved to a big city he was tested for the HIV infection and found to be negative. However, he drank and drugged heavily and had unsafe sex. After a few years he discovered that he was now HIV positive. Naturally he is filled with deep regret, but unfortunately nothing can change his HIV status.

AIDS education efforts met with great success initially. Gay men learned to change their sexual behavior. However, recently many older men have been reverting to, and a new generation of young people have begun engaging in, unsafe sex. The reasons are many: drug and alcohol use, depression, sexual shame and survivor's guilt. Unsafe sex is also being viewed by some as the ultimate form of intimacy.

Whether one has a single partner or multiple sexual encounters, the need for safe sex is still an absolute necessity. We have a moral responsibility to protect the ones we love as well as ourselves.

Recovery teaches us self-esteem. We value our new-found lives. We accept the principles of this program and engage only in safe sex.

Help me to develop a healthy attitude toward myself and others.

December 8

The world is a looking glass, and gives back to every man the reflection of his own face. Frown at it and it will in turn look sourly upon you; laugh at it and with it, and it is a jolly kind companion.

—WILLIAM MAKEPEACE THACKERAY

If we tend to find everything disagreeable and unpleasant and are easily irritated, we should not be surprised to find ourselves with few friends. We often forget that our moods affect other people. If we are grumpy and take it out on others, we will likely receive sharp words in return. On the other hand, if we make an effort to find the good in this world and strive to be as amiable as possible with everyone we meet, our bright attitude will be returned in kind.

Each morning, upon awakening, we ask our Higher Power for the willingness to help make this a better world. Even in recovery there are times when we all fall short of our high ideals and aspirations. If we have been short-tempered or wronged someone, we are quick to make amends. We strive to remain on the best possible terms with everyone. Our time here on earth is short—let us use it so that when we are gone we are remembered with a smile.

I will remember that what goes around comes around. Help me to touch those I meet in a cheerful and kindly way.

A lean compromise is better than a fat lawsuit.
—GEORGE HERBERT

D o we think that we must always prevail in every argument? Must we always be right and have the last word? Are we constantly battling everyone and everything around us? Knowing when to bend rather than break is a virtue that we need to cultivate.

Life is often a compromise between the ideal and the impossible. If we see everything in black and white and overlook the gray areas, we are setting ourselves up for disappointment.

We need to be open to others and try to see different points of view. Every encounter is a two-way street. When we are wrong, we admit it. Needing to be the winner all the time is a form of control. We may fear we are not going to get what we deserve or that we may be embarrassed or shamed for not prevailing. This program teaches us humility. We respect others and their right to voice their opinion.

By not shutting out reason or closing our mind, we leave ourselves open to learning and growing. Argument for its own sake no longer appeals to us. We avoid extremes. Without abandoning our principles, we can be agreeable and enjoy the benefits of the middle path.

Today I will be flexible and open.

December 10

To have a quiet mind is to possess one's mind wholly—to have a calm spirit is to possess oneself.

—HAMILTON MABIE

It is often said that alcoholics are not happy unless the drapes are on fire. This also holds true for almost anyone with a compulsive-obsessive personality. Many of us have become addicted to drama and dependent on an adrenaline rush for thrills. We purposely create chaos to avoid taking a close look at ourselves.

Setting aside a period each day where we can have a quiet time is a wholesome tonic. A good way to still the committee in our mind is to sit calmly and concentrate on our breathing. Some people find it useful to focus on the flame of a candle and let their thoughts pass by until their minds are quiet. Others may lie on the floor, count backward from five to one and visualize being transported to a safe space where they are free to allow their spirit to float unhindered by worldly concerns.

No matter what method we use, we reap immense benefits from practicing meditation. Centering ourselves each day prepares us to face whatever challenges arise.

Each day I will practice being quiet and allowing life's flow to wash over me.

December 11

The real significance of the homosexual temperament
is that non-warlike men and non-domestic women
sought new outlets for their energies and became the
initiators of the arts and crafts, spirituality, shaman-
ism and the priesthood.   —EDWARD CARPENTER

Many people say that gay people are just like
everyone else except for what we do in bed.
Some feel that we do the same things in bed as other
people but are different in a number of ways. There are
many who think that a gay sensibility sets us apart
starting in earliest childhood. In recovery we can affirm
this difference and our right to be recognized as people
of worth and value.

For some gay men, the organized sports and games
of our childhood were a nightmare. We rebelled against
the bullying and mean-spirited competitiveness. Playacting, books, daydreaming and the enjoyment of creative efforts exerted a strong pull on us.

However, our fears sometimes made us hide our
true nature, and we sought to conform. As recovering
people, we are free to express ourselves. We can
integrate our emotional, physical and spiritual lives into
one joyous celebration of our gayness.

**Today I will reflect on that which is different
about me and affirm my essential goodness.**

December 12

One doesn't discover new lands without consenting to lose sight of the shore for a very long time.

—ANDRÉ GIDE

When we first come into this program, many of us are reluctant to let go of our old ways. We find it frightening and difficult to imagine change. We are in uncharted territory and have no idea what will happen to us. Some of us are afraid the program is a cult and that we will lose our individuality. However, before long, we find that this is a program of suggestions, and no one is going to force us to do anything.

It seems that a lot is being asked of us. First we are told that we must admit our powerlessness. This leaves us feeling vulnerable and without defenses. Then we are introduced to a new way of life and advised that we need to work on eliminating our character defects if we are to stay sober.

At first this change of direction is overwhelming. We don't think we will be able to do it. We often have mental reservations and tell ourselves we will give up if it proves too difficult. Then we see people around us, working the Steps, making important changes and leading happy lives. This inspires us to give it a try. Good results follow. We see ourselves improve and feel better about our lives. We are motivated to continue working the Steps and look forward to continued growth and change.

Help me to banish my fears and increase my faith.

One is not superior merely because one sees the world as odious. —FRANÇOIS RENÉ DE CHATEAUBRIAND

Coming into the program was a big step for us. We had to admit that we could not get better on our own. Perhaps at first we felt superior to everyone else. We saw the people in the rooms as losers. For years we had held onto the notion that we were unique and what worked for others could not possibly work for us. We thought we needed special attention.

Some of us fell into the trap of rating ourselves and others, saying, "He is recovering faster than I am" or "Look how badly he works his program." Our attitude changed when we began to identify rather than compare. This meant swallowing our pride and accepting that we were here for the same reason as everyone else. We recognized it was time to let go of our willful self-centeredness. We all share a common problem and need one another if we are to recover. Very few people make their way out of the darkness alone.

When we feel that we are part of a group, our isolation and loneliness begin to fade away. Finding similarities and forgetting difference promotes a sense of comfort and unity.

I will take a leap of faith and surrender to the healing power of the group.

December 14

What gays experience is a rejection not of their actions but of who they are constitutionally, a rejection of their very nature and being. —ROBERT BAUMAN

A young man from rural Massachusetts who was sober for seven years told a meeting at a Roundup in New York that no one in his home group knew he was gay. His boss was also a member of his group, and he was afraid he would lose his job if it was known he was gay. He said that he felt so relieved to be able to speak openly in front of a group of people about his innermost feelings and concerns. He always limited his shares in Massachusetts because he was afraid he might forget to change gender when referring to a boyfriend.

Some have questioned the need for special interest groups for gay men and lesbians. Yet gay men have been told at meetings not to speak about their relationships, and others have complained about members using derogatory words such as "faggot." The rooms of recovery are usually safe spaces, but the members are human and they bring all their prejudices with them. When a gay man is in the company of peers, he can let his guard down and share more openly. Gay meetings provide a unique forum for gay men to be open and honest in a way that is difficult in most environments.

Today I will make a special effort to support the gay groups in my area by doing service and reaching out to newcomers.

December 15

The essence of pleasure is spontaneity.
                                        —GERMAINE GREER

Have we boxed ourselves into a restrictive routine? Do we get uptight when something interferes with our timetable? While it is important to plan, we do not try to manipulate every detail of an outcome. Being open to spontaneous happenings gives us the opportunity to be renewed and refreshed by the unexpected. Today let us look for opportunities to relax our control over everything around us.

Carrying groceries for an elderly person, graciously accepting a sudden schedule change or giving an unusually large sum of money to a beggar might hold pleasant surprises for us. When we accept a request to speak at a meeting at the last moment we can enjoy unburdening ourselves in an unrehearsed fashion.

Sometimes we need to make extravagant gestures. Buying a big bouquet of flowers that is beyond our budget might be the splash of color we need to brighten our lives.

We allow ourselves to be carried along by the process, enjoying the moment and turning the results over to our Higher Power. Sometimes the most decisive actions of our lives are unplanned.

Today I will trust that whatever happens is meant to be. I will enjoy the uncertainty of taking a chance on something new.

December 16

I like to think of nature as an unlimited broadcasting station, through which God speaks to us every hour, if only we will tune in. —GEORGE WASHINGTON CARVER

As human beings we have many needs. One of them is the need to make contact with nature. We live busy lives and are often enclosed in a cocoon of concrete and glass. Sometimes television, movies and computers are the chief sources we use to define our reality. Separation from nature makes us indifferent and even hostile toward it.

Our emotional well-being improves when we make contact with the living world around us. We gain satisfaction from direct experience of and contact with nature. We discover our interconnectedness to the rest of creation.

Taking long walks in the country, spending time near the ocean or camping out provides us with inspiration, harmony, peace and insight. In communing with nature, we open a deeper dialogue with our Higher Power. Confronted with the order and majesty of nature, we develop an affinity and kinship with the divine. Our lives gain new meaning and satisfaction.

Today let me find an opportunity to be a little closer to the natural elements around me.

December 17

Homosexual adults who have come to terms with their sexuality, who do not regret their sexual orientation, and who can function effectively sexually and socially, are no more depressed psychologically than are heterosexual men and women. —DR. ALAN P. BELL

A recent TV show featured a married minister who came out in his late forties. He said that most gay people would prefer to be straight if they had a choice.

Certainly many people remain in the closet for fear of censure or persecution. What would we choose if we could change our sexual orientation? Would we want to? Do we feel that being gay is acceptable? Do we believe we can find happy and fulfilling lives within the framework of this identity? What are some of the good things about being gay?

As sober people we are free to explore our sexuality with a clear mind. Many people find the courage to come out once they are in recovery. Others may feel that their past homosexual behavior was just a form of sexual experimentation. Some may feel more comfortable identifying as bisexuals. Sexuality is a continuum, and where we fall within it can only be defined by us. Prayer and meditation give us the courage to assert and affirm our true selves without considering other people's beliefs or opinions.

Today I will respect and accept myself.

December 18

Just as the false assumption that we are not connected to the earth has led to the ecological crisis, so the equally false assumption that we are not connected to each other has led to our social crisis.   —ALBERT GORE

We live in the "Age of the Individual," where personal freedom, mobility and individual rights govern the way we live. Each person, regardless of gender, color, sexual orientation or creed, has intrinsic worth. However, in our search for our self we can identify so exclusively with our bodies and persona that we ignore or deny our basic human need to connect with other people.

As the "lone wolf" is rarely found in the wild, so a hermit is unusual among humans. It is in our nature to be a part of a community. Yet our addictions isolated us from others and caused us painful loneliness.

Today we have a chance to commune with others and reap the rewards of social interaction. By participating as full members of this fellowship, we have an opportunity to cultivate a spiritual perspective toward those in our lives. Through nurturing relationships and mutual interdependence, we gain the support and love we need for growth and healing.

Today I choose to align myself with nature, other people and the joyful web of life's connections.

December 19

Relieve me of the bondage of self, that I may better do thy will.

—*THE BIG BOOK* OF ALCOHOLICS ANONYMOUS

In the past few years people have been told "This is a selfish program." But this distorts the original precepts as found in *The Big Book*. From the beginning, the emphasis has been on freeing ourselves from the bondage of self. When we were active, part of our problem was an intense self-absorption. A careful check of our motives revealed that even when we thought we were caring or attending to others, our ultimate goal was self-satisfaction.

In early recovery we are often overwhelmed with the immensity of our problems. We soon discover that there are others in the same boat as we are, and before too long we learn that we have something to give to other people. Being helpful to others starts us on a path of spiritual growth. When we listen to others when they share, converse with people before and after meetings and take a sincere interest in the well-being of other members of the group, our self-seeking slips away.

Let the love we all need today begin with me.

December 20

Responsibility is the thing people dread most of all. Yet it is the one thing in the world that develops us, gives us manhood or womanhood fibre.

—FRANK CRANE

In the past we often acted irresponsibly. We shirked our duties and obligations. We wanted to be carried because we believed the world owed us a living. Our fears told us that we would not get our share of what the world had to offer. As gay men we felt like outsiders and refused to play by the rules. It seemed as though the world had shortchanged us. This attitude closed many doors for us. Eventually we learned that everyone is given a different hand, and we have to play ours the best we can. No one has everything. Each of us has to work with what we have been given.

Being responsible is the mark of a caring and mature person. We all have duties to perform, work to carry on, obligations to keep and influence to exert. When we do a job well, keep our promises, act reliably or give a little extra, we discover that being accountable is not a burden. This might mean taking care of a pet, visiting a sick friend, working a little harder or doing service. Recovery teaches us to show up and keep our commitments.

Today I choose to be responsible for my destiny. It is a relief and a comfort to keep my word and do the best I can in all my efforts.

December 21

Oh Winter, ruler of th' inverted year,
I crown thee king of intimate delights,
Fire-side enjoyments, home-born happiness,
And all the comforts that the lowly roof
Of undisturbed retirement, and the hours
Of long uninterrupted ev'ning, know.
—WILLIAM COWPER

W inter is here and we are indoors much more than usual. We can read the books we have postponed reading, study a foreign language for our next summer vacation or master a craft. Now that the holidays are past, in this slow time of the year, we can savor everything we do and enjoy a different aspect of nature's wondrous palette.

Since the days are short and the nights are long, there is a chance that we will find the darkness depressing. Good insurance against the winter blues is a renewed commitment to meetings. We might plan our social life so that we do not fall into isolation, perhaps an evening of cards or a weekly date to see a movie with an old friend.

As the bear must hibernate, so too do we need plenty of rest to renew our bodies. When we lie in bed at night, let us be grateful for the warmth of our bed. We can also scatter some seed for those birds who have remained to share this season with us.

I feel the warmth of God's love in my heart of hearts.

December 22

We are quick enough at perceiving and weighing what we suffer from others, but we mind not what others suffer from us. —THOMAS À KEMPIS

Too often we have been quick to lash out at those who we felt hurt or offended us. We nurtured grudges and planned revenge. We wasted many hours rehashing real or imagined harms. Sometimes our entire life was controlled by the anger we felt toward others. Yet we were oblivious to our own actions and sought to justify each and every harm we did to other people. This self-centered view robbed us of our emotional balance and soured our outlook on life.

Through the practice of the Twelve Steps, we are free to have the best possible relationship with each person we meet. If we find conflict, we look at our own motivation and intentions. We search for the cause of any ill will and do our best to correct the situation.

If we still cling to resentments toward our friends or family, we pray for the willingness to forgive and let go. Sometimes we need to forgive ourselves for holding on to old hatreds for so long. Perhaps we have been the target of homophobic remarks or actions and bitterly resent it. Can we in all honesty say we have been completely tolerant and accepting of others? Am I treating others as I would have them treat me?

I pray for the willingness to look at my part in any conflict and let go of my resentments.

December 23

He not busy being born/ Is busy dying   —BOB DYLAN

D oes some old character defect keep slapping us in the face? Do our friends complain that we are grouchy? Do we often feel bored and depressed? If so, we might ask ourselves what Step we are working on.

As we work through the Steps, our lives keep changing. What once seemed impossible is now within our reach. New dreams and aspirations replace stagnation and hopelessness.

In recovery we surrender to a new way of life. Our faith is restored and we put our trust in our Higher Power. We take an inventory and share it with another human being. Willing to let go of our defects, we ask our Higher Power for help. We make peace with those we harmed. We use daily prayer and meditation to help us put what we have learned into practice. We carry the message of recovery to those who need it. We do our best to live a life based on spiritual principles.

Sobriety is a rebirth. Hope replaces despair. Our spiritual awakening has set us on an exciting course of change.

Today I am grateful for the second chance I have been given to grow and learn.

December 24

The only gift is a portion of oneself.
—RALPH WALDO EMERSON

In early sobriety we found ourselves frightened and confused. Recovery seemed strange, and we were not sure that it was for us. Then people reached out and gave us the gift of their time, experience and good counsel. They listened to us when we needed to talk to someone. At meetings we heard others share honestly about things we felt ashamed to admit. This gave us the courage to take a deeper look at ourselves. After meetings we went to coffee with others, and our spirits were brightened by the camaraderie we felt. Eventually we felt at home, a part of something larger than ourselves.

Do we make a point of talking to newcomers? Are we sponsoring someone? Now that our recovery has restored us to a productive life, are we too busy to take the time to help another person? Do we exclude strangers and only socialize with our friends? It is easy to forget how lonely and adrift most newcomers are. Making a special effort to share what we have learned will insure continued recovery and a happy, fulfilling life. It is good to keep in mind that our sobriety is a gift we were freely given. A sure way to keep it is to pass it on to others.

Let me never forget how much we need one another in this program. Today I will look for ways to give the gift of myself.

December 25

**Do we stand in our own light, wherever we go, and
fight our own shadows forever?**   —OWEN MEREDITH

At this time of the year when the day is at its
shortest, people around the world celebrate the
triumph of light over darkness. Candles and electric
illuminations remind us that our spirits can shine
through the gloomiest prospect.

Do we sometimes block joy by surrendering to negativity? Have we gotten into the habit of expecting
others to make us happy? Do we give up before the
miracle happens? If so, today we try to cultivate a
positive outlook. There is much that is wonderful and
exciting in this world. Without being Pollyanna, we
can look at the bright side of things. We work with
what we have and do the best we can. The results we
turn over to our Higher Power.

We choose today to stop getting in our own way.
We look around us and aim for what is worthwhile.
The promise of recovery in this program is a light
in our life. We make it a beacon to follow in all
our endeavors.

**Let the light of the season shine on me and
those I love.**

December 26

All my life I wanted to look like Liz Taylor. Now I find that Liz Taylor is beginning to look like me.
—DIVINE

All of us occasionally envy someone else. This only becomes a problem when we continually compare our "inside" to someone else's "outside." We rob ourselves of happiness by thinking our lives would be better "if only" this or that were so. We can never truly know what is going on inside someone else. There are always going to be people who are worse off or better off than we are.

One of the benefits we reap in this program is self-acceptance. We learn to value ourselves as we are. As we work the Steps, our old feelings of inadequacy fade and are replaced by a new sense of confidence. Our need to be validated by others lessens. We no longer deny our feelings or compromise our needs.

When we take our inventory, we must not forget to list our assets. Too often we concentrate on the negative and overlook the positive. As we grow and change, we find it becomes easier to acknowledge our worth. We accept the things about ourselves we cannot change and make an honest effort to improve what we can.

Today I accept myself as I am.

December 27

But oft the words come forth awry of him that loveth well.
— HENRY HOWARD

Many of us never learned to communicate properly. Some of us may act out in an angry or inappropriate manner when something is bothering us. Some of us resort to physical violence or vicious verbal attacks when we want to express our needs or feelings. Others withdraw into isolation and silence. There are those who keep secrets because they fear rejection or exposure. Behavior of this kind inhibits growth and understanding.

Effective communication is direct. We say what we mean. If we feel angry or hurt, we say so. We state our needs frankly. When someone is acting toward us in an unacceptable manner, we let them know as soon as possible.

If we are unclear about something our partner has said or done, we ask for an explanation. We also let the other person talk about whatever he needs and what is important to him. It is best to refrain from giving advice unless we are asked. We show that we are interested in others' feelings and experience. We take the time and patience required to settle differences in a kind and courteous way.

Today I will express my feelings in a clear and honest manner. I will sharpen my listening skills by being attentive and patient.

December 28

When you have closed your doors, and darkened your room, remember to never say that you are alone, for you are not alone; God is within—and what need has that power of light to see what you are doing?

—EPICTETUS

At this time of the year it can be difficult to be alone. At parties and family gatherings everyone seems to have a partner. If we are single, we sometimes wonder if there is something wrong with us. We ask ourselves why we are alone.

The most important thing to realize is that we are never alone. Our Higher Power is always with us. We do not have to be in a church or at a meeting to make conscious contact with our Higher Power.

We are no less worthwhile than others because we are not in a relationship. When we are single, we have a degree of freedom and flexibility not available to couples. Instead of bemoaning our fate, let us focus on how we can get to know ourselves better and on ways we can help others.

We seek to balance solitude and sociability. Too much isolation alienates us from society. On the other hand, we all need to occasionally retreat from society and rejuvenate ourselves by quiet communion with our Higher Power.

I am a part of this great Universe. Help me to realize I am connected with all of God's creatures.

December 29

It is a bad plan that admits of no modification.
— PUBILIUS SYRUS

When we make a plan, we should keep in mind that we have no control over the outcome. Perhaps we had our hearts set on renting a summer house and suddenly we need that money for a medical or other emergency. It is prudent to set goals. Once we do, however, we need to turn the results over to our Higher Power. If we set our heart too much on attaining one thing, we will be severely disappointed if we don't get it.

At the same time we must guard against perfectionism. Rarely do we achieve one hundred percent of any goal. If we are unrealistic, frustration and bitterness will certainly follow.

Depending too much on a particular person or job leaves us unprepared if the situation changes. If we are financially dependent on a person and that person dies leaving us unprovided for, we are in a difficult situation. The same is true if we are fired from a job and have no savings. It is prudent to plan several courses of action for every undertaking.

The important thing is not to be overwhelmed when things do not go our way. A boyfriend may leave us, friends may move or we may not get a job we fervently desire. We need to accept the situation and go on with our lives as soon as possible.

Help me to be open to the many possibilities in my life.

December 30

Every exit is an entry somewhere else.

—TOM STOPPARD

When we lose someone or something dear to us, it is difficult to see what lies ahead. We may lose a job and think we will never have another. A lover may leave us, and we are thrown into despair, imagining that we will be alone for the rest of our lives. Leaving old friends behind makes us unhappy when our career takes us to another town. Someone dies, and we feel an empty space that can never be filled by another. Inevitably there will be sad moments in our lives, but we cannot let them overwhelm us.

Change and closure are a part of nature. Like a flower that buds, blooms and then withers, we are constantly being reborn, growing and dying on some level. The secret to happiness is recognizing that life is a continuum and that we are always in the right place along it. If we are in a difficult spot, we look for the lesson to be learned. When we feel content and secure, we thank our Higher Power for the beauty of the moment.

We cannot stop time. Rather than clinging to the past, we look for the opportunities for expansion. What seems like a calamity can often be the beginning of an exciting, fresh experience. Retirement can be the beginning of a challenging new way of life rather than the end of our productivity. Defeat is a space where we learn our true strengths.

I will remember that when one door closes, another opens.

December 31

This time, like all times, is a very good one, if we but know what to do with it. —RALPH WALDO EMERSON

L et us pause and reflect on the year that is ending. Was it a time of growth and learning? Did we do all that we could to cooperate with our recovery? Perhaps we mourned the death of someone or the ending of a relationship. Maybe it was a time of new awareness when we shed some old unproductive habit.

Life is change. Accepting change helps us to move into new realms. We cannot cling to the past. Yesterday is over. Today is the first day of the rest of our life, and every hour is golden. We do not waste it by wallowing in self-pity or regretting what cannot be changed.

It is difficult to leave the familiar. Endings are painful, but we need not fear the future if we trust in our Higher Power. Let us resolve to put the principles of this program into practice this coming year, starting today. By being kind and courteous to everyone we meet, sharing our experience, strength and hope and being tolerant and accepting, we open ourselves up to a new way of life.

I will remember that the old dies to make way for the new.

Notes

Notes

Notes

Notes

Notes

Notes

Notes

Notes